Copyright

Benjamin Grey and the Cricklewood Mansion is a work of fiction. Names, characters, and events in this book are fictitious. Any resemblance to actual persons, living or dead, or events, is entirely coincidental and not intended by the author.

H Publishing

www.craighenebury.com

Benjamin Grey

And

The

Cricklewood

Mansion

A Novel

By

Craig Henebury

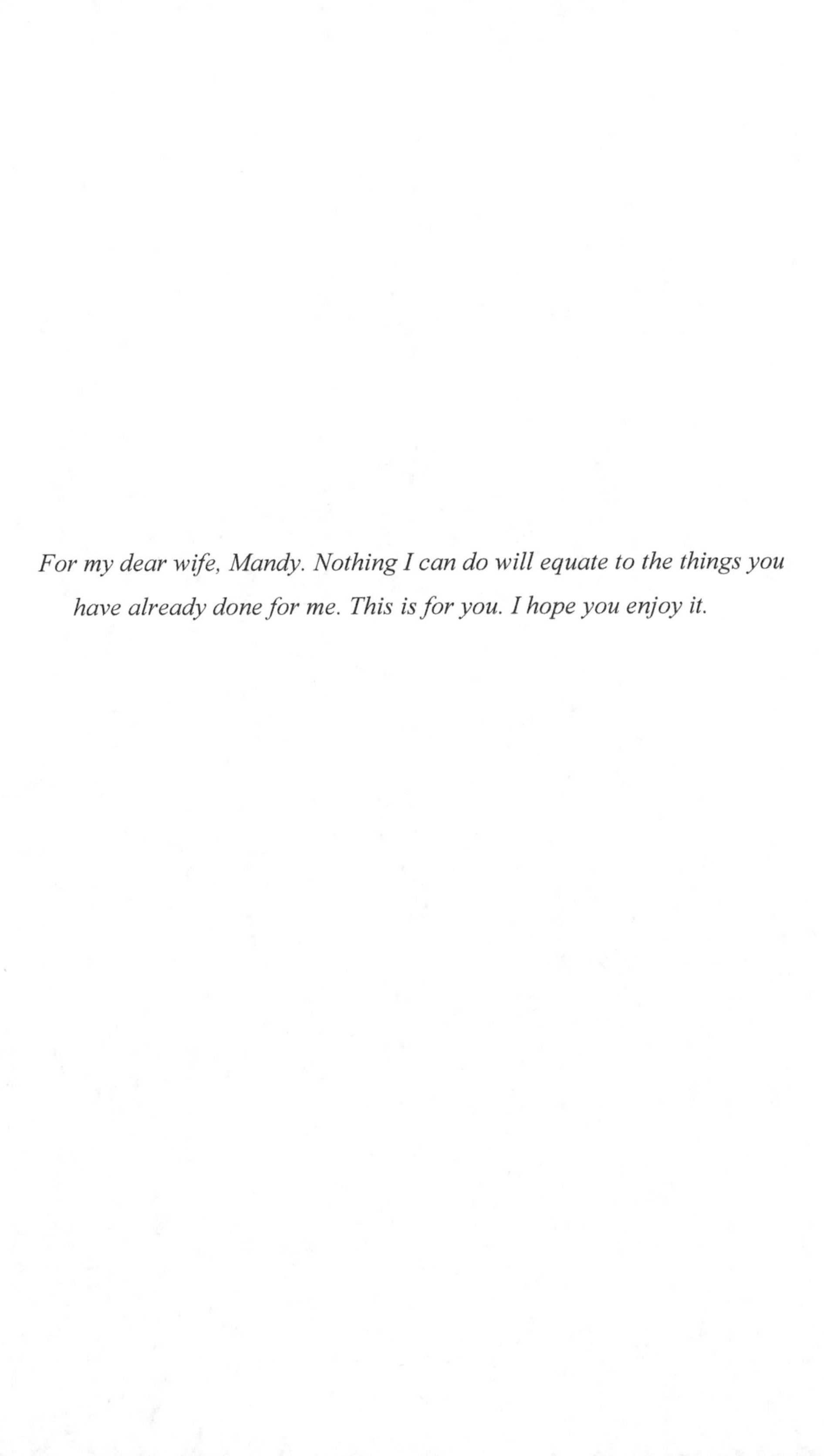

For my dear wife, Mandy. Nothing I can do will equate to the things you have already done for me. This is for you. I hope you enjoy it.

CHAPTER ONE

The phone at the front desk rang. Briggs jumped up to answer it.

"Good morning, this is Grey and Briggs Investigators. How may we help you today?" she said, brightly.

Ben looked up from his cell phone. He couldn't hear the phone ring, he had permanently lost his hearing at the age of eight, but he couldn't help noticing the speed at which Briggs moved. She turned her back to him. After a moment, she turned again, picked up a pen and began writing onto a notepad. Ben's lip-reading skills were excellent. *She was agreeing to something*, he thought. A smile broke across Briggs' face as she placed the phone on its cradle. *Okay, what has she agreed to?*

Ben looked at Briggs, waiting for her to speak. She continued to stand there, fiddling with the pen and grinning like the bird that had slept in but still managed to catch the worm. Ben gestured, opening his hands...*well?*

"That was Lady Havishem," Briggs declared.

"*The* Lady Havisham? Wouldn't she be a bit old by now?" Ben replied. His speech suggested an impediment but remained intelligible.

"Actually, it's Havishem with an 'e' and she didn't refer to herself as Lady. Her name is Olivia Havishem, elderly I guess, and she did speak as if I should know who she is, so my assumption is she must be quite well-to-do."

"Lost her poodle?" Ben asked, not attempting to hide his sarcasm.

Briggs' smile returned, broader this time. "No. She would like to employ us, to investigate a house next to where she lives."
Ben's expression softened.

"She's asked to meet with us so she can explain more fully. She did say the place in question has not been inhabited for a few years now since the owners died, and the property passed into Trust. She has observed 'goings-on' at the property," Briggs continued.

"Has she told the Police?"

"That's what I asked. Yes, she has advised the Police, but they dismissed her saying it's likely kids, homeless or travellers passing-through. They said they'd send someone to take a look."

"So why has she called us?" Ben asked.

"Because she doesn't believe them. And besides, it seems our Lady Havishem with an 'e', is not averse to doing some investigation of her own. She did say that she had seen lights on at the place at night, but when she went to look the following day, nothing." She said, with a magician's wave of the hand.

"A mystery worthy of Columbo himself to be sure. So, you agreed to go and see her?"

"Actually, we are going to see her this afternoon. So, get yourself showered and dressed to meet a Lady."

"You're kidding, right?" Ben replied, trying hard not to look down at his phone.

"Why? What else are you doing? We've only been open three days and you're already complaining? If you're going to be spending money on that game, you're going to need to investigate more than lost pets. She has agreed to cover any expenses and pay fifteen thousand up front, even if it does turn out to be nothing. It's a steal. Oh yeah, and she asked for you by name."

"She phoned us, she just asked to speak to Mr. Grey," Ben responded.

"No. She asked for *you* by *name*. She's heard of you. Asked if you were the one who caught those terrorists last year, to which of course I said 'yes', even though it was mostly me. So, get yourself ready as I don't want to disappoint the old lady."

Ben recalled his experience with the terrorists. His gift had led him to stumble across what he believed to be plans for a massive terrorist attack on the outskirts of London. Knowing he couldn't ignore what he had heard, but at the same time also knowing he had no way to explain how he came by such knowledge, he contacted the Police anonymously. A few days later, the intelligence services turned up, with the Police, at his mother's house. Sophie Briggs being the lead investigator at the time. It turned out, Ben's information corroborated the intelligence they already had. To avoid arrest, Ben had to disclose how he had obtained his information. His gift became known only to a few, Briggs included, and he was subsequently roped into the investigation itself. Using additional information that Ben was able to acquire, the terrorists were apprehended, billions of pounds and hundreds of lives saved, and everyone got to go home – except for members of a terrorist cell. Thanks to social media the sting operation had played out in front of the world, though Ben thought he had been very careful to avoid any publicity of his own.

How did Lady Havishem with an 'e', know that he had had anything to do with that terrorist operation? Ben mused.

Conceding, Ben pulled himself from the chair, checked his watch and saw that Briggs was no longer in the area.

"Where did she go?" he mumbled to himself. "Some investigator I am when someone can disappear in front of me. Lady Havisham, I will gladly take your money, thank you." He opened the door labelled 'Employees Only' and made his way up the stairs to the apartment where they now lived.

"We need to get that shower fixed," Ben stated, as he opened the car door.

"You know you can arrange appointments online?" Briggs replied as she slid into the passenger's side, though Ben couldn't tell if it was a statement or a question.

"Where does Lady Havishem with an 'e' live?" Ben asked.

"Cricklewood. Not really a village but more a collection of five substantial properties. Located near Church Stowe up the A5." Briggs replied.

"Sounds like the middle of nowhere."

"It is, if you were keen on walking. But by car, it's close to the A5. While you were getting yourself ready, jeans?" interrupting herself, wincing.

Ben looked down at himself, "What?"

In the car, Briggs continued, "None of the properties have been sold since the original buyers. And that was some two hundred years ago."

Ben started the car, and a wheel spat gravel as he pulled away.

Briggs shared the information she had gleaned while Ben and been showering. Ben would adjust the rearview mirror so he could see Brigg's lips while driving. Four of the houses remained occupied, the fifth and largest home is owned by the Henshaw family. The Henshaw's originated from Scotland and appeared to have had some connection to Prince William, the third son of King George II. Robert Henshaw IV and his wife Emily died when their helicopter crashed after attending the British Grand Prix at Silverstone. They left behind three children who had all grown up and left the family home by then. It turned out the listed property needed significant repairs and none of the siblings were willing to take on the cost. Several unsuccessful attempts had been made to sell the property, and the house has stood empty since.

The four other properties that comprised Cricklewood, had also been passed down the family line. The Havishem home, the smallest, Briggs seemed to want to point out, passed to Arthur Havishem four years before his father died. Arthur was already married to Olivia Travers, who had apparently had a mildly successful career in theatre. They have no children.

"Yet another fortune to be left to the Cats Protection League, no doubt." Ben mumbled.

Briggs, sat with her laptop open. "Googling the area, it looks like one of the homes might have a better view of the Mansion then the one the Havishem's have," she said.

"Who does that belong to?" Ben asked.

"To whom does it belong, to whom." Briggs replied, in her best Royal English, emphasising the 'm' with her lips. "The Stanley's," she continued, dropping the accent, "more specifically, Edwina Stanley the only child of Edward and Margaret Stanley. Edwina married James Gist.

They have two children, now grown up, Anne who married and moved away, and John who according to his social media accounts, still lives with his parents. Oh, it seems that Edwina passed away, cancer, several years back, and James has since remarried."

"And the remaining two Cricklewood properties?" Ben asked.

"The Loredan's, neighbours, if you can call them that, to the Havishem's, and the Bond's." Briggs paused. "What nothing to say about the Bond's?"

Ben shrugged, "Why would I have anything to say? It's a common enough name. Plenty of people are called Bond, and no doubt some are very wealthy. Any children?"

"Not any called James if that's what you're wondering. You do know James Bond isn't real?" Briggs added.

"He might not be called James, but the character would have been someone Fleming knew. Some flashy CIA spy." Ben replied.

Briggs signed 'Jerk'.

"Hey, it's dangerous to sign while driving."

"I'm not driving," she said.

"You know what I mean."

They turned off the A5 and onto Main Street, heading toward Church Stowe.

"We'll need to drive through the village and there should be a turning a bit farther up."

"How long do we have before our appointment?" Ben asked. Briggs looked across at Ben. "Gotta be a pub in a small English village." He added.

"On the way back. We are a few minutes early, but I was thinking we could drive up to the Mansion for a quick nosey round before meeting Mrs. Havishem," Briggs replied.

"With an 'e'," they both said in unison.

An aging road sign pointed the way to 'Cricklewood'. A winding lane, barely wide enough for two cars, disappeared into woodland. As they approached, the treescape opened up to reveal two substantial residences.

"This one on the left belongs to the Bonds," Brigg stated. "That one straight ahead is the Loredan's. Follow the lane around to the right and we should see the Havishem's on the left."

"These are huge," Ben remarked.

The road curved to the right and continued past the Loredan home, soon coming to small roundabout, with a statue of cherub at its centre, surrounded by shrubbery that suggested maintenance was only an occasional thought.

"The Havishem's is down there," Briggs pointed, off to the left of the roundabout. The Mansion is straight ahead," she said, though they could see only what they assumed to be the driveway.

"That means, this one to the right must be the Stanleys." Ben added.

Ben looked back at the Havishem home. The driveway wasn't gated and continued straight for perhaps two hundred metres before stopping at the property. The home itself was rectangular, from the road at least, with the long side facing them. The walls were limestone and the roof a reddish slate. It was clean and, even from here, clearly being well maintained.

"Keep going straight, let's take a look at the Mansion," Briggs urged.

Ben slowed as he navigated the roundabout, still peering at the properties while avoiding doing anything that might anger the cherub.

A large gate marked the entrance to the mansion property. The rusted iron gates were open and pressed up against the substantial conifer trees. More trees lined the first thirty metres or so, before the driveway curved to the left and created a vista of the house and grounds.

"Woah," said Ben, moving his head closer to the windscreen.

"It was last on the market for ten million, it didn't sell. The last tax assessment valued the property at eight million." Briggs said.

"Eight million quid and you still have to spend a fortune before you could likely live in it." Ben remarked, as they approached a large oval water feature. The statue of a lady stood, perhaps eight feet tall, at the heart of a pond. Sculpted in long, flowing garments, her head tilted toward the jug she held, which pointed down toward the pond. No doubt once very elegant, the statue and the pond had borne the brunt of the English weather. The pond overgrown with weeds and filled with water lilies and the odd beer can. The statue, grubby, covered in mildew and other fungi.

Ben stopped the car and stepped out onto the gravel driveway. His eyes scanned the front of the property. Three levels, he counted ten windows across the top and middle levels. At ground level, large double doors of reinforced wood and some intricate metalwork, marked the entrance. The entrance was in the middle to give the house symmetry. The windows at ground level were larger, and taller than those above. Nature around the house was in full swing, creepers extended up and along the walls like fingers that threatened to strangle the building. The bushes that lined the front, no doubt once uniform, now stood at differing heights and gave shelter to weeds and litter that would have blown across the countryside over the years.

Or perhaps not. Ben looked more closely. While some of the litter looked old, a beer can and a newspaper did not. He walked over to the newspaper. It was damp but not sodden, no visible date. It felt greasy, he smelled his fingers.

"Chips," he said.

"Any teenagers from the village will know about this being abandoned," Briggs replied.

Ben nodded. "Well, there are no lights of any kind, and I assume the statue is a fountain, which isn't working. Power must have been disconnected. By the looks of things, I doubt any of the utilities are working. What's the council tax on a place like this?"

"The highest band is 'H' so that in effect caps what someone would have to pay," Briggs replied. "Each Council applies its own charges to the Bands. This house would obviously be Band H. A few hundred every month I expect," said Briggs.

"Any way to avoid paying it?" Ben asked.

"Dunno. Don't think so, though I think the owners of empty properties get a discount. Why?"

Ben shrugged, "No reason."

Briggs started to walk towards another building detached from the main property. "This must be the garage and workshop or something." She reached a single door with a brass handle and small window. She tried to peer through the glass. "Can't see a thing," she said, though by now there was no chance Ben would have been able to read her lips. She tried the handle, "locked."

Ben walked past the garage block and to the end of the main building to take a look around the corner toward the back of the house.

"There's another wing to the house. You know what's weird?" Ben asked, turning to look back at Briggs.

"No security?" Briggs replied.

"You noticed."

"I don't mean to be rude, but I'm the one that's qualified to be an investigator."

"You don't need qualifications to be an investigator," Ben remarked. Returning to walking down the side of what was the west wing of the main house, "You just need to observe, and listen, use a bit of common sense, and maybe a dash of patience." He continued.

"Really?" Briggs responded, fully aware she was speaking to herself. "I suppose your criminal law degree and formal training taught you that," she muttered, as she walked around the garage block looking for another entrance.

As she arrived at the rear of the garage block there was yet another set of garage doors, and another single door, mirroring the configuration at the front. Again, she tried the single door. Locked. This time the rear garage doors, or what she still thought to be the garage, were not only locked but also padlocked. She checked the time on her phone and looked around for Ben.

Ben had reached the end of the west wing. At the rear of the house there was a substantial lawn, with a few mature trees, bordered by once landscaped gardens. Beyond that, it looked like pathways trailed off into woodland. Annexed to the end of the west wing was a conservatory, aluminium construction with what Ben assumed to be a digital control panel, not functioning, but the touch screen clearly visible through the windows. Inside, the place looked deserted. Some empty boxes scattered around the floor, a lone table and chair, a few open cupboards no longer housing anything.

Ben felt a tap on his shoulder.

"Come on, let's go see the old lady," Briggs said.

A couple of minutes later they pulled up outside the Havishem home. The long straight driveway, swept around to the left to a large, gravelled area, ending at a brick triple garage. In contrast to the Mansion, the borders were precise, bushes manicured, and the gardens landscaped with a mix of hydrangea, Japanese spirea, hemlock, lavender, and roses. An older model silver Jaguar XKR and a blue Ford Focus were parked in front of the garage.

Ben and Briggs got out of the car and made their way up the few steps to the porched entrance. The porch was framed in marble, the leaded windows recently stained, and the large arched oak door was able to look both old and new at the same time. Briggs pressed on the doorbell which returned a stately ding-dong. The door was opened by a young woman.

"Hi," Briggs said, "this is Benjamin Grey and I'm Sophie Briggs, we have an appointment with Mrs. Havishem."

"Oh yes, please come in, please come through to the sitting room, I'll let Olivia know you are here. Would you like tea or coffee?" the young woman asked. "My name is Alison by the way, I'm the help."

"Sure, a tea would be great," Briggs replied, "Ben?"

"Eh, yes, thank you." Ben confirmed.

Stepping into the entrance hall, Alison led them into a room off to the right. The walls were lined with books and a few pieces of furniture that provided cupboards and a place for ornaments. A two-seater love seat, and two individual armchairs framed a glass coffee table in the centre of the room.

"Please take a seat, I'm sure she won't be a moment," said Alison.

Briggs sat down into one of the chairs. Ben walked over to the back wall and started browsing the books. It wasn't long before an elderly lady entered the room.

Briggs stood, "Good afternoon, I'm Sophie Briggs we spoke earlier today…" her voice trailing off as she noticed the expression on the lady's face.

Briggs turned to see what the lady was looking at.

"Sorry," Briggs said, taking a step toward Ben so that she could give him a prod. "This is Benjamin Grey. Ben lost his hearing as a child."

Ben turned around to see Briggs glaring at him. He quickly realised they were no longer alone in the room. He turned around the other way to greet the lady.

"Hi, I'm Benjamin Grey," he said, holding out his hand.

Ben couldn't hear his own speech and so couldn't be sure of how he sounded. He had learned how to speak as a child before a virus robbed him of his hearing. He was pretty confident the words he had learned as an eight-year-old sounded okay, but the words he had learned since, he was much less sure about.

Accepting the explanation for Ben's rudeness, the lady stepped forward and lightly shook Ben's hand. "Olivia Havishem," she said, "nice to meet you."

Ben realised he was now standing on the wrong side of the room. He would now have to squeeze past Mrs. Havishem in order to take the other individual chair, or risk further embarrassing himself by taking the two-seater for himself. He glanced at Briggs. Quickly Briggs stepped forward and ushered Mrs. Havishem toward the two-seater. Ben moved around to sit in the chair just vacated by Briggs.

"You have a beautiful home Mrs. Havishem," Briggs said, once they were all seated.

"Thank you, and please call me Olivia," she replied.

"Well," Briggs continued, "what is it Ben and I might be able to help with?"

"Yes. Thank you for coming to the house. As I mentioned to you on the phone, I'm concerned about what might be going on over at the mansion." Olivia started. She adjusted her posture to face Ben a little more, though she continued to speak to Briggs. "I've been seeing lights. You see the place is supposed to be empty. It's horrible really. The Henshaw's own the house, we call it the Mansion because it's the largest of the Cricklewood properties, but its real name is Henshaw Lodge. None of us like the name 'Lodge', makes it sound rather like a bed and breakfast, so it became known as the Mansion. Anyway, Robert and Emily, the Henshaw's, were tragically killed in an accident, must be five years ago now. They had three children. They're all grown up and have their own lives. The Mansion has remained empty since. It's been in the family since it was built in seventeen-fifty. But there were rumours the Henshaw's had run up some debts and the house itself was in a state of some disrepair. Anyway, following their death, the council declared the property unsuitable for living in. It seems none of the children were able, or willing, to take on the renovation costs. Arthur, my husband, he believes it's asbestos."

"Do you know if the children live close by?" Briggs asked.

"Elizabeth is the eldest. She's lovely, went to Oxford you know. She ended up marrying a banker. They have made New York their home now, though I'm sure they have a several properties. Junior, Robert the fifth, has found some success in marketing. He lives in the city. The youngest, Rupert, was a bit of a wild child as I remember. He travelled Africa for a time, no idea how he actually earned a living, but yes, he must be back in the country because I know he's been to visit the Stanley's on occasion."

"The Stanleys? They own the house on the other side?" Briggs asked.

"Yes. The latest Mrs. Stanley, seems nice but I find the husband, James, a bit aloof these days."

"The latest?" encouraged Briggs.

"Number three," Olivia confirmed. "Her name is Monica. I've really only met her a couple of times. Polish or somewhere around there. Speaks with an east European accent."

"You mentioned Rupert Henshaw had visited them." Briggs said.

"Yes. Was a bit surprised at the time as I'd never seen Rupert really interact with the Stanley's, even as a child."

"Did Rupert visit recently? Were you able to share your concerns about the property with him?" Brigg asked.

"No. I happened to be out doing a bit of gardening when I saw them together, James and Rupert. It's important to stay active as you get older. It looked like they were just on their way back from a walk. Rupert didn't even say 'Hello', you see as a boy, Rupert and my husband never really hit it off. Rupert was a bit rambunctious, and Arthur believes children should be seen and not heard, if you know what I mean."

Briggs smiled and looked across at Ben.

"So, what is it you would like us to do Mrs. Havishem?" Ben asked.

"Olivia please. I want you to find out what's going on at the Mansion of course. It wasn't just a one off. I've seen lights on a few times over the months. That's partly why I don't think it's squatters or whatever they are called these days. I mean if there is someone staying there illegally, the lights would be on a lot more often don't you think? And if it was adolescents, there'd be noise, parties, garbage, that sort of thing, wouldn't there?"

"Can you see lights at the mansion from here?" Ben asked.

Olivia shifted in her seat before answering. "Well, no, the first time I saw them I had just arrived back from my bridge club. It was later than I normally get home and I happened to notice lights up on the second floor, as I was driving up you understand. At night, the light creates a halo effect above the spruces. I was curious of course, because the place is supposed to be empty. There's a break in the trees, so I went to have a better look." She clasped her hands together before continuing. "I saw a light in two of the rooms on the second floor. Not the regular chandelier lights, but something else. Not a torch, something bigger, I'm not sure, a lamp light I assume."

"Did you notice anything else Olivia?" Briggs asked.

Olivia shook her head. "I'm not one to pry. It's not like I stood there all night in the cold. I didn't see anyone, but a light was definitely on."

"Liv, have you seen my boots!?" a voice shouted from outside the room.

"Alison was cleaning them for you. Have you tried the laundry room?" Oliva replied

A moment later and the head of an elderly man, ruddy in complexion and bald but for two streaks of grey on each side, appeared at the door.

"Has she told you the old place is haunted?" the man said. "Oh! Err hello," more directed at Briggs,

"The is my husband, Arthur."

"Where is Alison?" Arthur asked gruffly.

"How would I know? Have you checked the kitchen?" Olivia replied.

"Humph. I'm going out with Loredan to do a bit of hunting. We'll get dinner at the club."

"You can tell Alison, when you ask her about your boots." Arthur disappeared from view. "Sorry about that," Olivia said, returning her attention to Briggs, "You'd think he'd never set eyes on a coloured woman before. You are very beautiful you know, you remind me of that British actress." Olivia added. Briggs blushed. "Arthur thinks I'm being silly and shouldn't be sticking my nose into someone else's business." Olivia continued.

"Alison is your housekeeper?" asked Ben.

"Yes. She has her own quarters here. She helps us around the house, prepares meals and helps with the shopping. She's lovely. Arthur and I can still get around, but we feel like we're giving back a little. I mean, houses are so expensive these days, petrol prices, taxes just keep going up, I don't know how the young generation survive. We thought we could help by employing someone, give them some accommodation, and hopefully enable them to save up something for a place of their own. Of course, the help is still welcome. Alison is our third. She's very capable, it'll be a shame to lose her, when the time comes."

Olivia stood. Briggs quickly stood too. "Oh, it's ok, no need for all that," Olivia said with a wave of her hand. "I'm just going to fetch my phone," Olivia said.

Briggs returned to her seat as Olivia left the room. She looked at Ben who just shrugged. "What do you think?" Briggs asked.

"We need access to the house," he replied, "and permission, if we're going to look around the property." Briggs nodded.

Olivia returned to the room, holding her phone in front of her. "I received your email," she said, looking at Briggs. "You said it's okay to make the transfer using that email address?"

"Before you make any payment, Olivia, we need to know that we have permission to access the property. I'm not sure there's much we can achieve without access to the premises." Brigg said.

"Of course," Olivia replied, "I had assumed you would want to take a look around. I contacted Elizabeth and she has given you permission. There's a security lock on one of the doors at the rear of the east wing. I've just emailed Elizabeth's consent together with the code for the lock. You'll be able to enter the house from there. Now, can I assume you are good to investigate this for me? The Henshaw's were good friends, and I hate to think what might be going on there."

Briggs looked over to Ben. Ben nodded as though bidding in an auction. "Yes, we'd be happy to look into it." Briggs confirmed.

"Very good," Olivia replied, pressing onto her phone. "There, I've made the transfer as requested. I've signed the contract and returned that to you. I understand you may also need to make a claim for expenses. I expect an update from you at the end of each week, or sooner if anything of note comes up. And sorry again about my husband, it's not that he's racist, he's just well, you know…"

"Ignorant?" Briggs added, standing.

Olivia looked momentarily taken aback before a rue smile broke on her face, "well, yes, I suppose he is. But he does mean well, and he has a good heart under that gruff façade."

Briggs smiled. "Thank you, Olivia, we'll do our best," holding her hand out.

"Naomi," Olivia stated. Briggs was quizzical. "I just remembered the name of that actress, the one you remind me of, Naomi Harris I believe her name is. I'm an actress you know, or at least I was. Not many parts now for women my age."

"I think you'd make a wonderful Miss Marple," Briggs replied with a twitch of her nose.

CHAPTER TWO

Ben again found himself looking up at the Mansion. Briggs had taken the car to return to the office to cover another appointment. He wondered what the house must have looked like, what it must have been like for someone to live in such a place. To call such a place, home.

Ben's own upbringing was much more normal, if normal is measured by majority. He grew up in a mid to lower class semi-detached townhouse in the Benfleet area of Essex. His dad left when he was thirteen, and his mum did her best to make ends meet. Ben hadn't been abroad until he was seventeen, and then it was only because one of his friends had invited him along on a trip to Germany.

He turned to face the garage, which alone covered more floor space than the apartment he now shared with Briggs.

"Ok, let's make a start," he said to himself, and started walking toward the east wing of the house.

The entrance to the house faced south ensuring it captured the most of what the British sun had to offer. The east wing was easily seen from the driveway as it swept in from the south. It wasn't until Ben looked around earlier that he realised the property also had a west wing, making the house from the air, 'U' shaped. As he walked around the corner, he noted that some of the windows along the east wing had been blacked out. The white paint peeled and barely clinging onto the frames. He wondered how much of the decay had preceded the deaths of the Henshaws.

About half-way down the east wing, access to the rear was restricted by an iron gate, which was fixed to a solid looking fence. The fence ran behind a line of trees which ended at the border of the property with the Mansion. The gate was ajar.

Ben pushed on the gate, it provided little resistance and squeaked less than expected. He walked through the gate. Before he reached the end of the east wing he saw another detached stone building, similar in size to the garage but twice the height. There was a circular concrete area in an open area a little distance from the stone building. It soon occurred to Ben what he was looking at, a helicopter pad and hanger. *Who has a hangar at their home?*

He turned the corner of the east wing, to find yet another detached building at the rear of the property. This one, even larger than the others, rectangular and a modern design. The body of the building was made of large glass panelling, atop of a short brick foundation. The glass reached up two storeys before curving to create a convex roof. It reminded Ben of a garden centre, but in this setting, it must be…*a pool.*

Returning his attention to the east wing, he came to the rear entrance door with the electronic lock that Olivia had referred to. The door itself was at odds with all the others he had seen. Weathered but not worn and splintered. As he got to the door, he could see it wasn't made of wood. He tapped on the frame, *steel.* The lock was a numeric pad with a few additional buttons. Ben looked down at the palm of his hand and entered the code. A click followed a short whirr. He tried the handle, opened the door and stepped in.

Sunset would not be until eight pm but inside the house, the available light diminished markedly. Ben figured he had a little over an hour to inspect the home. He had never set foot in a stately home before and realised he had no idea how he was going to refer to each of the rooms. He pulled out his phone and took some pictures. The room he was now in had used newspapers on a tiled floor, and several shoe racks. Cupboards lined the back walls, stopping only to allow for a door, which would continue into the house. Over to his right, was a deep ceramic sink, more cupboards, and separate washer dryer machines. Ben turned around and looked back toward the door he had just entered. There was a plastic box attached to the wall next to the door. A thin black wire made its way from the box the short distance to the door frame, and then up and along the top of the door frame, before disappearing into the frame itself. Ben walked over to the box and gave it a wiggle. The lid of the box flipped open and revealed some simple wiring and a nine-volt battery. Ben closed the lid. He noticed the metal sensors on the door, and a wire disappearing into the plaster. He scanned the corners of the ceiling for cameras or detectors but saw none.

Stepping farther into the house, a door to the left led to a washroom. He tried the taps in the washroom, but nothing came out. A bucket partly filled with murky water had been placed next to the toilet. He tried the toilet handle, still connected but there was no water in the cistern. He didn't want to look under the seat.

Opposite the washroom, was an office. A substantial oak desk sat underneath a double window that looked out into the grounds. A green leather captain's chair was beside the desk. Dust and cobwebs had collected on top of the desk. Underfoot, a Persian rug covered the hardwood flooring along the desk. There were twin metal cabinets against one wall. One closed but with the keys still in the lock, the other with an open drawer. A few empty boxes littered the floor, along with more cobwebs, a few pieces of stationary, and mouse droppings. A tapestry of a race car hung on the wall behind the door, and a large ornate wooden cabinet stood against the far wall. The cabinet had several drawers below large doors with frosted windows. The room had otherwise been cleared.

Beyond the office was another room, similar in size and shape but this time a wooden waist-height shelf had been built to run the length of the far wall. Several cut-outs provided access to electrical outlets underneath. This room might also have served as a study, giving an occupant a view into the rear courtyard.

He progressed through the first floor, capturing pictures of the 'games' room that still housed a full-size snooker table, its dust cover still intact, scattered snooker cues and blue chalk on the floor. A flash was needed due to windows being covered. There was a 'media' room with cinema style seating and a large projector screen, the projector affixed to the ceiling. Crisps, popcorn and other crumbs littered the area. There was the faint smell of beer mixed with the damp, musty cool air.

Ben entered another substantial room with hardwood flooring partially covered by two of the largest rugs Ben had ever seen. There were four coffee tables, two on each rug, and more than a dozen old style armchairs. Continuing, he passed an elevator before arriving at a grand entrance hall. The space was enormous with a double height ceiling in the foyer and an open marbled staircase the centerpiece. The foot of the staircase was a crescent, perhaps twelve feet across. The main stairway split left and right before connecting to the first floor. Double doors each side of the staircase provided access to the grounds at the rear of the house. Ben stood on the first step looking around a moment to take in the scale. The staircase faced the oversized front doors. His eyes were drawn to the door hinges that would not have looked out of place on a drawbridge. The front entrance was arched with its apex well above Ben's height. He tried the handle which was, to his surprise, easy to press down though the doors were locked.

Moving toward the west wing, there was another smaller staircase leading down, followed by a formal dining room, a substantial kitchen that would have graced any successful restaurant. Beyond the kitchen, another open dining area followed by an informal seating area. Farther into the west wing, were a laundry, another washroom, and another open space with an imposing armoire, one of the doors hung open and stacks of board lay inside. He passed a library with rows of books coated in cobwebs. A conservatory followed, which Ben had seen earlier from the outside, large enough for the most ambitious garden party. Clouds were gathering. He didn't have long.

Ben jogged back to the main hall and up the grand staircase to the second floor. He entered a bedroom above the main entrance. There were curtains up at the window. The bed made ready but covered in dust, and cobwebs hung from the posters – natures mosquito net. Ben stood at the window and looked across the driveway and out toward the Havishem estate. He wondered if he was standing in the room where Olivia had seen the lights. He took a few more pictures before entering the next room. The next room was larger. At first it appeared empty but then he noticed several things of interest. Floor mats, like well worn yoga mats, lay on the floor on one side of the room, sprawled, not uniform, and certainly out of place. There was litter on the floor, tufts of long hair in different shades, and a couple of hair bands. Signs the room had been visited by mice. There was a desk and chair in one corner. A mirror rested on the desk, which was otherwise clear. Too clear. For once, a piece of furniture that wasn't caked in dust or tangled in webs.

A door led into an ensuite bathroom. Again, a bucket filled with murky water was placed next to the toilet. This time there was a roll of toilet paper on the holder. Ben became aware of the smell. He looked around. On the floor were cigarette butts, loosely grouped under a shelf. The shelf itself displaying the marks of repeated stubbing. Ben continued with his pictures before deciding there was little mileage in continuing further as the afternoon gave way to evening. As he left the room, he searched his pockets. He found a mint which he unwrapped and popped into his mouth. He then folded the wrapper and carefully wedged it into the top of the door jamb, as he closed the door.

Back outside the property, Ben pulled up the Uber app on his phone and booked a ride. *Fifteen minutes.* He looked up at the clouds and hoped the rain would stay. He walked over to the pond for a closer look at the statue. It was full of detail and to Ben's untrained eye, quite exquisite. The girl, whoever she might be, was elegant, charming even, as she poured water from an amphora she carried into the pool. No water ran from the container and the stagnant water had turned green.

Ben checked the app again, the driver was still a few minutes away. He walked across the driveway, and up onto a grassy embankment, looking for the break in the trees that Olivia had mentioned. It wasn't long before he thought he had found it. He stepped into the gap and poked his head in a little farther, and sure enough, the Havishem driveway revealed itself through the branches. He looked down at the ground. It was covered in dead needles from the trees, soft and uneven. As he looked back toward the Havishem house, he noticed headlights coming up the lane. He stepped back out from the trees as it started to rain. He walked briskly back across the driveway and took shelter at the main entrance. A few moments later his ride pulled up.

"Nice house."

"Not mine," Ben replied.

"Really?" the Driver said, though Ben was unable to detect the droll.

During the ride back, Ben used his phone to video chat with Briggs and offered to pick-up dinner on the way home. They settled for pie on chips.

"What did Mr. Samir want?" Ben asked, once they were both settled at the table.

"He wants me to spy on his wife. He thinks she's cheating on him." Briggs replied, placing a blob of ketchup on the side of her plate and pouring some red wine for them both.

"Do we have any vinegar?" Ben asked.

"In that cupboard to the right of the stove," Briggs replied, with a wave of her hand in that general direction. She waited for Ben to return before continuing. "I am to undertake surveillance for two weeks. Mr. Samir believes that should be sufficient time to find out one way or the other. He's paying time and expenses."

"What do you think? Does it sound like she's stepping out on her husband?"

Briggs shrugged, "Dunno, he must be what, late fifties, and she can't be more than mid thirties. She's attractive, he's.... not, so may be. What about you? I assume you took a look inside?"

Ben nodded. He relayed the afternoon at the Mansion, room by room.

"It's not haunted," he said.

"I'm sure Olivia will be most relieved," Briggs replied, pouring herself another glass of wine.

"I'll go back tomorrow and spend some time looking around."

"I'll be out with my camera most of the day. I have a list of Mrs. Samir's appointments for the week, at least those her husband knows about. I'm sure I'll have time where I'm just waiting around, so if you need any help or background gathering, I can help with that."

"It is a bit odd. I think Mrs. Havishem likely did see something. The power is off, no water, I assume the gas and electric are off." Ben mused.

"Squatters?" Briggs suggested.

"Possibly, but I don't think so. Didn't see any sign of a break in, and there was this desk in one of the bedrooms. The only piece of furniture that I came across that wasn't covered in dust. And it was cold in there, but I didn't see any blankets or sleeping bags. And the place was clean, well kind of, I mean other than what you'd expect from a place that's been empty a few years."

"Are you trying to infer squatters are dirty bastards?" Briggs asked.

Ben smiled, "No, I would just have expected more mess that's all. I think someone has been in there, and frankly, kept the place better than my old bedsit."

"You said that as though your bedsit was a paragon of cleanliness."

Ben frowned. "I'll open a case file tomorrow and download the pictures I took. Do we have any motion cams?"

"Still in the box, try one of the boxes marked 'office' in the storage."

Briggs had left. Ben had spent thirty minutes rummaging around in the storage room for the cameras, and then some for batteries. He checked the time on his phone, grabbed the car keys, snatched the cameras and headed out the door. He realised he hadn't locked up or changed the sign to let any potential clients know how to reach them.

Briggs had taken the Tesla which left him with the Corsa. The Tesla had been a gift from Brigg's mother on learning she had started her own business. Her father was far less impressed that she had given up a promising career in MI5, to go into business 'with an uneducated yobbo'. She hadn't shared Ben's heroics in 'saving London' with her father.

Satisfied he had everything he needed, Ben drove off to the Cricklewood Mansion.

As Ben drove up toward the Mansion, Olivia Havishem was pruning bushes along her driveway. She looked up but seemed unsure who was in the car. Ben wound down his window and waved. After a moment, she waved back, clippers in hand.

Ben pulled up at the Mansion, the gloom of the house matching the clouds in the sky. His agenda for the day would see him complete an inspection inside, followed by a closer look around the outside of the main building and the external buildings. And if time, a nosey around the extensive grounds.

Starting back on the second floor, he examined the area in more detail. Upon reaching the top of the grand staircase, one was greeted with enormous bay windows on either side, allowing light to flood into the landing from the rear of the property, while providing a panoramic view of the grounds.

The area close to the property was flat and largely lawned, though now overgrown and wild. Discreet footpaths led away from the house, connecting to the pool, the other buildings – a gazebo, a covered stage, the helipad, and a footpath that morphed into a trail as it vanished into the trees beyond. A circular fountain centered by Apollo standing proud, naked and weathered created a focal point.

Ben turned around, he was standing across from the bedroom he had entered yesterday. The bedroom with the desk was to his right. To his left, were two smaller rooms, set back from the bedrooms, and another much larger room that would have taken up the whole south-east corner. The first of the smaller rooms was a laundry area, housing industrial looking washer and dryer machines.

Ben found his descriptions all to be relative. The laundry room was larger than Mum's kitchen. Between the laundry room and the enormous corner room, is a storage room comprised entirely of slatted shelving. Some of the shelves were clear, others had towels, bedding, curtains. As he stepped in, a mouse scuttled past him, out the door, along the skirting boards, and under the door into the corner room. Ben stepped back out and followed the mouse.

Double doors with glass panelling opened into the room. A mini-grand piano stood in one corner. A dusty white sheet covered the piano, but its features were unmistakable. Between windows that looked out to the front of the house, several guitars lined the wall. A mix of electric and acoustic, some with broken strings. Amplifiers were placed around the room. In another corner, a large rug covered the hardwood floor. On top of the rug were an assortment of different instruments. Ben walked in, the creaks from the floorboards echoed. Another pair of double-doors farther down led back out into the east wing.

Ben walked over to a window. From here he could just make out the front gate. He was trying to make sense of the house. A bedroom with a fully made bed that hadn't been touched. Untouched blankets and bedding. Those guitars must be worth a small fortune to anyone struggling for money. The piano, yeah okay, that's not going anywhere easily. But the mats on the floor in that empty bedroom, food crumbs and cigarette butts, the hair strands. Someone has been here and recently to, but limited their movements to that one room.

With only half the house explored, Ben continued with the second floor. In the east wing, that started with the Music Room, there were four more bedrooms each with its own bathroom, and a separate washroom presumably to service users of the Music Room. The beds remained made, and according to the webs, untouched. At the end of the wing was the largest bedroom, twice the size of the others. It also benefited from a grand balcony that opened to the rear. The closet, which made Ben laugh when he noted the space down, due to its size, still contained clothing – expensive looking dresses, coats, jackets, and ball gowns. A glance at some of the labels revealed these were not cheap knockoffs.

The west wing was dominated by an even larger master bedroom. Similar in design to its east wing cousin. The ensuite had been modernised. Flush speakers peppered the ceiling, LED lighting, jacuzzi, sauna, a shower for…perhaps six, and furnishings that would not look out of place in any

New York penthouse. This too, had a balcony leading to the rear gardens. Ben took pictures of every room saving them under names he hoped would allow him to reassemble them into a collage of the whole house.

As he walked back down the stairs, his phone vibrated. A text. Briggs saying, she was parked outside a hot yoga class. Ben replied, *'still looking round. Place is enormous.'* At the foot of the grand staircase, Ben headed to his right and down the small stairway to the basement.

With no natural or unnatural light, Ben reached into his jacket and took out a torch. He had come prepared. At the foot of the stairs a corridor ran left and right. Like the other floors, several doors lined the corridor.

A door led into an open living-kitchen space. Some natural light entered the area courtesy of rectangular windows across the top of the facing external walls. The space was furnished, tidy but as with the rest of the house, uninhabited for years. The kitchen had appliances. A tall cupboard housed a mop and bucket, a sweeping brush and various cleaning items. A cupboard next to the fridge freezer still had cereal boxes and a few soup tins. A door, only accessible from inside this living room, led into a bedroom and a small ensuite. Ben labelled the area, 'housekeeper quarters.'

Back out into the corridor, Ben shone his torch in both directions. At both ends, light reflected back at him from what he assumed must be glass doors. Exploring he came across more storage, another laundry room, a wine cellar empty but for a few bottles, a walk-in freezer – not functioning but the walls were lined in steel and several meat hooks hung from the ceiling. There was another commercial-sized kitchen fit.

On the other side of the hall, a washroom, a separate shower room that connected to changing rooms. Concrete steps went up to a door that must provide access to ground level. Heading back toward the staircase he had used, he passed the elevator and carried on down the hallway to the glass doors at the other end.

He pulled on a glass door. The hinge creaked either from the weight or the lack of use, possibly both, and swung open into another hallway. Light from the torch was swallowed by the darkness as Ben pointed it into the space beyond. He walked in, lighting his footing as he went.

The flooring had changed from the tiles in the hallway, to the familiar hardwood flooring of the upper floors. This space was huge, even making the Music Room seem small by comparison. Swathes of fabric adorned the wall that would have been at the front of the house. A tapestry of the Mappa Mundi centered the wall.

Opposite to where Ben had entered the room, were chairs stacked up against the wall, fifty, a hundred, maybe even more, all stacked up along the eastern wall. As he moved the light around, he made out tables, lots of them, folded and neatly arranged along the south wall under the tapestry. The rest of the time in the room revealed a stage fitted with lighting, curtains, mics and speakers. And a cloakroom, empty but for the railing and hangers for a hundred guests. Ben was in the Ballroom.

The remainder of the morning was sent checking the remaining rooms and spaces. As with almost all the rest of the house, these spaces had not been used in years. With nothing further of note, Ben went to explore the grounds.

Outside of the house, Ben looked for any signs of a break-in. In the two years since the 'London Saved' incident, Briggs had spent most of it trying to convince Ben to work as an investigator and give purpose to his gift. But Ben was no investigator and while his gift had contributed to the saving of hundreds of lives, he had no idea how it would help him in the more mundane. He still didn't.

He eventually gave in when Briggs approached him with the idea of a partnership. She would leave MI5 and they would set up as private investigators 'Grey and Briggs'. She had even conceded that his name be placed first, even though she was the one with all the training, expertise and contacts. While looking for premises and applying for a business licence, Briggs put Ben through several months of training. With several months training under his belt, he saw no sign of forced entry.

He wandered over to the garage block. He knew Briggs had tried to gain entry before but armed with his torch he figured he could at least peer in through a window. He pressed the torch up against the glass door and looked in. He could make out a covered vehicle, a car, though what model he had no idea. Then another. And behind the cars facing the rear doors, was a sit-on mower and some other types of machinery. He moved the torch around trying to get a view of the sides. Rows of shelving contained all kinds of materials and containers. Ben walked around to the other door. The light revealed a row of gardening tools, placed on hooks and arranged across the length of the far wall. Empty the building would have had ample space for several vehicles.

Not far behind the garage, stood a greenhouse. Aged and needing repair, some of glass panes had broken and a part of the aluminium frame had bent. Whatever plants had been benefiting from care and attention, were now withered and long passed any form of recovery. Weeds had taken root.

Walking parallel to the Havishem property border, Ben came to a basketball court. He didn't know if it was full size or not, but it did have a hoop at either end. The lawn area continued past the court and on for maybe another hundred feet before hitting trees.

A path meandered west from the basketball court, and Ben soon noticed a metal pole in the ground a few inches across. The grass was overgrown, but it was still possible to make out the shape of a tennis court.

Now at the rear of the property, Ben was drawn to the indoor swimming pool. As he approached, he could see the entrance doors had been chained and padlocked. The building itself was largely glass and making it was easy to look in to see the general layout. The doors would have opened into a lobby area and opposite the entrance were doors marked male and female changing. Adjacent to the changing rooms, was an open area carpeted in thick blue mats surrounded by a series of various weights, dumbbells, and exercise machines. Ben walked along the southern edge. Opposite the weights were a line of differing cardio machines, two treadmills, two ellipticals, a pair of rowing machines, and exercise bikes. An archway leads through into the pool area. The pool was empty and some twenty metres in length. On the far side, a hot tub and next to that an odd-looking tube disappearing from the floor off into the ground. Even at seven million, Ben was beginning to think this place might be a bargain.

By the time he reached the end of what had now referenced the leisure building, he could clearly see the helipad. The concrete rectangle cracked, and its edges overtaken by grass and weeds. Flaked white paint marked out an 'H'. Ben turned back to the house, a huge 'U' shape. To his left, the hangar. Two track lines were visible along the ground. Two lines of cement a foot wide running from the pad to the hangar. Ben had no idea how a helicopter might be moved but assumed whatever the solution was it had to involve wheels.

Ben picked up his pace and walked over to the hanger. The two lines disappeared under an oversized double garage door. A regular sized door provided side access into the building, and there several windows along the side wall. Ben shone the torch into the building.

Any hopes of seeing the helicopter were dashed. The building was empty. As a child he had dreamed of owning a helicopter. He remembered being fascinated that they could fly straight up, circle around and lean this way and that. His mind flashed back to himself playing with the black helicopter that shot orange missiles at 007's white Lotus Esprit. One of his last memories of his mother's voice was her asking, 'Isn't James Bond supposed to win?', as he blasted the spy's Aston with the missiles.

Ben checked the time and had a toss-up in his mind between heading back into the house or seeing if the Stanley's were at home. His stomach won and he chose to head back into the village for some lunch.

The village of Church Stowe is centered around St. Michaels church and falls within the Stowe Nine Churches parish. Given the parish only benefits from two churches, the origins of its name are unclear. What was clear to Ben, the local pub, the 'Mort & Pestle', had steak and kidney pie on the menu.

Inside was cozy and traditional. He was greeted with a smile from the barmaid who, like Ben, appeared to be in her late twenties.

"Menu, love?' she asked.

Ben nodded and looked around for a table to sit at.

"Anything to drink?" the woman asked. Ben was still looking around, and unaware she had said anything. She repeated herself, just as Ben turned to look at her. He caught the last word.

Pointing to his ear, Ben said, "Sorry, I'm a bit deaf. Yes, please, err, Porter?"

She gave a faint nod of understanding. The smile returning, she asked, "Fuller's, okay?".

"Sure, thanks."

The only customers were two gents playing cribbage at one of seven tables, and another sat alone at the bar looking into his almost empty glass. Ben took a stool and sat at the bar. The customer at the bar tipped his head.

The woman handed him a menu. "You're not from around here," she stated, making a point of looking Ben in the eye.

"No," Ben replied, hoping that was sufficient. It wasn't. The woman remained next to him, *go on* written on her face. Ben took a moment to weigh his options.

"I've been asked to take a look around the Mansion," he said, convinced she wasn't leaving until he had said something.

"The Henshaw place? It's been empty for years now."

"Yes, I'd noticed."

"What's to see there?" she asked.

"Er, do you mind if I get the steak and kidney pie?"

"Chips, boiled or mashed potatoes?"

"Chips please."

"Gravy?"

"Sure."

"Anything else I can get you love?" she asked.

"No, that'd be great, thank you."

Ben took out his phone and texted Briggs to let her know he was having lunch and asked how she was getting on. *Sat outside a shopping mall,* she responded, *thinking to grab a wrap or something before she comes out.*

"Here you go love. You speak to Rupert yet?" she said, placing the pint down.

"Not yet, no. You know him?" Ben replied.

"Occasionally he'll come in here. He's an IPA man and rather partial to our fish. It wasn't Rupert then that asked you to check on the house?"

"No, Mrs. Havishem. She thought she had seen lights on at the property. Asked me if I'd look into it."

"You an investigator or something?" she asked.

Ben nodded, "Yeah."

She looked him up and down. "You seem a bit young?"

"How old am I supposed to be?" Ben replied.

"Alright, just sayin'. Do you have a card or something? I can let you know if I hear anything."

Ben felt a sudden pang of guilt as that wasn't a bad idea. He reached into his jacket pocket and handed her a business card. She took it and looked at the details.

"Which one are you, Grey or Briggs, or do you just work for them?"

"I'm Grey, Benjamin Grey," he replied.

She raised her eyebrows, seemingly impressed, "Well, I'm Marina and if you need anything love, just holla."

While waiting for his food to arrive, Ben browsed the news across the internet. Fears of another Covid outbreak, China tightening its stronghold on Taiwan, seemingly impervious to international sanctions, the first black PM grappling with the collapse of the NHS and rising inflation. He switched to more local news and the tragic murder of a black teenager, Caroline Walters, in Milton Keynes, which had sparked a protest outside Bletchley Thames Valley Police Station. Another report of a missing teenage girl had reports asking if the two incidents could be connected. Ben followed the Caroline Walters link. The teenager was fourteen, an immigrant from Nigeria. The other missing teen was white Caucasian, Louise Larke, the fourteen-year-old daughter of Romanian parents who had settled in nineteen years earlier. The protests against the Police claimed they were guilty of taking the missing white teenager more seriously than the murder of Caroline Walters.

"Here you go love," the barmaid said, placing the meal in front of him. "Ketchup? Vinegar?" she added.

Ben looked down at the thick brown gravy over his pie. "No, I'm good, thanks. Do you know how Stowe Nine Churches came by its name?" he asked, attempting to be more social.

The woman stopped and smiled.

"Most people don't ask, I think they just assume we have that many churches around here. But we only have two. The official reason has something to do with the Lord of the Manor of Stowe having the authority to recommend people to be the Rector of nine churches around Stowe."

"Stowe Manor?" asked Ben

"It's a posh school, now. The one over near the circuit."

"And the unofficial reason?" Ben asked, feigning interest.

"Well, there are several, but my favourite is the builders of St. Michaels failing eight times to complete the church. Only on the ninth did they succeed."

"How did they manage to fail eight times?" Ben enquired.

"The Devil," she said, with a little too much enthusiasm for Ben's taste. "Each time they began to build the church, the Devil himself would come and destroy what they'd done. Not to be put off, the builders persevered, and defeated their enemy on the ninth attempt."

Ben nodded, "Yeah. That's a good one."

"Best be eating your food now, love, before it gets cold."

Ben took a swig of his beer and tucked into the food.

Stomach satisfied and now on his way back to the Mansion, Ben noticed a woman in the Stanleys' driveway, petite with blond hair tied in a ponytail. She looked in her late thirties and was unloading groceries from the back of the Range Rover. She turned and looked at him, as he drove around the roundabout to the Mansion. Ben pulled up just outside the gate and walked back toward the Stanley's property.

"Hi!" He called out to the woman. She placed a heavy looking grocery bag back into the boot of the car, then turned back toward him. "My name is Benjamin Grey, I'm a private investigator," very much hoping he was speaking clearly. "Mrs. Havishem has some concerns that there may be people hanging out at the Mansion. I wondered if you might have seen anything?" Ben continued, walking toward the woman.

"You don't look like a private investigator," she said.

"I actually thought this was my best private investigator look," he replied.

She smiled, "Then I think you need to try harder," she said.

Ben held out his hand as he approached, "Benjamin Grey, nice to meet you."

The lady glanced over her shoulder toward the house. "I am Monica Stanley. James Stanley is my husband." She didn't shake Ben's outstretched hand.

Monica Stanley stood just a couple of inches shorter than Ben, making her five feet eight in her trainers. She had striking blue eyes and the red lipstick she wore, popped from her pale white complexion. She wore light blue jeans, a white blouse under a red pullover.

"Sorry for the interruption, but I just wanted to ask if either yourself or your husband may have noticed anyone at the Henshaw place over the last few weeks or months?" said Ben.

"The house has been empty for a few years now, even before James and I got married. Rupert checks in on the house occasionally, but other than that, no, I haven't seen anyone there. I assume you know who Rupert is?" she said. Ben nodded. "Wouldn't be much of an investigator if you didn't," she chuckled.

"So, nothing at all? No noises, no vehicles, no lights or anything? Ben asked.

"Who are you?" came a voice from behind the car. A stern looking man approached, dressed in a tweed jacket and blue jeans, an inch shorter than Monica, at least ten years older and twice her weight.

"Benjamin Grey sir," Ben said, holding out his hand.

The man looked Ben up and down. "What are you doing here?" he asked, ignoring the hand in front of him.

"Sorry, I was just saying to your wife that I have been asked by Mrs. Havishem to follow up on some concerns that she has regarding the Henshaw property." Ben replied.

"Busying herself in other people's business," the man stated.

"Mrs. Havishem has seen lights inside the property, several times in the last few months. Given the property is supposed to be vacant, she was concerned that someone, perhaps squatters, may have broken in and taken up refuge."

"Of course, they haven't. And if they had, it would be a matter for the police, not some… Who are you, anyway?"

"I'm a private investigator, hired by Mrs. Havishem."

"You don't look like a private investigator," the man responded sharply. Monica turned away, grinning.

"Yes. I'm sorry for the interruption, I just thought there would be no harm in asking if you had seen anything at all."

The man paused, then let out a breath. "We haven't seen anything unusual. Probably what Olivia saw was simply Rupert who on occasion comes over to check in on the property. I take it you've had a look around?"

"Yes sir."

"And no sign of a break-in?"

"No sir," Ben replied, now feeling like he was responding to his old school headmaster.

"Well, there you go then. Your job is done Mr. Grey."

"Thank you. Mr. Stanley, I take it?" Ben asked.

"Yes, this is my husband James," Monica replied, before Mr. Stanley could respond.

Ben took out a business card and offered it to Mr. Stanley. James Stanley made not attempt to hide the disdain as he looked down at the card.

Monica reached out and took the card, "Thank you, Mr. Grey. If we do see anything, we'll be sure to let you know," she said.

Mr. Stanley rolled his eyes, turned, and went back to the house, leaving Monica to continue unloading the shopping.

"Thank you," Ben said, "I don't suppose I could help you with those?"

"I don't think that would be a good idea, do you?" she replied.

Ben smiled awkwardly, nodded, and made his way back up the driveway to his car.

Sat back in the car, Ben checked himself in the rear-view mirror. *What the hell is a private investigator supposed to look like anyway?* He asked himself.

Ben spent the next two hours walking the Mansion grounds. He discovered the trail that led from the gazebo into the woods, did in fact continue for about half a mile before coming to a pond, though Ben had no idea of what the distinction between a pond and a lake might be. He also had no idea if he remained on the Mansion grounds or not.

Walking back, he took a different path through the trees. One he expected would take him closer to the rear of the Stanley property. He eventually came out of the woods, some distance from Stanley property, and found himself standing at one end of a made road. The road headed off in the direction of the village. A locked gate with a 'Private Property' sign blocked the end of the made road from the unmade track that continued into the wood. Ben looked around and felt fairly confident of his bearings. The Mansion grounds behind him, a field and no doubt the Stanleys to his right, the village ahead. He leaned against the gate.

The air was cool and fresh except for the faint but unmistakable whiff of manure. Ben pulled a soft mint from his jean pocket. He looked down at his boots, a pair Briggs had bought him for his birthday a couple of years back. He kicked them against the metal gate to shift some of the mud that had collected. He noticed cigarette butts on the ground. A concentration of them. He took a picture of them with his phone. Returning the phone to his back pocket, he looked back toward the field and could see signs of a trodden path. Subtle, but the long grass had definitely been pressed forward, leading from the gate, across the field and into the woods. He followed.

Ben soon realised the track he was following was curving around and away from the Stanley House, and more to the direction of the Mansion. He continued and reached the woods. He stopped to see if there were any indications as to where the trail went from there. None, at least not to Ben's untrained eyes. But he did feel like he was facing more toward the Mansion. He continued into the woods and came across a chain fence to this his left that must mark the edge of the Stanley property.

Ben continued, and the fence veered off away from him. Continuing farther, it wasn't long before he stepped out from the woods and found himself standing within sight of the helipad.

Rain drops started to patter against Ben's leather jacket. He made his way across the grounds, around the house and back to his car. He took the cameras from the car and headed back to the house. At the back door he looked around for a suitable placement. Nothing. He entered the code, stepped inside, and again looked around for somewhere suitable. Again, nothing, that would give a view of anyone passing without making the presence of the camera obvious.

The cameras were self-contained two-inch cubes that housed the camera, a motion detector that turned on the recording, a sim card for storage, and a rechargeable battery. It was quick and easy, but not exactly the stuff of spy films.

He wanted a camera somewhere near this entrance, but where? With no obvious place, he went into the house and upstairs to the bedroom with the desk. He looked around and understood why proper spy cams had to be so small. He walked over to the desk and had an idea. Feeling under the edge of the desk, he thought he could attach the camera underneath. He bent down and played with the positioning of the camera.

The small box he had been using to carry the cameras around in also contained a few items to help fix them to different surfaces.

Five minutes later, Ben emerged from under the desk, sore but satisfied with his work. The camera was well hidden under the desk and pointing toward the bathroom. Unlikely to capture the face of anyone going into the bathroom, unless they were a small child, the camera would at least confirm the presence of someone.

Back at the rear entrance, he placed the camera discreetly behind the top edge of a cupboard. He had to use a chair from the office for elevation. Checking the time, he messaged Briggs with '*all set*' and left the property.

Outside the Havishem home, Ben pressed the doorbell. Alison answered and after exchanging pleasantries invited Ben in, asking him to wait in the same sitting room as before. It didn't have to wait long.

"I wondered if you might come here, after I saw you earlier," she said, "Is your lady with you?"

"Er, no. Sophie is working on another case." Ben replied, unsure what she might be implying.

"Then I guess you will have to do. How can I help?"

"May I ask, what made you contact us?" he asked, trying to ignore the earlier remark.

Olivia breathed in and straightened her back, "You mean, why did I specifically ask for you?" Ben nodded. "I remembered you from that terrorist attack. As I was led to believe, it would have been a terrible attack were it not for you. But I think what you are really asking is, how did I know to ask for you?" she said with mischief.

Ben smiled and shifted in his seat, "It was really a team effort, I'm not sure I had that much to do with the outcome."

"You are too modest Mr. Grey," she chastened, "Arthur has a friend in the Met, well he used to be, Retired Assistant Commissioner. I don't think he'd ever met you, but he had certainly heard the rumours."

"Sorry, what rumours?" Ben asked.

Olivia's eyes tightened, "There were rumours that you had some sort of *gift*. What it might be was open to speculation. But what people were sure about was that you had something. Something that gave you access to information the police and the intelligence services, did not. You have an advertisement on the notice board near the bus stop outside Lewis' in Milton Keynes. I don't use the bus of course, but Arthur drops me there occasionally when I want to do a spot of shopping. Grey, with an 'e', and Briggs Private Investigators, it wasn't hard to connect the two." Olivia paused for a moment. "I don't know what your gift might be. I guess it's possible you might be connected to some hacker group or something, but it really doesn't matter to me. I know your partner was an experienced MI5 officer. She must see something in you, and I am satisfied with that. All I want to know is Mr. Grey, will you find out what is going on at the Mansion?"

Later that afternoon Ben arrived back at the office. He let himself in, made himself a cup of tea, sat down and scanned through the pictures he had taken.

Eventually he got up and went into one of the offices where a glass eraser board hung on the wall. Browsing through the pictures again, he made a start, writing words on to the board: 'Desk', 'Cigarettes', 'Field', 'Guitars', 'Yoga Mats', 'Bedding'. He logged on to the computer and printed pictures of each and stuck them up next to each word.

A light in the corner of the office came on, someone had opened the front door. Ben came from the office to see Briggs closing the door behind her.

She smiled, "Cup of tea?" she asked.

Over dinner Briggs shared her day, concluding there was nothing so far that suggested Mrs. Samir was cheating on her husband. Ben shared how Olivia Havishem had come to ask for Benjamin Grey, with an 'e', by name.

After dinner, Ben showed her the case he had opened for 'the Cricklewood Mansion' and the words he'd placed on the board. She sat in the office browsing the pictures on Ben's phone, while he stood at the board. She looked up to see Ben staring at her.

"Okay, so tell me why you've written those words." She said.

Ben visibly sighed, "I thought I was the one with the hearing difficulty." He started over. "I've written 'Desk' because it's the only piece of furniture that isn't covered in cobwebs. It's clean, relatively, which means someone has been using it."

"Or it's been recently placed there," Briggs added.

Ben frowned, "Why would someone put a desk in the room?"

Briggs shrugged, "I don't know. But I also don't know why someone would specifically want to keep that desk clean. Obviously, the desk serves some purpose and given the mirror, someone is likely checking their appearance or something."

"Right," Ben agreed.

"Okay, why 'Cigarettes'?" she asked.

"I found these in the ensuite of the bedroom that the desk is in. I could still smell them, so someone was smoking in there not long ago. Also, I found another pile of butts at this gate at the end of a road at the back of the properties. And when I say the back, I mean hundreds of metres away."

Briggs was looking down at the phone. After a moment, the printer whirred into action and spit out a piece of paper.

"You can print from the phone?" Ben asked.

"Of course, it's all networked," Briggs replied. "Here's the other picture you took of the cigarettes at the gate." She passed it to Ben who stuck it up next to the picture from the bathroom. They both peered at the two pictures.

"Okay, the same brand," she said.

"I wrote 'Field' because there seemed to be a trail from the road going off into the woods at the back of the houses. See, here," he said, pointing to the downtrodden grass. "Why would someone be walking there?" Ben added.

"Where does it go once you hit the woods?" Briggs asked.

Ben shrugged, "Couldn't be sure. There's a chain link fence that encloses the Stanley property, or you can head another way and eventually come out in the Mansion's rear gardens. I couldn't determine where the trail might have gone. To be honest, the whole thing could be part of the Mansion's grounds."

"Easy enough to check," Briggs replied.

"Okay, Guitars?" she asked.

"Well, here's the thing. When someone comes to you and says they've seen lights in an abandoned building, you think squatters. The Stanley's clearly do, and likely Olivia would have had the same response from the local police. If it were squatters, there's no sign of a break in, and why would they leave something of value like the guitars behind. They would be easy enough to pawn. Squatters wouldn't ignore them."

"Yoga mats?" Briggs encouraged.

"They're also in the bedroom with the desk and rolled out as if in use. But the bedrooms still have made-up beds in them. Again, if you're just bunking in the house, why wouldn't you just crash on one of the beds?"

"Bedding?"

"There's a storage room the size of this one that contains blankets and bedding. Again, it makes no sense that these haven't been touched, if we were talking about squatters. The place is cold enough not to ignore the bedding."

"So, what are the options here?" Briggs asked. She grabbed a pen from the board and started to write, away from where Ben had placed his words.

She wrote: 'Squatters', 'Nobody', 'Rupert/Family', 'Known Someone'. "I'm inclined to agree with you, I don't think this is squatters or a stranger looking for a bunk for the night. They wouldn't know the code to get in, they wouldn't ignore the beds or the valuables in the house. Olivia doesn't strike me to be someone easily mistaken and the desk room shows someone has been there recently. That leaves a family member, we've been told Rupert visits so it could be him, or someone a family member may have shared the code with, a 'known someone'. Either of these might visit but not need to stay overnight."

"Rupert would explain Olivia seeing something, it would explain why the valuables remain untouched. But what would he be doing with the yoga mats or that desk with a mirror?" Ben replied.

"You're going to have to ask him? Or it's someone they have given the code to, that may have needed a place to crash." She said. "You met with the Stanleys' then?"

"Yeah. I saw Mrs. Stanley unloading the car as I arrived. Mr. Stanley came out as I was just asking Monica if she'd seen anything."

"Monica, huh?" Briggs teased.

"Being rich must be attractive. She's half his age, and yes, somewhat pretty. But as you know, blonds are not my type."

"Olivia mentioned she is Polish."

"I couldn't tell," Ben replied, smiling.

"So, what are you going to do next?"

Ben considered his next move. "Clearly, I'm going to need to talk to Rupert."

"And what about the other thing?" Briggs asked.

"What other thing?"

"Your gift. Couldn't you stay somewhere nearby and see what you can uncover?"

"I don't see how that's going to help."

"You always say that. You don't know what you might stumble across. If it's not squatters and the family or someone known to the family is using it, you should…do your thing. Tune-in to whatever the neighbours might be gossiping about. You don't have to be onsite."

"I could get a room at the Pub in the village, that'd be within range," his enthusiasm moving up a notch from zero to one.

"What are you waiting for?" Briggs asked.

"What? You mean now?"

"Sure, why not?"

Thirty minutes later, Ben was putting his sleepover bag into the back of the Corsa. Briggs gave him a hug and politely kissed his cheek.

"Good luck," she said.

CHAPTER THREE

Ben pulled into the car park at the back of the Mort & Pestle. It was dark and raining. He waited a moment for the wipers to clear the drops from the windscreen. Briggs had booked him the room and told him he can enter through the Guests door at the rear if he didn't want to walk through the bar. As the screen momentarily cleared, he saw the entrance at the corner of the building. Grabbing his bag from the passenger seat, he trotted over to the door.

Inside, a long corridor ran the length of the building. Off to his right, a carpeted staircase led up. A desk stood near the foot of the stairs, with a closed Guest book on it, and a sign that read 'Please Check In at the bar'. Ben sighed. Leaving his bag at the desk, he took the corridor which led to the bar.

The place was busy, the tables were occupied, and patrons lined the bar. A short, older woman was serving at the bar. She saw Ben enter from the back.

"You checking-in love!?" she shouted across from her position.

Ben nodded. The woman said something to a customer before walking over to him.

"Marina, can you cover the front for a moment!?" the woman shouted over her shoulder, toward an open doorway. The woman wiped her hands on a cloth and headed over, past Ben and down the corridor he had just come from. Ben followed.

At the desk, the woman turned and looked at him, seemingly waiting for something.

"Sorry, did you say something?" Ben asked, "My ears don't work. I can read lips but I need to be able see your face."

"Oh, sorry." she said, with a giggle, "Could I take a swipe of your credit card please? Or you can tap."

Ben paid for his room and after receiving directions and other essential information, made his way up the stairs. The room, like the bar area, was cozy. The building was old, he wasn't sure how old, but the walls on the outside were stone, and large exposed stained beams ran through the ceilings anchoring the walls. The carpeted floors creaked underneath. The door to his room creaked. Even the faucets creaked as he turned the taps on to wash his hands. Ben checked the time, nine p.m., and decided he should get work.

Laying on the bed, Ben closed his eyes and regulated his breathing. Deep breaths, slower, slower, slow. He would focus on the phosphenes behind his eyelids. He was looking for a place.

After losing his hearing, Ben started to hear voices. The voices would enter his head as he drifted toward sleep. He was terrified at first, so was his mother when he first told her about them, thinking they were imaginary. Turns out they were not.

But over the years, in secret he learned how to utilise this ability. The voices only came as he teetered on the edge of sleep. Too far and he drifted off to sleep and the voices disappeared. If he was disturbed or stirred from his semi-conscious state, the voices were lost. The voices were only at the edge, the place between awake and asleep, this was the place Ben was trying to get to.

Ben drifted. He imagined the lights he could see at the back of his eyelids, were stars in the expanse of space, moving and fleeting as he travelled at speed through the universe. And as he did, voices began to emerge, like they might as one tuned into one an analogue radio. It had taken countless hours to master. At first, the voices flooded in, overwhelming him and threatening to drive him mad. But he persevered, the curiosity of youth prevailing over his fear. Ben gradually and with the practice required to master any skill, learned how to filter through the crowds and isolate any voices of interest. To focus and discard at will.

Through the years, he discovered several other things relating to his *gift*. There were different *types* of voices. Regular voices like those he heard before losing his hearing. But also, those he had come to call *whispers*. The whispers were different to the voices of those merely speaking quietly in that warbled, the sound like the light from a lighthouse, would come close only to spin away before briefly returning again.

He came to understand these whispers were the unspoken thoughts of people. He also learned his gift had a range, a limited range. Still not sure of its exact limits, he had figured it to be a radius of between ten to fifteen miles.

Why he had this gift, where it came from, he had no clue. Over the months and years, listening seemed to bring him only sadness, a revelation of all the hate and wickedness in people's hearts. The fallen state of mankind. Rarely would he stumble across the light in people's voices. The sacrifice one would make for another, their wealth, assets and even parts of themselves, given without hesitation and condition. Usually for a loved one, but on a singular occasion, a stranger.

But love, compassion, and sacrifice, were, in Ben's experience, qualities much rarer than gold.

Two years ago, while Ben was scanning the airwaves, he stumbled across a conversation between men plotting an attack. A few months later, a massive terrorist attack on the Queen Elizabeth bridge and its tunnels averted, and the mastermind captured. London had been saved.

Ben's role in the success of the operation went largely unknown, or so he thought. A Vancouver based detective reached out to him shortly after the event for assistance in tracking a young girl, and now Olivia had revealed that there were rumours.

Ben had also learned he could hear nothing from the unconscious. He cannot not hear dreams or whatever thoughts the sleeping might keep. Timing was important. The nefarious might be busy during the night, but regular folks slept. And this evening, Ben was interested in the regular - the gossip, the rumours, the mundane, were where he would start this search. Totally relaxed, Ben raced through the stars.

The voices flooded in. Ben wasn't sure what he was searching for. Words, phrases, or the names of people. He had mastered the ability to filter the voices, like looking through hundreds of photographs, quickly discarding the irrelevant ones and leaving only those of interest.

It wasn't long before he caught a break. A conversation, one voice male the other female. The male accent was archetypal English, what Ben had come to think of as 'BBC English' from his memories of how BBC presenters all seemed to sound. The female voice was heavily accented, she was speaking English, but she was *not* English.

"His name is Benjamin Grey," the woman said.

"I know what his name is. What the hell was he doing here?" the man snapped.

"He said he has been employed by Olivia. We knew there was always a chance someone might notice something going on at the house." The woman replied.

"Yes, yes, but hiring a private investigator! Contacting the local police, okay, but hiring an investigator. What the hell is she thinking? Who hires a private investigator because they see some lights on at a house?"

"The house is supposed to be empty. They should have been more careful."

"You'll have to call Rupert. He'll have to come over and explain to Olivia it was him. That he has been at the house and on occasion may have had a damn light on. Get her to stop wasting her money on an investigation."

"He doesn't seem like an experienced investigator. A bit young for a start," the woman replied. "He'll come to the same conclusion as the police."

"That he might, but I don't want anybody snooping around. No mistakes am I clear?" said the man, more of a statement than a question.

It seemed the man was clear as the conversation changed topic and soon their voices fell silent, and Ben drifted off to sleep.

Ben was stirred from his slumber by his phone vibrating. A text from Briggs –

'Anything?' she asked

'Yes, I think so,' he replied.

'Video?' she suggested.

Over a video call, Ben shared what he could remember of the conversation the prior evening.

"Stanley and his wife," she said

Ben agreed, "What do you think they're up to?"

"Could be a number of things or may be nothing really at all?"

"Drugs? You think the Stanley's are drug dealers?"

"Well, we do know that whatever they are up to, it involves Rupert. And we should probably give Olivia a heads-up that she's about to get a visit from him."

Ben showered, changed, and went down for breakfast. Briggs had suggested he book himself in for another night and pay the Stanley's another visit to try to rattle their cages.

Breakfast, served in the bar, was a full English to be washed down by coffee. He was served by the same woman as the previous evening. She introduced herself as Esther and revealed she was Marina's mother. Ester was a lot less inquisitive, keeping her questions to what Ben wanted to order, and if his room was okay.

"Why is it called the Mort and Pestle?" Ben asked, as Esther returned to top up his coffee.

"I think it's more a play on words than anything, but the rumour is that some people lost their lives here, before it became a pub of course," she said, with the same giggle he had seen from Marina.

"How does that explain the name?"

"Sorry, it explains the mort part. The rumour was that they were killed in their sleep by a madman that would smash their faces with a pestle. So, Mort and Pestle," Esther explained, adding the actions with a little too much enthusiasm.

Ben looked down at his half-eaten breakfast, wishing he hadn't asked. Looking back at Esther he asked, "Some people were murdered here?"

"In your room as a matter of fact," she replied cheerily. "Just the one extra night?" she asked.

Before leaving the pub, Ben had asked Briggs to call ahead to see if it would be all right for him to drop by Mrs. Havishem's. He pulled up at the house. Arthur Havishem was loading golf clubs into the back of the Jaguar and acknowledged Ben's arrival with a polite nod. Olivia was standing on the doorstep. She waited for her husband to drive off before showing Ben into the house.

This time, Ben was ushered farther into the house, and into the kitchen. It was a farmhouse style kitchen with an island that could comfortably seat eight. The pantry wasn't merely a walk-in but rather a disappear into. Knotted pine cupboards lined the walls, the splash backs were yellow and white tiles, and a tiled replica of van Gogh's sunflowers featured above the stove.

"Beautiful home," Ben remarked as they took their seats at the island.

"Thank you," Olivia replied. "It was passed down to Arthur from his father, and from his father before that." She said, her attention seeming to wander to a different time. Ben remained silent. "Don't know what we'll do with the place," she added, returning her attention to Ben.

"No children?" Ben asked.

"No. Not that we didn't want them, we did. We tried, but it just didn't happen for us."

"I'm sorry," Ben replied. "Did you consider adoption?"

"Of course, but you live in the hope that you are going to have your own. Then when you realise it isn't going to happen, adoption just seemed like too much work. You've seen how Arthur is, he would only consider a white baby, and then it would have to be a boy of course. We argued about it to the point where it became a subject we stopped speaking about. Time just disappears and before you know it.... Well," she said, interrupting herself, "You didn't come here to listen to my regrets."

"Sorry, yes, I wanted to come by to make you aware of something, provide a heads-up so to speak." Ben said.

Olivia frowned.

"We think something may well be going on at the Mansion," Ben started, unsure how to start.

"Yes, I told you that," Olivia interrupted.

"Well, we've reason to believe that Rupert is aware of whatever it is, and that the Stanley's may also be involved."

"That's awfully vague. What is it you believe they might be involved in?"

"We're not sure yet. But we are expecting that Rupert will be reaching out to you. To try and persuade you to drop the investigation, by reassuring you that what you saw was simply him at the house."

"And was it?"

"We don't know," Ben admitted. "I'm sorry this all sounds a bit vague. The Mansion is being used for something. Rupert and the Stanleys are in some way involved and it would seem they don't want anyone to know what they are up to."

Olivia's frown gave way to frustration. "What do you think might be going on? If what I saw was Rupert snooping around his own property, then there is no need to investigate further. If he tells me it was him, what am I supposed to tell him? I don't believe you and I'm continuing the investigation?"

Ben took a breath. "We overheard the Stanley's talking. They are concerned that we are investigating the Mansion. They made reference to Rupert, and they want Rupert to say it was him that you saw. But it wasn't. You saw something and whatever it was, it wasn't Rupert innocently spending time in the property."

"You're spying on the Stanley's?" Olivia asked, with a crafty smile breaking on her face.

"Err…yes, well, not exactly. But yes, I overheard them talking." Ben replied.

"With all due respect Mr. Grey, *you* did not overhear them talking. You've been spying on them. But you haven't answered my question Mr. Grey," she said.

"We're not sure what is going on or what the Stanley's might be involved in. But I doubt it's legal and we will need to continue if we are going to find out. We are expecting Rupert to ask you to stop. It's up to you of course. You are perfectly entitled to ask us to stop, not a problem. But we do believe the Mansion might be being used for something criminal."

Olivia paused for a moment, taking a sip of some tea that she had poured them both. The smile dropped from her face. "Criminal? You're thinking it might be drugs? You think I might have a drug cartel setting up shop, or whatever it is they do, next door."

"Possibly," Ben admitted.

Oliva took another sip of her tea. Ben likewise. "Well, we can't have that sort of thing carrying on. You'll have to get proof, something that we can use to engage the proper authorities."

"What will you tell Rupert?" Ben asked.

"Oh, don't worry about that. I have Elizabeth's number. I'll call her and figure something out. She's very sensible and will be able to help, if Rupert is in fact up to some no good. What are you going to do?"

"I'm going to pay the Stanley's another visit, try to rattle some cages."

"You are a little naughty Mr. Grey," Olivia responded, grinning.

"Ben please. It might encourage them to share more information."

"Share? I very much doubt that. You mean to throw a grenade and see what goes off. I must say, I find it almost amusing that you're spying on them, and so soon. It's not that James is a bad man, he's not. And that awful business with Edwina passing away, was simply horrible. It would have been very difficult for all of them. The money came from Edwina's side of the family you see. Not that James wasn't from stock, he was, his family had made a small fortune in mining, tin I believe. James went to Imperial College but then, his family lost much of their wealth, leaving him with very little. I'm sure Edwina would have made provisions for her husband before her passing."

"Sorry, wouldn't James have inherited everything?" Ben interrupted.

"Oh no, you don't do things like that. The wealth was from her line. You don't allow that wealth to go outside of the blood line. Oh no, she would have ensured that the majority of her wealth passed to her children, especially the boys. She was a fair woman and I'm sure would have made proper provision for James."

"So, James wouldn't have inherited everything."

"I expect an allowance would be paid to James with the majority going into trust for the children until certain conditions are met."

"Conditions?" Ben prompted.

"My boy, you are going to need to do your homework. Conditions such as when they reach a certain age, if they marry, get employment, have children of their own, that sort of thing. Any conditions would have been specified in Edwina's will long before the cancer prevailed. Her own parents likely placed a number of conditions on her. The point is, they are designed to keep the majority of the wealth within the blood line. James is not blood."

"So, the house might not belong to James Stanley?"

"Of course not! It's not some two-bed semi just to be handed off. Edwina wasn't heartless, far from it, James would have been allowed to continue in the home, even with that fancy foreign woman of his, but it *belongs* to the children," she stressed. "Surely, you've heard of prenuptials?"

Ben nodded but remained silent for a moment digesting what he had just heard.

"Now, tell me what you have learned so far," Olivia encouraged.

Ben spent the next twenty minutes drinking tea, eating shortbread, and sharing with Mrs. Havishem what her pounds had so far bought.

Waving goodbye, Ben drove back to the Mansion. He sat for a moment considering his next move, or rather what he was going to say should the Stanley's be at their home. He got out of the car, swept his hair back, and walked back up the driveway and toward the Stanley home.

The front entrance to the Stanley's home faced west toward the Mansion. A stone wall and mature conifer trees, however, blocked the view, affording each property privacy. Ben approached the side door that he had seen James Stanley use the day before. There was a single concrete step up to the door. The door looked solid with brass fittings. An old-style push-button doorbell was conveniently positioned just to the right of the door.

Ben pressed the button. And waited. He stepped down away from the door, unsure if anyone was home. He looked right and then left. He noticed the Range Rover parked farther down the gravel driveway. With renewed confidence, he stepped back up and pressed the doorbell again. And waited.

Opening the door, James Stanley said, "What do you want?"

"Sorry for the interruption, again, but I wondered if I could just ask a couple more questions?" Ben replied.

"What?"

"I wondered if you know the purpose of the lane at the back of the properties, in that direction," he said, pointing.

Mr. Stanley frowned. "What does that have to do with anything?"

"I thought it a bit odd that the road appears to have benefitted from a recent relaying. It looks like new tarmac. Odd don't you think for a road that doesn't go anywhere?" said Ben.

"A lot of the land around here used to be farmed until around twenty years ago. The road is a service lane for farm vehicles."

"So, it is odd then? That the road should be so well maintained?"

"How the hell should I know? What business is it of mine? Now if you don't mind, I have better things to be doing." He said, with a slight push on the door.

"Sorry, am I to understand you don't actually own this property Mr. Stanley?" Ben asked.

Blood flushed in James Stanley's cheeks.

"You damned impertinent swine. If you mean did this property belong to my dear late wife, yes. And it will eventually pass to our children. In the meantime, this property continues to be my home, and you are now trespassing. Please get the hell off my property before I call the police."

Ben took a step back as Mr. Stanley slammed the door. Ben smiled.

Back at the Mansion, Ben walked around the perimeter of the house for any signs of disturbance. He retrieved the memory cards from the cameras and downloaded the footage onto his laptop, though saw nothing of note. He put the memory cards in a pocket.

Then his phone vibrated, a text from Briggs, '*What have you done!?*'

Rather than type a reply, he called her. Her face immediately appeared on the screen.

"What have you done?" she repeated.

"You said 'rattle some cages', so I rattled the cage," he replied.

"I've just had a call from an Inspector from Northants Police telling me he had received a complaint that you have been harassing a prominent member of society."

"A prominent member of society!" Ben scoffed. "James Stanley, doesn't even own the property he's living in."

"You should probably stay away from them, for now at least," Briggs suggested.

"You were the one that suggested I go and poke them."

"What did you say to him?"

"I just said that I understand he didn't actually own the property."

Briggs laughed, "Yeah, that would do it. Did you mention to Olivia that Rupert might try to persuade her to drop the investigation?"

"Yes."

"How'd that go?"

"It got a bit awkward. She was more interested in how I knew than what I knew."

 "So, what did you say?"

"I let her believe we had been spying on the Stanley's, then I let her believe he might be running a drug cartel with the Stanley's."

"Well, he might be for all we know. Is she good to continue?"

"Yes, the thought of any drugs passing back and forth across her doorstep seems to have strengthened her resolve." Ben said.

"What's she doing now?" she said, confusing Ben for a moment before he realised, Briggs was still driving. "Sorry, I need to drop I was expecting Mrs. Samir to turn left towards the hairdressers. She told her husband she would be going to get her hair done but instead she's continued straight on. I'll speak to you later, okay?"

"Sure," Ben replied.

"And Ben?" Briggs quickly added, "Well done."

Ben leaned against the car thinking now would be a good time to listen in on the Stanley's. But there are limits to one's ability to force oneself into slumber. Ben was wide awake.

He got back into the car and drove the short distance to Olivia Havishem's.

"Oh! Hello again," Olivia said, as she opened the door.

"Alison not around?" Ben asked.

"This is my house. I'm allowed to answer my own front door should I wish," she chastened. "She's out getting the groceries. Arthur too and I was having a quiet time doing my tapestry. Are you coming in?" She said, leading the way into the house and leaving Ben to close the door behind him.

Ben followed Olivia down the hall, past the kitchen, and to a living space that looked out onto the back garden. The lawn looked good enough to host championship bowls. Landscaping created curves with pristine edges, and banks of rose bushes, lavender, lilies and hydrangeas adorned the sides. A tall hedge with trellis, partitioned the garden from whatever might lay beyond, accessed via a painted wrought-iron gate.

"You're just in time," Olivia said, turning away from the patio doors to look directly at Ben. "There, over there," she now pointed, "you see? There's a hummingbird at the feeder."

Ben peered out of the window at the brightly coloured bird hovering while it drank.

"Seems you bring luck, Benjamin Grey. Fascinating creatures. Did you know they can fly upside down, if they so wished. Remarkable. I've spent many an hour looking but have barely seen a thing. The moment you walk in, and we're graced with this beautiful little creature. Cup of tea?" she asked.

"No, thank you," Ben replied, only catching some of what Olivia had just said. "I didn't mean to bother you again, not so soon, but I wondered if you might have contact details for Rupert Henshaw and perhaps Elizabeth too, should I need to speak to them?"

Olivia turned around and back toward the kitchen. She soon returned holding an address book open. "Do you need me to write it down for you?"

Ben took out his phone as Olivia handed him the book.

"Okay if I take a picture?" Ben asked.

"Go ahead," Oliva replied.

Ben snapped a picture. "Thank you."

"I never told Rupert that I had hired you," she said.

"No, you said, you had cleared things with Elizabeth," Ben replied.

"That's not what I meant," Olivia said, tilting her head forward and her eyes up. "You were here earlier to give me a 'heads up' that Rupert might contact me to try and persuade me to drop the investigation."

"Yes," Ben replied.

"Well. I didn't tell Rupert that I had hired anyone. How does Rupert know about you and Miss Briggs?" she asked.

Ben took a moment to try and recall what he had said to her earlier.

"It must have been the Stanley's who told him," Ben replied. "I had introduced myself to Monica and told her then that I was being employed by you. Like I said, we've reason to believe that the Stanley's, Mr. Stanley at least, is involved with Rupert with something it would appear they both wish to keep quiet."

"She's attractive, isn't she?" Olivia asked, changing the subject.

"Who?"

"Monica, Monica is attractive."

"Yes, I suppose she is. How do you think she met Mr. Stanley?" Ben asked.

"No idea. She's number three you know. After Edwina passed, things weren't the same. I've no doubt James loved her very much, but after Edwina's passing, he…changed. He withdrew, seemed to travel more, married some Asian woman that I expect he picked from one of those catalogues. That didn't last. Then Monica came along. She seems pleasant enough and he seems happy."

"Would she know about the home?"

"You mean it not belonging to James? Yes, I expect so. Why? You think attractive women only marry for money?" she asked.

Ben felt a flush of embarrassment. "No, sorry. I mean there is a bit of an age gap, and you have to admit, she could probably do better."

"Which probably goes to show she hasn't married him for his money. Now, if it's all right with you, I'd like to use the rest of the time I have, working on my tapestry. Here," she said, opening the inside cover of the address book. "I assume you have one of those social Apps or whatever they're called?"

"Yes, I do," Ben replied.

"Well, take note, you can message me next time you have a question. Save you some time and you won't have to bother Miss Briggs."

"Thank you," said Ben. "Sorry, just one more question. You wouldn't happen to know the dates you saw things at the Mansion?"

"Actually, I do. Arthur and I still make use of a calendar. It's more for him. He's not comfortable with technology, you know." Olivia turned and walked back toward the kitchen. This time Ben followed.

"Here we are," she said, turning to Ben. She lifted the calendar off it's hook and set it down on the island. "These are the dates, they coincide with my bridge nights, not all of them of course. Here I've marked the ones where I saw something with a red dot, see."

Ben peered down at the dates. Three had been marked. All Thursdays. "Thursdays," Ben mused.

"Yes. As I said, I play bridge and so have a tendency to come home later than I normally would."

"This is four weeks apart and then five weeks, then four again," Ben said.

"Well, there could be more. It's not like I'm out there every night."

"Thank you, that's very helpful," Ben replied.

Ben returned to the Mansion and fetched his bag from the trunk of the car. He found what he was after in a side pocket. At the back door, he placed shoe covers on and put on latex gloves. He let himself in and peering up at the camera, remembered he still had the memory cards in his pocket. Replacing the cards, he headed to the bedroom with the desk.

Back in the bedroom, his fingers fumbled to replace the camera's memory card. He bent down and searched for the hair fibres he had noticed the day before. Using tweezers, he placed them into a plastic bag. Down on his hands and knees, he took a closer look at the yoga mats — more hair fibres, differing in colour. And some nail clippings, some coloured in nail polish.

Still using the tweezers, he took a look closer at the clippings. His near sight wasn't great, but he could tell the nails were on the small side. He bagged the clippings too.

Ben examined the desk and the area around it more closely, not sure what he was looking for. Then the bathroom. Deciding he had collected enough hair, not even sure why he was even collecting it, he bagged a couple of the cigarette butts. He was careful to avoid taking too much material. Should the Smoker return, he would expect to see the pressed butt ends on the windowsill and floor, where he (or she) had left them.

He sent a text to Briggs, 'done here' then waited to see if she would respond. After a couple of minutes, he headed out, got in the car and drove to the Mort and Pestle.

Briggs followed Mrs. Samir's car. She drove for another twenty minutes, heading out of town, before arriving at a large single-story building on the outskirts of town. The red brick building looked new. The window frames gleamed, and there was no sign of moss on the tiled roof. Mrs. Samir had pulled into the car park and parked in a space close to the entrance. There were not many parked cars, so Briggs pulled up just short of the parking entrance. But close enough to watch as Mrs. Samir entered the building. She walked briskly, with confidence – *she's been here before, a regular*, thought Briggs.

Briggs checked her watch and made a quick voice recording. "The time is just after one fifteen pm, and Mrs. Samir has entered a building about two miles south-east of Buckingham, just off London Road. The building appears to be new and there's no obvious signage from my current position at the entrance to the car park."

She paused the recording and drove into the car park, choosing a space that afforded her some cover should Mrs. Samir make a quick return. Briggs got out of the car and walked toward the entrance. Some of the cars parked all had the same type of permit – 'The Rural Idyll'. It was then Briggs noticed preparatory work for signage to go above the entrance. Brackets and fixtures had been placed ready to receive whatever letters were about to go up. *A hotel?* Briggs thought, "Naughty Mrs. Samir," she said to herself.

Later that day, Rupert Henshaw pulls up outside the Cricklewood Mansion.

CHAPTER FOUR

Rupert Henshaw grabbed a coat, torch, and balaclava from the backseat of his car. He glanced around, put on the balaclava and made his way around the side of the house. He punched in the code at the back door and entered.

Once inside, he immediately turned to the door, shining the torch, inspecting the frame. *Nothing*, he thought. He moved the torch along the line of the ceiling. As the light moved across the top of one of the cupboards, a flash of light reflected at him. *Glass.* Rupert walked over and reached up for whatever it was. A moment later he was inspecting the camera in his hand. "Bloody amateur", he said, placing it into a pocket. He scanned the remainder of the room, and satisfied there were no further camaras, he made his way farther into the house.

Ben sat watching football in his room when his phone lit up and started vibrating.

"How did you get on today?" Briggs asked. Her black hair curlier than usual.

"I'm watching the footie in my room at the Mort and Pestle. I looked at the cameras but there's nothing on them. I did find something of interest from Olivia."

"Oh yeah?" Briggs encouraged.

"It turns out there appears to be a pattern to the happenings at the Mansion. Seems the ghosts party on Thursdays, limited to once a month."

"When's the next one?" she asked.

"Good question. If the pattern persists, it'll be this Thursday. The pattern looks to be four weeks followed by five."

"It's Wednesday tomorrow. I doubt they'll hold a party this Thursday when they know we, and by we I really mean you, have been snooping around."

"That's what I was thinking."

"We have to expect them to search for the cameras."

"I thought of that too," Ben replied.

They were both silent for a few moments.

"Is that pizza?" Briggs asked, as she caught a glimpse of the box next to Ben on the bed.

"Yup. It's a local one, pretty good."

"You know, technically, we've done our job." She said.

Ben paused for a moment as he read the speech to text at the bottom of the screen. He had gotten used to reading her lips but occasionally she would still surprise him with certain words.

"What are you suggesting?"

"I'm just saying. Olivia asked us to find out what was going on at the house, and we know that it's not ghosts, but Rupert Henshaw using the property for some nefarious activity."

"Allegedly," Ben added. "And I don't think she's going to feel any better knowing her own house is on the silk road for drugs."

"You think it's drugs?" Briggs asked.

Ben shrugged, "Most likely, but something about it seems, I don't know, off to me. I can totally see them doing it but I'm not seeing any signs of that, and it doesn't explain the bedroom."

"Perhaps it's not drugs then but prostitutes or something?"

"If Rupert's entertaining women at the house, how would the Stanley's be involved in that?"

"They don't have to be using the women themselves, maybe they're pimps."

Ben made a face.

"I'm just saying, Olivia hasn't asked us to solve some sort of major crime, she just wanted to know what was going on at the Mansion."

"And we still don't know what it is," Ben replied.

"Is she still happy to continue paying?"

"I think so. She gave no indication of stopping after I shared the news about Rupert. I think she's even more concerned now."

"Very well then," Briggs said, "I'll leave you to enjoy your pizza and the football. What's the score?"

"Two nil."

"Well, that should cheer you up a bit then," she said cheerily.

"To them. We're losing two nil."

"Sorry. Look, call me if you want to chat otherwise, I'll see you tomorrow, yeah?"

"Sure, see ya," Ben replied, the screen returning to the home page.

A cheer went up on the tv as a third goal went in. Ben was happily spared the raucous, but the pictures of celebrating fans and quick show of VAR confirmed the updated score line. He switched the tv off, grabbed his phone, and lay back on the bed. As he opened up his mobile game, he felt a pang of guilt at not having asked Briggs about how her case was going. He pictured her face as he answered her call, bright and cheery. Guess it *can't be going too badly*, he thought, and returned to the game.

After checking the house, Rupert Henshaw arrived at the Stanley's. Monica showed him into the dining room where several take-out containers had been spread across a table. James was seated, sucking on a chicken wing.

"Hungry?" he said.

"Sure," replied Rupert, taking a seat a few chairs down from James.

Rupert had been in this house on many occasions. To him, it stank of old money, worn out tapestries and oversized oil paintings of nobody's. The chandelier that hung over the table was the only thing of real value in the room, and he would have sold that years ago.

"I'll get you a drink," said Monica from behind him.

James wiped his face, then his fingers on a napkin, the sauce staining the cloth. "You've been to the house?" he asked.

"Of course," Rupert replied.

"And?"

Rupert drew a camera from a pocket. "Just this piece of junk."

"Where was it?"

"In the boot room. Not very well concealed. Bloody amateur as you suspected." Rupert said.

James placed the spoiled napkin down, "Well it's a good job it's the yobbo doing the investigation. The other one isn't a damn amateur, she's ex-MI5."

Rupert lifted the lids on the various containers. He grabbed a fork and pulled a container of beef noodles closer.

"You've checked the rest of the house?" James asked.

"Of course, I'm not an idiot. I'll go back in the morning and check the outside. It was too dark earlier. I'll double check the inside then."

"I doubt even that imbecile placed only one camera around the place."

Monica returned with a glass of beer. She placed it down next to Rupert and took a seat next to James.

"The next delivery is on Thursday. It's too late to stop it now. If we tell them, we can't accept the delivery they'll have to go elsewhere. And that would be very bad for business gentlemen." She declared.

Rupert sighed, "I know it would be bad for fucking business. Why is the old bitch sticking her nose into our business anyway?"

"Because your people screwed up!" James shouted.

"Now, now gentlemen, there's no need for us to fall out," Monica said, calmly. "Firstly, are we still agreed we want to take delivery?"

The two men, nodded.

"Can't we alter the schedule to Friday or something, may be next week?" Rupert asked.

"If we try to change anything, they'll become suspicious. They will start asking questions and we risk losing the whole operation." Monica replied.

"Do your damn job and make sure the house is ready and isn't being watched," James remarked, searching for more food.

"They know we have influence in the police, but I doubt it will put them off. And it won't mean a great deal if they get any evidence of what we're doing." Monica said.

"I've called a couple of guys over for tomorrow. We'll go over the house and make sure it's ready. I'll have dogs there on Thursday."

"Good," Monica replied, "Are you going to talk to this Benjamin Grey?"

"I expect so. I'll try to convince them it was just me at the property, mooching around and just looking in on the place." Rupert responded.

"I said we needed better cover," James said, "all we needed to do was tell that busybody that Rupert was going to be at the house. A pretence for renovations."

Rupert rolled his eyes.

"How did they get access to house?" Monica asked.

"Elizabeth of course," Rupert confirmed. "The old bat and her are close. She must have shared her concerns with Elizabeth, and Elizabeth must have agreed to give them access."

"Have you spoken with Elizabeth," Monica asked.

Rupert sighed again, "Not yet. I'll try and get hold of her tomorrow. Perhaps I can convince her it's just me and get her to agree to removing access."

"You can change the code without needing her permission." James added.

Rupert looked at James. The man he knew when growing up had lost his virility. He was old, the nip and tuck his face had received over the years couldn't hide the skin that now collected around his neck. Nor could the tan he was so proud of, hide the increasing number of liver spots. Rupert knew that Monica's relationship with James was one of business, but still, how could she sleep in the same bed as this guy.

"I've done it." Rupert said.

"Well then," Monica declared, rising from her chair, "we're all good. We have our orders. I'll confirm the delivery. Rupert will get the house ready and try to halt the investigation and you," she said turning to look at James, "well, you can book a round of golf with the Chief Constable. I'm going to retire for the night. Good night."

Both men watched as Monica left the room. Smiling James returned his gaze to Rupert. Rupert stared at him for a moment before returning to the food.

"How old are you now Rupert?"

"Thirty-one," he replied. "Why?"

"Another year of this and you will have made enough to retire."

"What about you? Have you made enough? Do you think she's going to…retire?" he replied with a nod of his head in the direction Monica.

James stood. "Don't worry about cleaning up, I'll have the maid do it in the morning. You can find your way to your room, I take it. Do lock the door, there are some nasty people out there," he said, smiling as he left the room.

Rupert filled his mouth with more food before washing it down with the beer. His thoughts wandered into tomorrow and what needed to be done, unaware someone had been listening to the evening's conversation.

The next morning Ben awoke to daylight shining in through the gap he had left in the curtains. Though he had been late for work a few times, sunlight, even in England, was still a reliable way of waking himself up. His employers had typically been understanding of his occasional tardiness however, he had hoped working for himself would remove the anxiety of trying to wake at a set time. It didn't.

He checked the time on his phone. In eleven minutes, his phone would start to vibrate, and the alarm app trigger the light to flash. Pointed at his face on the side that he usually slept, meant, in time, the flashing vibrating combo would cause him to awake. Of course, this method was far from perfect. If he was facing the other way or just dead tired, he could easily oversleep.

He texted Briggs, 'Where are you?'

'Still at the office,' she replied.

'Stay there, I'm on my way.'

'You have an hour before I need to be out.'

Ben checked the time again, 'K'.

He got dressed without showering, stuffed his remaining clothes into the overnight bag and left the room.

"No breakfast?" Marina asked, seeing him at the bottom of the stairs.

"No thanks. Need to dash," Ben replied.

"Everything alright?"

"Yes, perfect, thank you. Must go."

Ben arrived home with fifteen minutes to spare. He left his bag in the car and entered the office. Briggs was on the phone. Ben waved his hands and nodded his head…*wrap it up*. Briggs raised her eyebrows and wiggled her head…*okay!* She soon put down the phone and followed Ben into the Case room where the earlier words remained up on the board.

"What's going on?" Briggs asked, once Ben had closed the door and turned to face her.

"I heard them last night," he said. "James, Monica and Rupert. They are going to take a delivery on Thursday.

"Delivery of what?" Briggs asked.

"I don't know. Whatever it is that they are involved in."

"You haven't put them off then."

"They said something about it being too late to call off and then they seemed concerned they would lose business if they did."

"We could try the Police again?" She said.

Ben shook his head, "We don't have any evidence of anything and besides James is friendly with the Chief Constable."

"Well then, we'll need to gather some evidence ourselves. If we have proof that something is going on, the Chief Constable won't be able to ignore it." Briggs stared at Ben… "What?" she added, seeing the concern in his face.

"What am I supposed to do? They'll be people there, watching for us. And dogs."

"Dogs?" Briggs repeated.

"Dogs. If I'm anywhere near that place I'm gonna get chewed on, and hospitalised by some crony, if I'm lucky."

"We have to do something. How about you go and take another look around, see if there's somewhere we can stake the place out. Look I have to go, I have something I need to check."

"Rupert is going to be there," Ben replied.

"You don't have to go to the house. Just go the grounds, see if there's somewhere we could set up, may be somewhere on Olivia's property."

Ben visibly relaxed. Briggs turned and opened the door to leave before Ben tapped her on the shoulder. She turned.

"How is your case going?" He asked.

Briggs smiled. "I think I know what's going on, but I need to confirm something this morning. I'll call you when I'm done. Let's try to meet up for lunch. Talk to you later."

She turned and left.

Ben slumped into a chair and stared up at the board. He cast his mind back to the walk around the grounds of the Mansion, trying to think of a safe spot from which to view the house. The property was surrounded by trees but anything close to the house would surely attract the attention of trained dogs or untrained dogs for that matter. He began running various scenarios in his head.

Rupert arrived at the Mansion and told the two men equipped with surveillance detectors to make a start. As they walked away, Rupert walked across the driveway to the trees that bordered the Mansion and the Havishem properties. He stopped and waited for a moment. With no visible sign of activity, he continued out of the trees and down the driveway toward the house, brushing off needles and leaves as he went.

As he approached the house, the front door opened. Arthur appeared at the door holding a pair of shoes.

"Oh! Hello Rupert, how are you?" Arthur asked.

"I'm very good thank you Arthur. Golf?"

"Oh yes," he replied cheerfully, waggling the shoes in his hand. "Trying to get a few more rounds in before the weather turns again. The joints don't like the cold and the damp even less," he added as though he were sharing a secret.

"Very good," Rupert replied. "Then I won't keep you. Look I'm sorry to bother you but perhaps I can speak to Olivia if she's around?"

"Yes, of course. Alison!"

Moments later Alison appeared at the door.

"This is Rupert Henshaw, his family own the Mansion. He grew up here you know. Please show him inside to meet Olivia."

"Of course," Alison replied, tipping her head in acknowledgement. Rupert reciprocated having met Alison on several occasions. She showed Rupert into the study.

"Please take a seat in here. I'll let Olivia know you are here, she won't be a moment. Thank you."

Rupert walked over to the window and looked out onto the driveway in time to see Arthur backing out of the garage.

"Hello Rupert, so good to see you," Olivia said as she entered the room. "Please have a seat. Can I ask Alison to get you anything, tea perhaps?"

Rupert smiled and sat down, "Sure, why not."

After getting settled, Olivia said, "It seems so long since we last saw you. How are you?"

"I'm very good thank you. I have some business interests in London. Things have picked up again after all that Covid kerfuffle. I see Arthur is still golfing, is his handicap improving?"

"I don't think so, but it's good exercise for him, and it keeps him out of my hair for a few hours," she chuckled.

"I'm trying to remember the last time we saw you. It must have been Guy Fawkes a few years back now."

"Yes, I think it probably was."

"That was nice. It always is nice to see everyone together and have a bit of fun. I seem to remember you getting in on the action letting off the fireworks. And who was it, oh yes, Rose number two, running the barbeque."

"Rose number two?" Rupert repeated.

"Oh sorry, that was naughty of me. Yes, Rose, James' second wife."

"Ah yes, Rose. She didn't seem to last very long did she."

"Yes, that was strange how she just seemed to leave all of a sudden. But I guess that must be a risk, you know, with her being from Taiwan."

"Vietnam, I think it was," Rupert corrected. "A risk how?"

"I mean with her family being in, Vietnam, there must always be a risk that she might want to return there."

"Oh, I see," Rupert replied. "Yes, I'm not sure what happened, but James seems very happy with Monica, number three," he added jokingly.

"Makes you wonder how he meets these women. Rose being from Vietnam and Monica being Polish."

"Albanian," he corrected.

"What?"

"Monica is from Albania, not Poland. She's Albanian."

"Oh, I'm getting it all wrong today. Nevertheless, still curious how one would run into these women."

"Yes, well I expect Rose was somewhat of an arrangement. I know James took Edwina's loss very hard. As for Monica, he could have easily met her while on business or anywhere. People are everywhere these days."

"Yes, I suppose. He does seem to travel a bit. I'm too old for that now, the hips not being what they used to. Cruises are our thing now. A lot more relaxed, everything close by."

After a moment, Rupert said, "Olivia, I'm here to talk about the little investigation you have going on."

"Oh, yes. You know I did try to contact you. I've been seeing lights on at the house, and I became concerned. You know, what with squatters and their rights these days, I wasn't sure what to think."

"Er, yes, you really should have spoken to me first. I could have saved you the time and the money. I have been spending a bit of time there on occasion. Checking on the house, sorting through a few things we have stored there, that sort of thing. I had meant to drop in and say hello to let you know I would be around."

"Oh, now I am feeling rather silly. I didn't know. I mean it wasn't just the odd occasion, it was a few times. Now I do feel a little embarrassed. I was just concerned it might be something else, you know."

"Of course, no need to be embarrassed. Thank you for being…neighbourly. It's my fault, I really should have stopped by to let you know that I was going to be visiting the place."

Olivia sipped her tea.

"So, you'll ask the investigators to stop?"

Olivia took another sip before answering. "Yes, of course. Arthur thought I was being silly from the outset. Sticking my nose in and making something out of nothing. He'll enjoy this."

Rupert picked up his tea and leaned back into the chair. "Perhaps I should pay something toward your costs you've incurred. Afterall, if I come by like I had meant to, that would have prevented all of this in the first place. I do feel partially responsible."

Olivia waved dismissively, "No, thank you, but there's really no need. I hadn't offered them very much anyway. I think they're new and rather young to be doing this sort of thing. I can't imagine they have much experience. Anyway, the job is done. I asked them to find out the reason for the lights, and here we are - it was you." She said cheerily.

For the next twenty minutes, Olivia brought Rupert up to speed on what had been happening in the village, her perspective on the impact of recent political upheaval, and the fond memories she had of the children growing up.

Two hours later, the phone rang. Olivia was sitting in the conservatory, the tapestry on her lap, when Alison brought her the phone.

"Sophie Briggs," Alison whispered, handing over the phone.

"Sophie," Olivia said.

"Hi Olivia, I was just calling to ask if Ben might stop by this afternoon. We'd like to set up external surveillance at the Mansion and we thought there may be a suitable spot on your side of the border."

"Surveillance? External surveillance? Does that mean you already have surveillance inside the house?" Olivia asked.

At the other end of the conversation, Briggs smiled awkwardly. "It's probably best we don't share the details. But yes, if we want to know what's really going on at the Mansion, we'll need to obtain some evidence. The best way to achieve that is through surveillance."

"He came by this morning you know," said Olivia, changing the subject.

"Who did? Rupert?" Briggs replied.

"Yes. Like Mr. Grey said he would. Told me the lights that I saw were him doing a bit sorting through storage. Asked me to stop the investigation."

"And what did you say?" Briggs asked.

"I told him 'Of course'. There was no need to continue now we know it's nothing to be concerned about." Olivia stated and then paused. "Oh, don't worry, I've no intention of asking you stop. I've known that child since he was born. He's always been a little different. Must stem from being the youngest you know. I mean, having to compete all the time with older siblings, especially when they have talent, and one does not. Understandable in a way, that he would be the mischievous one. Easiest way to get attention, you see."

"I see," Briggs replied, though not sure she did. "So, it's okay for Ben to come by a little later today?"

"Oh yes. I will let Alison know to expect him. Does he need access to our house?"

"No, I don't think so. He'll just be looking along the border for somewhere suitable to fix some equipment."

"Well, tell him he needn't knock. He can just do what he needs to do. How much longer do you think you will need? For the investigation."

"Well based on your observations, we think something might happen this week. If we can collect some evidence, we might be able to work out what is going on, and then it's up to you what you'd like us to do next." Briggs confirmed.

"I may need an excuse for when Rupert finds out I haven't in fact, stopped the investigation. For now, I can just say I had forgotten to tell you, there are some advantages to being old, everyone assumes you are losing your memory. But I can only use that excuse once. I'll need something better if this going to last beyond this week."

"Well, let's see what we can find out and take things from there. We'll let you know as soon as we have any further information."

"I did say it was all right for Mr. Grey to message me directly. His impairment must place a greater burden on you."

"Thank you for your consideration. Ben is really no burden at all, quite the opposite. But yes, there are some things its just easier if I do them. Thank you though, I will remind him."

Ben had been at the Havishem's property more than hour when he saw Sophie's blue Tesla approach. The wind had picked up and the temperature had dropped. His fingers were starting to seize up as he fixed the last camera to the branch. He watched as Briggs pulled up behind the Corsa. After getting out, she was quick to zip up her jacket.

"Up here!" Ben called out.

Briggs looked up and met his eyes. She continued walking until she was standing below the branch Ben was standing on.

"You all right up there?" Briggs asked.

"One moment, just finishing up."

Briggs stepped further into the trees to assess the line of sight to the Mansion.

"You sure you're going to see anything," she said. She looked up again as Ben tightened a screw. He hadn't heard her of course.

Finished, Ben tiptoed along the branch like a gymnast in training before climbing down the rest of the way.

"Can you see the house from there?" Briggs asked again.

"A bit," Ben replied, panting. "Do you know how many trees I've been up and down in the last hour?"

"Where's the receiver?" Briggs asked.

"At the Havishem's. Here," he said, taking his phone from a pocket.

Ben brought up the surveillance app that connected his phone to the cameras he had just affixed to the trees. I'm using the long-range IR cameras. We can see the front of the house okay, and we might get the number plates depending on where they park."

"What's that?" Briggs asked pointing to a blur at the bottom edge of the video.

"I have to break a few branches to clear the view."

"Any sign of the dogs?"

"Not yet. Though I did see some guys leave the house earlier."

"Rupert?"

"Could have been. You know people rarely look the same as they show themselves on social media. They always appear older."

"You mean like yours?"

"I like that picture. I don't have many with my Mum."

"You were fifteen years old. Anyway, what I meant was, Rupert came by to visit Olivia this morning, so I expect he has been at the Mansion throwing our cameras away."

"What did she say?"

"She told him she'd tell us to stop the investigation," Briggs replied.

"Is she going to?"

"No. She wants us to continue and find out what he is up to."

"Olivia lied, nice. But that won't hold for very long."

"Which is why we need to uncover something quick. Or Lady Havishem is going to find herself in an awkward situation."

Briggs looked at the images showing on the phone. "We can only view the front of the house, and these cameras aren't going to show us anything that might be going on in that bedroom if the other cameras are removed."

Ben waited for her to look up. "We need something that covers the back."

Briggs looked down at the box laying open on the ground. Wires and various equipment were tangled up inside. She bent down and untangled a camera.

"Come on, let's get it done before the dogs do show up." She said.

They spent the next best part of an hour trudging around the estate trying to locate a suitable spot for the equipment. They had not quite finished when they heard vehicles approaching the Mansion.

Quickly they grabbed the unused equipment, and Briggs signed to Ben, 'we need to get out of here.' Then she heard the excited bark of a dog, a large dog, and the voices of at least a few men. 'Quickly!' she signed.

They headed directly away from the house and down toward the lake. Once at the lake, Ben motioned for them to take a trail leading away from the lake and even farther from the Mansion.

Briggs signed, 'I think it's okay. I don't hear anything.'

'Then why are you still signing?' Ben replied, also signing.

Briggs pulled a face, "Come on, idiot, they could still find us if they decide to check this way."

Ben and Briggs had ended up walking some three miles from the rear of the Mansion, down to the pond, across the countryside and back out onto one of the country roads, before heading back as covertly as the route would allow, to the Havishem's property. From there, they drove their cars to the Mort and Pestle.

"You know we could just turn up at the place tomorrow night," Briggs said, a moment after depositing some steak and kidney pie in her mouth.

"You do know, you eating while you are talking doesn't make understanding you any easier." Ben replied.

"Sorry," Briggs said, bringing a hand up to cover her mouth. "I'm just saying, we do have the option of turning up at the place tomorrow night. We'll probably be able to gauge what is going on from that."

"And how are they going to react when they see us turn up? I don't think your kung fu is going to be enough to protect us. And what if we can't tell what's going on?" Ben replied, adding, "If we do walk into some drug's ring, they're not just going to let us walk away."

"Are you going to sleep here tonight?" she asked.

"Not tonight, I wasn't planning to. I'm thinking I'm going to have to stay tomorrow night."

"I've picked up another case."

"You haven't finished the one you're on, the cheating wife one."

"Work isn't serial, we going to need to take on more than one case at a time. And she's not cheating, at least not from what I've seen," Briggs replied.

"What's this other case?"

"Industrial sabotage," Briggs said, leaning in as she spoke.

Ben also leaned in, though unsure why. "Mysterious," he said, "How come I don't get to work it?"

"Because you have your hands full here."

"How much is that one worth?" Ben asked.

"Time and expenses at the moment, but if a settlement gets agreed, we'll get a percentage."

"What is it?"

"There's a company in Milton Keynes specialising in commercial printing. They have recently lost some large contracts due to what they believe is a manufacturing defect from one of their suppliers. They say the defect resides in a chip, and they believe the supplier knew the chip was faulty."

"Don't they have lawyers for that?" Ben asked.

"Sure, it was their lawyer that contacted us. Lawyers don't get their hands dirty. That's our job." Briggs said, smiling as she stuck her fork back into the pie.

Briggs looked up as a man approached. The complexion on the man's angular face was pale, almost sickly. His mousey brown hair was thin and had the appearance of being glued to his head. He stood no taller than Ben at five ten at the most. He was wearing a checkered brown tweed three-piece, white shirt, and a Manchester United tie. Rupert Henshaw pulled up a seat, removed his flat cap placing it on the table and sat down at the table.

"I presume you know who I am," Rupert stated.

"You look younger online," Ben replied.

Rupert made no attempt to hide his disdain for the remark.

"You are Rupert Henshaw," Briggs replied, smiling, and holding out her hand. "I'm Sophie Briggs and this is my partner, Benjamin Grey. It's a pleasure to meet you."

Ignoring Briggs' gesture, Rupert continued, "I know Olivia hired you to snoop around my house. I informed her today there's no need for her to be alarmed, the activity she has seen going on at the house, was just me. So, there's no longer any need for you to be snooping around."

Briggs and Ben glanced at each other. It had been established early on in their relationship that Briggs would take the lead in any conversation.

"We're not snooping," Ben said.

Briggs gave Ben a look. "What my partner means is, Mrs. Havishem was simply concerned that the property may have squatters given the property is not in use. She asked if we check things out on her behalf. Elizabeth, your sister, and joint owner gave us permission. I have it here if you'd like to see it?"

"Yes, well as that may be, I can assure you no one is squatting at the house. Not that it's any of your business but I'm doing some preliminary sorting with a view to getting the property back on the market."

"Yes, we understand, and we are sorry for any inconvenience." Briggs replied.

Lifting a large grocery bag up onto the table, Rupert added, "I believe these are yours."

Ben had to move his plate quickly.

Briggs grabbed at the handle before the bag tipped its contents all over their food. "Yes, thank you. We could have come by to retrieve the equipment. But thank you."

"No need. Let me be clear, I will treat any further encroachment on my property, as trespassing," Rupert replied curtly.

"It's not your property." Ben stated, wiping ketchup from his mouth.

"What?"

"I mean, technically it's not your house, is it?" he repeated. "As I understand things, while you were named within the Will, the administration fell to Elizabeth. She is the executor, the one in charge."

Rupert's face flushed pink. He glanced around before resting his gaze on Ben. "I trust your costs are in keeping with your incompetence," he replied, struggling to maintain his composure. He stood up and leaned on the table, "Get back to whatever circus you came from and stay off my property."

Rupert turned and left.

"Ass," Ben remarked.

"You were a bit of an ass yourself. There's no need to provoke him, it'll only make things worse for Olivia." Briggs replied.

"Well at least he didn't make a comment on how I'm supposed to look."

"What? What are you going on about now?" Briggs replied.

"Nothing. Pass me the bag."

Briggs obliged.

Ben rummaged through the bag. "They are not all here. He's missed one."

"He might have missed one or just not bothered to pack it."

"Hopefully he's missed the one in the bedroom. He's up to something at that place and his sister must suspect it too."

"Well perhaps finding these in the house might mean he thinks he has them all. Might make him a little less cautious going forward. Come on, eat up, you could use a shower."

Ben spent the remaining hours of the afternoon stationed in the office, facing the front desk in case anyone walked in. Briggs had shut herself in an interview room with her laptop.

At five o'clock, Ben closed the office and peaked through the glass at Briggs. Images of various electronics and printers were spread across the table. She was a good student, disciplined, thorough, a proper investigator. She had completed University a year early, was recruited by MI5 and placed on the fast-track. Ben recalled their first meeting. She was standing at the door of his mother's house a few days after he had placed an anonymous tip about a potential terrorist threat. Turned out it's not easy to remain anonymous and that meeting led to him being brought into the investigation.

Investigator Sophie Briggs was black and attractive, attributes Ben assumed had helped her on her way – promoting diversity being the latest fashion, unless you were deaf that is, in which case you were considered hard-work. But it soon became clear, that she was smart, tenacious, and a terrific officer. Those were the attributes MI5 were after. She never flinched when he shared with her how he came by the information that he had anonymously shared, neither did she show any sign that his disability made him anything less than ordinary. To Ben, Sophie Briggs was remarkable.

Briggs looked up from her laptop like she sensed she was being watched and smiled over her shoulder. Ben suddenly felt embarrassed. He returned her smile and turned away. Stretching his tired joints, he made his way upstairs to their apartment.

The office and apartment were part of a converted barn. The property was owned by a private construction company, the owner of which now lived in Henley. Two other businesses ran out of the same premises, an estate agent, and the other a self-employed architect, though they had offices only. Ben and Briggs shared the only apartment. A modern, spacious twelve hundred square feet of living space, according to the advert, with a bedroom and ensuite for each of them.

Ben cared little for the finances, happy to leave that to Briggs whom he had already trusted with his life. Though not religious, Ben had come to understand the truth of money being the root of all evil. 'Don't ever share your money with anyone,' his mum had told him. His dad had controlled the family finances and emptied all the coffers on his way out. Ben understood the warning but not the finality of it. The idea that two people see it as normal to share children and yet keep their money apart. Briggs had risked her life for his, and he had no doubts she would do it repeatedly. To Ben, not trusting her with the money seemed asinine and besides, if she did want it all, she was welcome to it.

The challenge now was to make the business work. Briggs had given up a high-profile career and weathered the wrath of her father to join him in this venture. She trusted him and his 'gift'. Ben felt the pressure, but the chance to live and share his life with Briggs, meant it was it. They were not a couple in the traditional sense – no intimacy, not yet anyways, but just being around her brought him a sense of security that he hadn't felt since being a child. Somehow, he thought, when he was with her, everything would be all right.

Ben grabbed an apple juice from the fridge, slumped into his favourite chair and flicked on the TV. He checked the time on his phone and brought up the local TV news. It was Briggs that had encouraged him that it would be good if the local private investigators kept in the know about what was going on in their neighbourhood. Captions were always on.

While waiting for the adverts to clear, he signed into a mobile game. He didn't smoke, tried to refrain from swearing and consumed little alcohol. Gaming was his vice. He tried not to think of the number of hours he had poured into games, or the money spent in this 'free-to-play' activity. Still, it was a distraction and helped to keep someone employed.

Local news was headlined with the murder of teenager Caroline Walters and growing concern for missing teenager Louise Larke. The report started with a focus on Caroline Walters, whose body had been discovered on a popular trail close to the H3. She had been strangled having been reported missing only two days earlier. She was last seen getting off the bus on Grafton Street, less than three hundred metres from her home. Comparisons were being drawn to Louise Larke who had been reported missing only the day before Caroline's body had been discovered. Louise was last seen, captured on CCTV, leaving IKEA on Bletcham Way.

Peaceful protests had resulted from the perceived difference in priority that Police were giving the murder of Caroline Walters and the disappearance of Louise Larke, and the potential racial discrimination. A Detective was being asked why a Child Rescue Alert, which had been issued for Louise Larke, had not been issued for Caroline Walters. His answer, though expected, would likely do little to assuage tensions.

The news report switched to the parents of Louise Larke making an impassioned appeal for any witnesses that may have seen their daughter to come forward, no matter how incidental. A reporter, standing outside a school, shared Louise was considered an exemplary student, captain of the school netball team and known to the community through the volunteering she did at her church.

Since acquiring his gift, Ben had on occasion wondered how it worked or why he had it. Was he unique, the only one or were there others in the world like him, and like him, keeping it secret. Was there a God behind it, perhaps one with a sense of humour – I've taken your regular hearing but let's see what you can do with this. But why Ben, he had often wondered. The only thing more exceptional than this gift, was how normal he was. His current view, until he comes across a better explanation, is his gift has its roots in some dormant human abilities – like mind reading, levitation or some such. It didn't matter, he had it and so what did matter, was what to do with it.

His thoughts returned to the two girls as images of concerned family and teachers appeared on screen. A pang of guilt twisted in his stomach as he wondered whether he should be doing something to help Caroline, instead taking money off an old lady.

Briggs bounced up the stairs, laptop in hand. "You okay there?" she asked, once Ben had looked up.

"Huh?"

"You seemed lost in thought, everything all right?" she repeated.

"Yeah, fine. A local news report on a missing teenager. A girl who doesn't sound like the type to have just wandered off. Police seem concerned.

"And…you wonder if you should be doing more to help?" asked Briggs.

"You know, your perception can verge on creepy." Ben replied. "You must have faced the same situation some point. Working for MI5 and then learning a friend needs help."

"Of course, but you soon learn that you can't help everyone."

"But if this is a gift, as you keep referring to it, then who gave it to me? And for what purpose?"

Briggs walked over and placed a comforting hand on Ben's shoulder.

"I believe what you have *is* a gift, from whom is anyone's guess. But I do know it is something that can help anyone and everybody. Think of the people you helped save in London. What about that family you told me about in Vancouver? You are doing what you should be doing. Helping people while bringing scumbags to justice. Now, do you want a cup of tea?"

"There's a sprite in fridge, please." Ben replied, returning his attention to his game.

That night Ben lay down staring out off the skylight above his bed. His thoughts wandered drifting from the Mansion to Rupert then to James

Stanley, and Monica. *How does someone like him hookup with someone like her, and from Albanian?* Wealth must be a powerful attractant.

Ben yawned as his thoughts shifted again to Caroline Walters. Images of her mother sobbing as she pleaded for anyone with information to come forward. He quickly got out of bed, threw on some clothes, and scrawled a note on the pad on the lounge coffee table – *Gone out, will be back soon, trouble sleeping. Phone.*

The report had mentioned Caroline Walters told her parents she was going for a walk to the Abbey Hill golf course. Ben punched in the address into the GPS.

Traffic was light and it wasn't long before the navigation was instructing Ben to make a left turn into the car park. He chose a spot near the 'Foot Golf' sign, he didn't know there was such a thing. Ben angled his seat back and closed his eyes.

It wasn't long before the voices poured in. Over time and with use, his ability to filter them had improved. The initial scan, as Ben thought of it, was always the toughest. He was never sure of what he was scanning for, having no real idea of what a particular person's voice might sound like. He depended on words, phrases, or names. Subsequent scans for the same person were easier as the persons voice provided a point of reference.

Ben scanned the airwaves, filtering out voices he thought to be male or too young. Discarding those that seemed happy, focussing on those he thought to be female, and broken. He listened, switching between the remaining voices for clues. Then…a whisper with its distinctive warble.

He had experienced three types of voices. The first and most prevalent were the voices of people speaking. These were conversations he had tuned into, unseen and unnoticed, the proverbial fly on the wall.

The second were the whispers. These were not the regular voices of someone simply speaking quietly. These whispers held there own quality – a warble, a connection fading in and out, an audible flicker.

The third type, he had only come across once to date. A voice, deep and guttural, otherworldly, filled with hate and profanity. Ben referred to this as a Demon. Voices, whispers and the demon.

Ben stopped at the whisper and listened in.

'Please God, if you exist, please bring my baby home. I realise I have no right to ask anything of you, I don't even know if you exist. But many people do, and I believe my Caroline did. So, if not for me, oh God, please do it for my Caroline. She is sunshine, bringing light to everyone fortunate enough to know her. She's gentle, she wouldn't harm nobody and never refused to help anyone. Please God don't let anything happen to her. Bring her home to me, please God.'

A prayer. Ben had heard many over the years. Rarely were they given in thanks and often made in desperation. The whisper changed to a regular voice. Ben broadened the reception so he could hear any other voices that might be very close by. He heard another voice, a male voice, it too sounded fractured, its cadence uneven, faltering.

He listened as the conversation moved from expressing the anxiety they both felt to the mundane of life continuing – discarding clothes into the laundry, brushing teeth, and searching for a charger. Then the sobbing returned. Ben couldn't see the tears of course but, the words were filled with heartbreak - the tremor of the lower lip and the inevitable slurp as the person reached for another breath. A sorrow deep enough that they would forget to breathe until their bodies forced it. The conversation stopped. Then separate whispers and then…nothing.

Ben was rocked from his slumber. The car was moving, and a light was shining into the car. He looked out of the window to see man leaning up against the car, saying something.

Ben slid the window down a little and told the guy he was deaf but could probably read his lips if he lowered the torch. The man responded. It was then Ben could see the man's private security uniform.

"You can't be sleeping here sir," the man was saying.

"Sorry, I just nodded off. Sorry, just needed some quiet time. I hadn't intended to sleep. I'll be on my way."

"Thank you, sir. Have a good rest of your night," the guard said, backing away from the vehicle.

It was after three a.m. when Ben returned home. He crept back into his room, removed his sweatshirt and fell asleep.

CHAPTER FIVE

It was almost eleven when Ben emerged from his bedroom. Briggs had left the door to her bedroom open, the usual pile of clothes strewn across the floor. She wasn't in there. Walking over to the coffee table, he saw his note from the night before to which Briggs had added – *'Figured you had a late night. I have an appointment at the printers, Imagearium. Get me on my cell. Don't forget tonight. And pick up some groceries if you can. S.'*

After coffee and dry toast, Ben went into the office. They had both decided against employing a receptionist until they were sure they were getting enough business. Right now, Ben was regretting the decision. The office was beginning to look cluttered even to his eye.

He looked across to the entrance door. Briggs had placed the 'We are not here currently' sign up. It shared Briggs' cell phone number as the primary and his own as an alternate. His own phone utilises a speech to text app for audio calls. Video calls allow for lip reading but also provide the caller's text as an overlay in case the person is hard to read or the video quality drops. And there was always the virtual receptionist, voicemail, should Ben miss the call or choose against answering.

It was a few years after his hearing loss that Ben found the courage to resume using his own voice in conversations. His dad, before he left, always told him to be quiet saying he sounded retarded. His mother tried to encourage it more after his dad left, she said she liked the sound of his voice.

Ben, no longer sure of how he sounded, figured people would likely lean toward his father's view than his mothers. It was a girlfriend from his fifth year at secondary that really encouraged him to use his voice, and his mother paid for some elocution lessons – she never liked the term 'speech therapy'. Not that they had money, they didn't, not after his dad left, but she was keen for Ben to present as 'normal'.

Staring across the office and out of the window his mind turned to the camera missing from those returned by Rupert Henshaw. He was regretting not having placed wireless networked cameras. Briggs had made him aware of the more expensive technology, the cameras linked wirelessly to a receiver that could be placed some distance from the surveillance. The receiver being a larger unit connected to the cellphone network and enabled remote access to the cameras via a phone. The cheaper internal cameras meant he would have to go back to the house if he wanted to retrieve any footage. He brought up the app for the external cameras, there was no activity at the mansion.

Olivia Havishem appeared at the office window. Ben saw her waving and then started tapping on the window like it was going to make any difference. Ben remembered he hadn't changed the sign and walked over to let her in.

"Mrs. Havishem, how are you?" he asked.

"You'll not get a lot of business if you advertise yourself as closed at this time of the morning," she pointed out. "The forecast is good for the day and Arthur wanted to attend some of the racing at Towcester. I don't mind horses but have no love for racing them so I made my excuses and thought I'd take a chance on seeing if I could catch you."

"Well, you caught me," Ben replied, stretching out his arms. "How can I help? Please come in."

Ben ushered Mrs. Henshaw to the lounge seats, intended for anyone waiting to be seen. Olivia seemed hesitant to sit.

"Oh, it's okay. We can move to a private office should anyone come by." Ben assured.

Having seated herself, she placed her handbag on her lap and looked at Ben.

"Rupert came by as you said he would. He said you had agreed to stop snooping around the Mansion. He also wanted me to agree I would stop the investigation. He said it was just him sorting a few things out in readiness for selling the house."

"What did you say?" Ben asked.

"Like I told Sophie, I lied to him and agreed. I thought his explanation a bit odd actually. I mean, Elizabeth has made no mention of preparing the house for sale. I'm sure she would have mentioned it, if that's what they were intending. He's an odd boy, always has been…" Olvia drifted, seemingly searching for the right word. "Odd," she finally repeated. She paused leaving Ben unsure if he should be saying anything. "But I'd like to know, what do we do now?" she added.

Ben sat back, he had been asking himself the same question. He was sure Rupert and James Stanley were involved in something illegal but didn't know what, or what to do about it. He looked at Olivia. She did have a quality about her, an elegance, like she only needed to glide whereas everyone else had to walk. Her grey thinning hair would have been blond and bustling in her prime, while those blue eyes likely possessed even greater potency. Olivia cleared her throat.

"Sorry," Ben said. "We have external surveillance in place, and we think Rupert may have missed one of the internal cameras. The external cameras are linked to my phone but if I'm going to see what is on the internal camera, assuming it is still in the house, then I'm going to need to get back in there. Rupert will have certainly changed the code."

"He has," Olivia replied. "But I spoke to Elizabeth last night. She called me saying that Rupert was quite irate. I told her there's no need to continue the investigation if it was only Rupert cleaning the house but reminded her it would be easier for everyone if one of the neighbours could still access the property in the event of an emergency. She agreed and shared the new code with me. I've written it down," she said, opening her handbag.

She passed Ben a slip of paper with a six-digit number on it.

"Thank you, that makes things easier. I'll be able to check on the internal camera. You know it really could just be something innocent or not very illegal."

"Not very illegal?" she replied. "Something is either legal or it is not." Then her shoulders relaxed, and she sighed. "But yes, I suppose it might not be anything worth creating such a stir over. Are you religious Mr. Grey?" she asked.

"Er, no, not really," Ben responded.

Olivia frowned, "It seems less and less are with every new generation. I don't pretend to be devout or anything like that, in fact I restrict my church visits now to only the main holidays. That's where the word comes from you know – holiday, holy day. But there are some things that I do know. There is a God and one to whom we must answer. And He helps you know, he has given us a wonderful gift."

She paused leaving Ben wondering if he were required to provide the answer.

"A conscience," she stated. "It's what sets us apart from the animals you know. We have a choice in what we do and our conscience is our guide. Well, my conscience requires confirmation. If he's smuggling stolen televisions or some such then we can leave him to it. He can have that on his own conscience, but if its something more, then it would remain on my conscience were we not to have done anything about it. Please find out what he's up to and I will be able to sleep better at night."

Ben nodded. "We will do what we can," he assured.

Olivia stood and after bidding Ben a good remainder to his day, she left.

Ben put the coffee pot on and spent a few minutes tidying up while the coffee brewed. A light switched on, one of several they had installed. The lights were triggered when someone entered the premises. Ben went to the reception desk where a woman with mousey shoulder length hair stood waiting. She was wearing a sports visor and a pink sleeveless top. She was looking down toward the ground, speaking to someone or something.

"Hi, I'm Benjamin Grey, how can I help you?" he said as he approached.

"Hello, I'm Tanya Birkhead and this is my daughter Lola, she's six. "We've lost our rabbit and wondered if this is something you could consider taking on?"

Ben looked at the young girl who looked back at him. She had been crying. He returned his look to the mother.

"I don't mean to sound insensitive, but our rates would appear high compared to the cost of a rabbit." Ben replied.

"It's a Dwarf Hotot, white, quite rare and not at all a common breed. We bought it just a few months ago. Lola misses her very much."

"I'm sure it's a lovely rabbit. Our rates start at a hundred an hour plus any expenses incurred."

Looking down at her daughter the mother said, "Baby, these people are expensive with no guarantee they will be able to find Mr. Snuggles. It would be easier if we bought a new rabbit."

"But it wouldn't be Mr. Snuggles," the girl replied.

"No, it wouldn't be Mr. Snuggles," the mum agreed. "But you could give the new one a new name? We don't know where Mr. Snuggles has gone and this man may not be able to find him. And we would still need to pay this man even if he doesn't find him. Then if we don't find him, we won't have any money to buy another one."

"Why does the man sound funny?" the girl asked.

The mother smiled uncomfortably, "Sorry," she said glancing up at Ben. "Some people speak a little differently," she said, returning her attention to the child. "It doesn't matter, we still understand what he's saying. Now what do you want me to do?"

The child seemed to be considering her options. "Okay," she eventually said, "We can get another one. This time I want a girl rabbit, a pink one."

"Okay baby, come on, you can look and choose the one you'd like." Returning her attention to Ben she said, "Thank you and sorry for the interruption." She held the child's hand and turned to face the door.

"You're welcome," replied Ben as the two of them left the building, now wondering how funny he sounded.

Ben returned to the kitchen and poured himself a coffee and slumped down onto a chair. From his phone he checked the external cameras at the Mansion. Nothing. He fingered the slip of paper Olivia had given him. He checked the time and took a gulp of his coffee, grabbed his keys, closed the office and drove away.

Ben parked at the rear of the property. He had left the car partially hidden and still some distance from where he was now standing. Familiar cigarette butts on the ground. He couldn't see the Mansion from here but from his earlier scouting, he knew it was there. Ben set off through the Wood.

The route to the Mansion seemed shorter than he remembered and the trail more worn. Familiarity might breed contempt, but it also made the world smaller. He skirted around the Stanley's property keeping one eye out to make sure he wasn't seen. He soon arrived at the lawned border of the Mansion. He checked the external camera's again and looked for himself to make sure the coast was clear. Walking briskly across to the rear entrance door he kept thinking of Alsatians.

The code worked. He cautiously stepped inside, wondering if Rupert might have installed his own surveillance. Entering the hallway, the dank smell once again greeted his nostrils. Ben conceded that most of the cameras he had positioned would not have been too hard to find. He bet on the one hidden in the bedroom to be the one Rupert had missed. If indeed Rupert had missed one.

Quickly he climbed the stairs and entered the bedroom. He immediately suspected someone had been in the room given the wrapper was now on the floor. His pulse picked up a few more beats. The mats were positioned differently, there was more rubbish on the floor and a couple of drops of blood. Ben crouched down to look more closely. Near a corner of the room, there were scratches in the floor, a broken fingernail, bloodied. Someone had been scratching at the floor. From the shape of the fingernail, Ben assumed it was a woman, someone with slender fingers, much smaller than his own. He grabbed his phone and took some pictures.

Turning on the balls of his feet, he looked at the desk hoping to spot the camera he had placed a few days earlier. The camera was still intact. He quickly swapped out the micro-SD card. Though he had only been at the property minutes, he had no intention of staying longer than absolutely necessary. If he had been caught at the property earlier, he would have been able to fall back on the invitation from Olivia. Now, however, it had been made clear to him that he would be trespassing, and he was under no illusion that Rupert would insist on nothing less than a Police record. Taking a few more pictures of the room, he departed and headed at pace back out of the house and through the Wood.

That evening, Briggs brought home take out beef noodles in cardboard cups. After dinner Briggs shut herself away writing up a report for Mr. Samir on the situation regarding his wife. Ben sat in an office and transferred files from the SD card and his phone, over to the company computer. Once complete, he started viewing the camera footage on the monitor. He soon realised that while the camera's location made it harder to detect, it also compromised a lot of the footage, showing mostly legs from the thigh down. On the Thursday evening, multiple people had been in that bedroom and none dressed in tweed.

Ben watched as occasionally legs wandered across the lens of the camera. Some heading into the bathroom, some just seemingly loitering around. Ben found himself counting legs. Four different people. Then…

The camera switched on and started recording as a figure slumped down into the corner. The person was covered by a blanket large enough to cover the head and shoulders down to the person's waist. The person wasn't moving. After a few moments the camera stopped recording. "Bollocks," Ben said out loud and quickly selected the next recording.

The figure was barely moving but just enough to trigger the camera. The head and shoulders remained covered. Ben looked at the timestamp, almost two a.m. on the Friday morning. A hand slowly appeared from under the blanket, painted fingernails on slender hands. The hand scratched at the floor. Ben tilted his head to see if it helped him see the scratches more clearly. Recording continued as the hand picked at the wooden floorboards. Small pieces splintered off creating the scratches he had seen himself earlier in the day. The finger moved around picking at the boards, then the nail broke off. Ben winced as he watched. The hand shot back under the blanket, and the person under the blanket started to rock back and forth. The motion kept the camera recording though nothing else happened for the next couple of minutes.

The hand reappeared, specks of blood clotted around the balance of the remaining nail. With a different finger, the scratching resumed. Again, Ben found himself unconsciously tilting his head for a better look. *A 't'?* he thought as the hand continued picking. He then remembered he had taken a picture. He paused the playback and brought up the picture he had taken with his phone. He zoomed in.

Briggs suddenly appeared in front of him. Getting used to people appearing suddenly was one of the many things one had to get used to after losing their hearing.

"What do you have?" she said, after confirming she had his attention.

"Look, what do you think this is?" Ben asked, nodding at the screen in front of him.

"Scratches?"

"Yeah. I took this picture earlier today. And here, this is footage from the camera."

Ben switched views back to the camera recording and selected resume. They watched the video as the scratch made by the hand from under the blanket, morphed into the picture Ben had taken with his phone.

"What the fuck?"

"Yeah, that's what I said," replied Ben, glancing between Briggs and the recording.

Briggs reached for the mouse. "When was this?" she asked. "Just last night? You didn't update the year on the timestamp," she added, answering her own question.

She scrolled the recording back. "Well, we haven't scared them off."

They watched the fingernail break in double time in reverse, then forward again. Briggs brought the footage back to the point it was at before rewinding it. She let it run as a muscular arm reached down grabbing the person's wrist, forcefully yanking the arm away from the floor and up. They watched as the person still covered by the blanket, is forced to their feet. The figure stands and then stumbles out of sight of the camera, the blanket falling to the floor.

"What the fuck?" Briggs repeated.

The footage ran for another thirty seconds before ending. Her hand reached the mouse before Ben's, and she scrolled the footage back. They watched it again, this time at half normal speed as the covered figure is forced from the corner of the room.

"Is there anymore?" Briggs asked.

Ben shook his head, "No, that was the last entry. It shuts off when there's no movement. What do you think is going on?"

Briggs was shaking her head. "Prostitution? Kidnapping? Not sure, but I don't like it. It looks like they were going to scratch an 'H', look, see how they have made this line, then the hand goes here and moves down before the nail breaks."

"A name or initial?"

"Or H as in Help," Briggs responded, her hand leaving the mouse.

Ben reached for the mouse and replayed footage slowly backwards and forwards. He paused on specific frames and used the software to enlarge certain parts of what was being displayed. The hand was smaller than his own, smaller than Briggs' but larger than a small child's.

"A teenager?" he asked.

"Yeah, could be," Briggs replied.

He moved the footage on. The powerful arm enters the frame.

"White male," Ben noted. "Look, scratches along the forearm, some scarring around the knuckles," Ben continued, pointing at the area on the monitor.

He went frame by frame as the person is lifted and the blanket falls to the floor. Hoping for a glimpse of who might be underneath. Nothing.

"Take it back a bit, to the arm, take another look at the wrist," Briggs instructed. "There, look, a tattoo. Take a screen print and send it to me. Ben didn't move but remained looking up at her from his chair. Briggs looked directly at him. He shrugged his shoulders. Briggs rolled her eyes. "Function and Print Screen," she said, reaching across and pressing the keys on the keyboard as she spoke.

"Okay, what now?"

"Now, we have some proper investigative work to do. I'm going to see if I can do anything with this tattoo and you," she paused.

"Missing children?" Ben prompted.

"About a hundred thousand are reported missing in the UK every year. Perhaps fifteen hundred of those in this county alone."

"Kids?"

"Yup, about half will be girls." Briggs confirmed. "We're going to have to ramp up surveillance of that place. Get some proper evidence that will engage the authorities."

"This is proper evidence," Ben protested.

"No. It won't be sufficient for any arrests and if the Police blunder in there, Rupert will simply move the operation elsewhere. Look, we think there's a pattern to them using the premises. Thursdays? Over the next couple of days, see what you can do with the surveillance and try to get some damn audio."

"I thought this was going to be teenagers messing around or something. This is serious." He said.

Ben spent the next hour researching surveillance, the do's and don't, though much of it were simply adverts for various private investigators and surveillance firms. It made him realise, Grey and Briggs Investigators didn't have a website. He wondered how his gift would headline – 'Grey has to fall asleep on the job to get things done', or, 'Grey the man hears nothing and everything'.

Ben typed 'Missing children in the UK" into the search bar. After a few more clicks, he began reading about one parent's ordeal. A male teenager was reported missing by his parents after not arriving home after going to his local badminton club. Club members confirmed Jayden was at the club and left around ten p.m. He was cycling home. CCTV at a local store showed him pass by six minutes later on what would have been his usual route home. Jayden didn't arrive. His dad had stayed up to wait for him, assuring Jayden's mum that he had probably just bumped into other friends on the way home. She went to bed. By midnight, the father was concerned and took the car to go out looking for him. He returned before two a.m. and woke his wife. They in turn called relatives who lived nearby and Jayden's friends, some of whom came out to help search. *Nothing.* Jayden's body was discovered a few weeks later, discovered in a river and too badly decomposed for a visual identification.

'We're devastated,' his mum was reported saying, *'he was such a good boy, caring, funny, and stayed out of trouble. I'm heartbroken. I still look at his picture on the wall, I can't believe he's not coming back. We need to know what happened. We feel let down by the Police. We've not been given any answers. We don't know how we died, when he died, or why. We need answers.'*

Ben recalled his own childhood when a girl from his secondary school, a grade above him, had been reported missing. He remembered her friends at school, all bunched around in the playground, red-eyed and sombre. Her body had been discovered a few days later at the back of someone's garden, apparently dumped over the back wall. Ben's thoughts returned to the figure in his footage.

There was a change to the lighting. Ben looked up and turned around to see Briggs switching off some of the lights. She walked over and signed, 'I'm heading up. I'll see you in the morning.' Ben nodded. He sat there in the room, his back to the computer, staring out into the office space where Briggs had been standing moments before. Playing through various explanations for what he had seen, none of them were innocent and all of them were varying degrees of troubling.

Ben was turning south onto the M40 by seven fifteen the next morning, the GPS navigating him to an upmarket spy store in Beaconsfield. Traffic was heavy with London commuters, but the drive was at least picturesque as the motorway carved its way through the Oxford countryside. Ben yawned and reached for his coffee.

An hour later, Ben was turning off onto Amersham Road. The traffic flow abruptly changed to the other side of the road. Ben drove past the football and rugby clubs on his way north. A few moments later he was turning left into the Ledborough Lane, but a lane it was not. The road was wide and smooth. Mansions sat in their acreages on both sides. Modern versions of the Cricklewood Mansion, each one architecturally different but all equally enormous. Another minute and another turn, into Wilton Road. The store should be just down here.

As he pulled up outside the store, he could tell he was too early. The sign confirmed he had some thirty minutes to kill. Taking his phone from its cradle on the dashboard, he searched for local coffee shops and selected the Flying Bean. It wasn't long before he found himself parking at the train station and looking around for the coffee shop. He saw a line up at a red van and there it was, the Flying Bean coffee truck. With a quick look at the clouds above, Ben got out and joined the back of the line.

Ben thought it odd that a specialist spy store would be tucked away in a quaint village. He had driven past Beaconsfield on many occasions but never through it. The small part of the town that he had now driven was sufficient to work out the answer. The train station would be only minutes away at most for anyone living in the town. Most residents could likely walk the distance if so desired and weather permitting. The London tube awaiting less than thirty minutes away and Heathrow airport very accessible from here. Throw in a Waitrose, a decent secondary school, and a few boutique shops and the multi-millionaire's checklist was complete. The people here had homes worth protecting.

Ben watched as the next three customers ordered and then received their coffee, extrapolating how long he was going to have to wait. He checked the skies again then regretted not grabbing the umbrella from boot, but he wasn't about to leave the line now. The line progressed faster than he had estimated, and the coffee proved better than expected. As he walked back to the car, rain started to fall.

Ben was able to park right outside the spy store which was just as well as the heavens had opened – the kind of rain that made you think Noah might sail by at any moment. He clambered into the store drawing a concerned look from the elderly proprietor. Ben smiled.

"Sorry, it's raining pretty hard," he said, pointing behind him.

The man's stare lingered longer than Ben considered friendly. He stood with a stoop, a couple of inches shorter than Ben, with grey willowy hair. His complexion fair with skin that had seen many an English winter, or summer.

Ben glanced around the store. There were no other customers. The man turned his back to Ben and moved slowly around a counter at the rear of the store.

Posters advertising all different types of equipment lined the upper part of the walls. Beneath the posters stood a line of metal shelving filled with boxes of all shapes and sizes. Three further lines of shelving occupied the floor space between the walls, creating four aisles. Ben wiped his feet and commenced down the closest aisle. He was no expert but the sheer variety of products on display made him confident he was in the right place. But he wasn't sure what he wanted.

"Need anything?" the man said as Ben approached the end of the aisle.

"Er, yes, I'm hoping you can help me?" Ben replied. Ben moved closer to the counter. "Hi, my name is Benjamin Grey, I'm a partner in a private investigation firm. We're in need of some equipment for a," Ben suddenly wasn't sure what to say. "A delicate operation," he added.

"Spying is a delicate matter," the man replied. The man's eyes drifted toward a stool next to the counter. Ben sat down.

"I'm running surveillance on a substantial property. Thing is I can't get that close to the property. I'm after getting quality images and audio."

"From what distance?" the man asked.

"I'm not sure, a hundred metres or so."

"Images won't be a problem at that distance, but audio will require specialist equipment. Are you looking to buy or rent?"

"Er, what's the difference?" Ben asked.

The man sighed. "You can get decent images from mobile phones these days for that kind of distance, but for audio you'll need a parabolic. The cheapest parabolic starts at around a hundred but don't get one of those, they're shite. I can let you have a proper one for three hundred, or you can rent one for fifty quid a week."

Ben considered his options.

"New to this?" the man asked.

"Yes, I guess. We opened just the other week."

"Any previous experience?"

"Well, it's my partner that has all the experience."

The man nodded.

"Could I take a look?" Ben asked.

"Next aisle, half-way down, second shelf from the bottom. The Sound Shark might be a good option for you."

Ben went to look and returned placing a box on the counter.

"No, don't open that one." The man turned and disappeared for a moment into a room at the back. He returned holding something similar to an oversized handgun with a glass collar around the muzzle.

"This is similar to the Shark, though its not nearly as good. They all have the same basic design. Directional microphone, parabolic dish, storage media, monocular, then you're into features like Bluetooth and auto-record."

"It links to my phone?"

"Not this thing, but that one yeah. Next price bracket has you buying individual components, the microphone and dish separately giving greater distance and recording options but for more money of course. After that, your best bet is drones, but then you're up into the thousands for those."

"I'll take this," Ben confirmed, trying to sound like he was following the conversation.

"Purchase or rent?" the man asked.

"Purchase please."

"It comes with a basic media card that'll store about forty minutes of decent audio. You need something bigger?" the man asked.

"Sure," Ben replied.

"I'll throw this in for free," he said, with a hint of a smile.

Driving back, Ben's phone flashed a text message from Briggs, "How are you getting on?"

"Siri, reply, 'Good. You?'" Ben stated as clearly as he knew how. Siri converted his speech to text and waited for further instruction. Ben glanced at the message, "Siri, Send," he said.

The motorway was clear with the commuter traffic still a few hours away. The rain petered out and stopped, and Ben did too, at the Ardley Services. Opening the boot, he opened the Shark box and inspected each piece. The battery was rechargeable. He placed the battery into the 'gun' wondering if it would indicate the level of charge remaining. It did. Three of the five bars were lit amber. According to the manual, that charge was good for about an hour. He took the battery and charging cable and headed into the motorway services. The early morning start had likewise shifted his lunch time and a ten-thirty burger felt very appealing right now.

Inside the Services, Ben chose a table away from the entrance and a seat that allowed him to see the majority of people coming and going. Not because he was particularly interested in the people, he wasn't, but he had learned it lowered the potential for embarrassing moments – the spectre of someone talking to him from behind and thinking him rude for not responding.

Burger in one hand, he scanned the news on his phone with the other. Rumours of war and growing unrest, politics and celebrity mishaps were staple for the media, and today didn't disappoint. He was about to open the mobile game when the phone vibrated, Briggs.

"Any joy? She asked.

"I think so," Ben replied. "I explained to the guy what I was wanting to do and followed his advice. He seemed to know what he was doing. It's a mic with a parabolic that connects to a phone."

On video Briggs was nodding. "Okay, it means a stakeout. I know the patterns have been Thursday but with the footage you got from yesterday, I'm wondering if they brought things forward a day."

"You don't think they'll be there tonight?" Ben asked. "Where are you?". Briggs was holding her phone close to her face, wind and rain photo-bombing the video.

"I'm bloody freezing," Briggs replied. "I'm stood outside the Imagearium offices and its just started raining. I have some interviews to conduct this afternoon. I'll be back before five. Let's meet up and I'll come with you to the Mansion tonight."

Ben nodded, "Okay, I'll let you go, see you later then."

He closed the call and placed the phone on the table. Twirling a chip pierced to this fork, Ben looked around the service station. Truckers, construction workers, white collar employees, and families. He watched them line up, order their food, pay, find a place to sit. Just as Ben had done. All seemingly perfectly normal.

And yet, Ben sat knowing he could fold his arms, rest his head and likely within minutes start tuning into any and all of their thoughts. How many secrets were being kept by those around him right now. He estimated around forty adults were at the services, meaning at least four had criminal convictions, a few more probably should have criminal convictions, and at least one person in here right now will have multiple convictions, most likely for violent crime. Perhaps even one or two are paedophiles. What really is normal? If we could peel back the veil, the facades, and strip everything back, what would we really see? We go about our lives in the knowledge that darkness exists but believing it to be somewhere else – not near us. The sad truth is its all around us and everywhere. Ben was all too aware. His gift gave him a glimpse under the covers, perhaps more than a glimpse, and the hours clocked had nurtured the cynicism of a homicide veteran.

And still Ben found himself returning. At first it was curiosity, curiosity in its power, the wonderment of losing ones hearing only for it to be replaced in a different form. Then came the practicing, the realisation that he could improve his skills, perfect them. But once perfected, the gift seemed shallow, a novelty. Until the London terrorist attack. Ben watched as a young girl dropped her ice cream. Stumbling onto the terrorist plans had given him purpose, and stopping the attacks had made him believe he can make a difference. Purpose and Belief, two of the most powerful forces in the universe, he had once been told.

A woman rushed to help the child that was now tearing up, staring down at the spoiled cone. A man picked up the cone and placed it in the bin while the woman used a tissue to wipe the floor. There was an exchange between the man and woman, the man reassuring the woman the child was fine. The man ushered the young girl back over to the counter where the employee seemed happy to replace the order.

Ben was interrupted from his musings as the wind outside picked up and rain hit the window next to him. He checked the time on his phone, cleared the remaining chips from his plate, and headed out.

Bluetooth on Ben's phone has a range of around thirty feet. They had driven up in the Corsa as it was less conspicuous than the Tesla and parked inside the Havishem's garage much to the displeasure of Arther Havishem. From the very brief exchange between Olivia and Arther, it was clear that while Arthur was initially supportive of finding out what had been going on at the Mansion, he was now of the opinion that it should be left with Rupert. Ben wondered how much of the investigation Olivia had shared with Arthur.

Ben and Briggs were sat in camping chairs under the cover of the tree line, within range of the mics for the Bluetooth function. But for the light from the house, it was otherwise dark. The earlier rain had ceased, and the wind settled to a light breeze.

"Not our first stakeout," Ben stated as he opened the container of beef teriyaki.

"No, but it is the first where it has felt more like camping." Briggs replied.

They were both skeptical anything would happen at all tonight, and were certain if anything did, it wouldn't be for a few more hours. It wasn't long before they heard the sound of footsteps approaching across the gravel driveway.

"Oh, that's lovely," Briggs said, as Alison approached holding a full tea tray.

"Olivia thought you might need it," she replied. "A pot of tea, some sugar and milk on the side if you need it. There's some digestives there too. Hopefully the rain stays away but if you need more umbrellas Olivia said to help yourself from those in the porch."

"Perfect, thank you, that's really nice of you." Briggs confirmed.

Over tea, Briggs shared where she was at with respect to Imagearium and the interviews she had conducted earlier.

"Where are the chips manufactured?" Ben asked.

"Taiwan."

"Aren't you going to need to go there?"

"Probably," she said, cleaning a spot of sauce from her lip. "There's a bit more background information needed from this end, but yes, I'm expecting to have to meet with the supplier."

"If they are at fault, they're not just going to admit it."

"Of course not. Showing up will put some formality to the claims but the hope is I'll find a disgruntled employee willing to share information with me."

"Does that really happen?" Ben asked.

"Sometimes."

"Well, how useful can that be?

"This is very unlikely to go to court. The chip supplier is huge, there's no chance of a local printer bringing a successful action against them. It's about reaching a settlement. I just need a whiff of something to help the companies settle."

"How's your Chinese?"

"About as good as yours," she replied. Waving her phone, "I'll have my translator."

They had agreed that if nothing had happened by midnight that Briggs would go home. Ben would then stay until two a.m. and call her if anything did subsequently come up. Evening became night and a little after ten, the internal lights at the Havishem property turned off.

"Time for bed," Ben remarked, pacing around.

"Do you think they are keeping the outside lights on just for us?" Briggs asked. "Are you okay, do you need the loo?"

"No." Ben replied, in a tone that made it sound like the word had bounced off a wall. "Just bored and my legs are seizing up."

"I can stay if you want. It doesn't look like anything is going to happen tonight anyway." Briggs said.

"Don't you have to be up in the morning? How is Mrs. Samir?

"I don't need as much sleep as you. She's not cheating on her old man, she's doing charity work for the homeless. I don't know why, but it would seem she didn't want to let her husband know what she was up to. My morning meeting is with Mr. Samir to let him know what she's up to."

"You don't think you should tip Mrs. Samir off first?"

"The thought had crossed my mind, but Mr. Samir is the one paying. I think he'll be quite relieved when he finds out, so whatever objection he may have to her doing charity work might no longer be important. And besides, then I would be the one effectively telling her that her husband is spying on her."

"Is it always like this?" asked Ben, marching in a circle while raising his knees up.

"Like what?"

"Well, it's awkward. We don't know why she hasn't told her husband, and you are about to drop her in it."

"I'm not dropping her in it. I've been hired, we've been hired, to do a job. I'm doing the job. It could be worse."

"How?"

"She might actually have been cheating on him." Briggs replied, her smile barely visible in the dim light.

Ben stopped with his marching in preference to standing on the spot, crouching up and down.

"You know you can relieve yourself in the trees or do you need me to look away?" Briggs teased.

"I don't need the toilet. I just..." Ben's voiced tailed off as he noticed vehicle lights approaching up the road. Briggs stood to look.

Multiple vehicles approached.

"Quick, move this stuff," Briggs said in a hushed voice.

They collapsed the chairs, and Briggs grabbed the tea tray and a shoulder bag before heading back toward the Havishem place. Ben climbed the tree in which the mic had been affixed.

The vehicles, a white transit van followed by a black Volkswagen saloon, drove past the Havishem entrance and down the Mansion driveway. Ben opened the app on his phone and popped in his ear buds.

Briggs placed the tray and the bag down on the ground at the side of the house. Unzipping the holdall, she grabbed a taser and slide it down part-way down the back of her jeans. On her phone, she opened the surveillance app to which the cameras and mic had been connected. After the vehicles had passed, she made her way back across the gravel and over to Ben. She put her ear buds in.

"Can you hear me?" Briggs asked, almost in a whisper.

Of course, Ben couldn't hear her, but text appeared in a small window open on his phone.

"Yes," he replied into the mic connected to his ear buds.

"Ok, going silent." She said,

From his position up the tree, Ben watched the vehicles pull up at the front of Mansion. As people started getting out, he turned his attention to the view on the phone, the night vision camera providing a much better view. Sound waves started to appear on the app.

As the driver of the Transit got out. The first to appear from the rear of the van was a tall figure, presumably male, handling a dog. The dog was large and immediately attentive. The word 'shit' appeared on Ben's phone. Ben nodded.

Two figures exited the VW, and Briggs could tell from the voice one of them was Rupert. The other figure from the VW was shorter, and slender. *Monica?* Ben thought. *What's she doing with Rupert? Where's James?*

"Ok, get them out," the figure assumed to be Rupert instructed.

From the back of the van three smaller figures emerged each of them covered. They were shepherded into the house by another, larger figure that emerged from the van. Dog Man closed the van doors.

"Make sure we're alone," Rupert said to Dog Man.

The figure with the dog held on to dog's lead and headed up the driveway, away from Ben's position.

Below Ben, Briggs watched as Dog Man led the dog away from their position, and the remaining figures went into the house. It wasn't long before lights on the second floor appeared. Briggs licked a finger and pointed it into the air and moved it around before deciding the slight breeze was in fact, blowing their scent away from and not toward the Mansion. She let out a deep breath. She checked the time, quarter to eleven.

The dog barked briefly then stopped. It was still some distance from Ben and Briggs' position. Ben kept switching his attention between the second floor of the house and his phone, hoping for a view of the smaller figures taken into the house.

"This isn't working," Ben whispered.

'It's fine' came a reply.

"What about the dog?"

'The wind is blowing our scent away from the house. I think we'll be fine.'

"You think?"

'Be quiet.'

They both watched as Dog Man came into view. He was getting. A bead of sweat slid down Ben's face. Below, Briggs had curled up in the foliage, the taser now in her hand. The dog barked though not incessantly.

Dog Man held on to the lead as the dog tugged. Closer. They moved along the tree line. The dog barked again. Seemingly satisfied, Dog Man pulled the dog from the trees and continued past Ben's position.

Briggs heard Ben's sigh of relief.

Ben watched the second floor. Shadows and light moved in the room with the yoga mats. His shoulders slumped.

"We're not going see anything," he said.

'Be patient and shut up.'

After giving Dog Man time to get further away, Briggs sat up and brushed off the leaves. They waited.

After some ten minutes, the figure they assumed to be Rupert appeared at the steps to the house. He stopped.

Dog Man reappeared from the side of the house and walked to ward Rupert.

"Anything?" Rupert asked.

"Nah, just some wildlife," Dog Man replied. Briggs recognised the accent as east European, though which country she had no idea.

"Okay, put the dog in the van, they'll be here shortly." Rupert instructed.

The dog continued to look in Ben's direction as it was pulled then pushed into the back of the white van. Briggs checked the time again.

It wasn't long before more headlights approached. Two cars pulled up and parked alongside the white van. A single figure exited the car in front while four figures got out from the car behind.

"Let's go inside," the single figure said in a male voice.

Ben watched the portly single figure and assumed he was looking at James Stanley. James, followed by the four other people, entered the house.

"James Stanley, the fat one." he said. Briggs responded with a thumbs-up emoji. Again, they waited.

Again, they didn't have to wait long before the lights from upstairs moved downstairs and people gathered at the entrance. The three smaller figures, still covered in what looked like blankets, were escorted to the back of the same white van. The dog barked when the van doors were opened.

"Can we expect a delivery next month?" One of the figures asked in a thick east European accent.

"No, we're going to have pause for a couple months. We'll confirm things to your boss in two weeks." Replied Rupert.

"Trouble?" the man asked.

"Nothing we can't handle."

The two figures shook hands and soon the van and one of the saloons had driven away. Three figures remained, Rupert, James, and Monica. James and Monica returned to the car that James had pulled up in, while Rupert returned to the other. Both cars drove the very short distance to the Stanley's property.

After the cars had left, Ben climbed down from the tree. He looked around for Briggs but couldn't see her.

"Where are you?" he said into the mic. No reply. He took a few steps away from the trees and toward the Havishem house, then noticed someone walking up the driveway. Briggs emerged from the darkness covered in twigs and leaves.

"Where were you?" Ben asked.

"The cameras won't get the licence plate."

"How did you get half the Wood on you?"

"Oh," she replied, looking down at herself. "I thought I had better lay low when the dog came close," removing more foliage.

After gathering stuff back into the car, Ben sat with his hands on the steering wheel.

Giving Ben a poke in the side Briggs asked, "What?"

"Those were kids," he replied.

"Yes, and we're going to help them."

"How are we helping them? We just let them drive away."

Briggs placed a reassuring hand on his wrist. "We are going to help them. I'll run this plate down and we'll figure out how to approach Rupert."

"This is bullshit," Ben responded, the profanity feeling strange in his mouth but nonetheless justified.

"If we go to the Police with what we have, its circumstantial at best. Yes, it looks dodgy and yes, they'll probably go ask some questions. Then what? Rupert is spooked, moves the operation, and we still don't know where those kids have gone."

"How long... how long do those kids have?"

Briggs sighed. "Forty-eight hours perhaps a bit longer. Depends what's really going on."

"They're bloody paedophiles. What else would they be for? And how the hell do they get them?"

"Runaways, kids looking for shelter, food. It's possible they could be being moved out of the country."

"What? Then we'll never find them!"

"I know, but the bit of good news is, if that is the case, it will probably take them longer and we'll have a bit more time to find them."

Ben checked the time. "I won't be able to get a room at the pub. Do you mind getting an Uber? I could stay here in the car and see if I can find anything else out."

Briggs looked at him for a moment. "Sure, let me call them now."

She leaned over and gave him a polite peck on the cheek. "Don't do anything stupid. You need me, you call me."

Ben nodded as Briggs got out of the car and made the call.

"About fifteen minutes. I'm going to walk up to the main road. You get started." She said, leaning her face to the window.

"Can you close the garage?"

The garage door closed and soon the automatic light went out. The car, and Ben were enveloped in darkness. He tilted the seat back, took a deep breath and closed his eyes.

CHAPTER SIX

"What's the address again?" James asked.

"sakwlvm7z2lcfa96," Monica replied, pronouncing each character. "And it's onion." She added.

"Yes, I know that. Just so damned hard to keep track of these stupid addresses."

"Well, that's the point old boy," Rupert interjected. "It would be stupid if they were easy."

"What are you looking at?" Monica asked.

"I'm just checking the last shipment." James responded. After a minute he said, "We are going to need more. They're bidding on them. Multiple bids."

"That's good, it will keep the price up." Rupert replied.

"If we expanded the operation, we'd be able to sell more."

"Honestly, your whining is becoming such a bore. As with any enterprise, if one grows too quickly one runs into supply and quality issues. We don't all need the money as much as you. Perhaps you should have looked after your investments a little better."

"You can be a prick, Rupert," James responded sharply.

"Boys, please," Monica interrupted, "You are both right. Yes, we are in this for the money, but Rupert is right, if we screw up again like the other week, we'll put the whole operation at risk. And our continental friends wouldn't be very happy with that at all. That kind of fallout would be bad for us all."

"I'm going to bed." James confirmed.

Ben continued to tune in and after a brief silence, Rupert spoke again.

"What do you see in that man?"

"Rupert, I thought boys were more your thing?" Monica replied. "He's not all that bad," Monica replied. "And besides, what else am I going to do while I'm sat around here. A girl needs to find some pleasure."

"I think people would understand if you…ate at a different restaurant occasionally."

"Who says I don't?"

"I could see why Edwina tolerated him. Fitting into her social circles, attending the same country clubs, make a speech here and there like the good lap dog he is."

"You are cruel," Monica said.

"Yes. The next thing you know I'll be rounding up unwanted children and selling them to the highest bidder."

They both laughed.

In the silence, Ben struggled to remain listening and fell asleep.

He was awoken by the light from the garage door opening. Despite looking at Arthur, Arthur proceeded with rapping his knuckles against the window.

"I'm deaf not blind," Ben said, though more to himself.

Ben slid the window down and peered up to make sure he could see Arthur speaking.

"What are you doing here?"

After a brief exchange and an apology, Ben reversed the car out and drove away from the Havishem's house, only to pull up again near the village. He was just in time to see '6:45' appear on the car's clock. He sat with his head resting on the steering wheel, playing back the conversation from the night. *What the hell did she mean by "onion"?* he thought, desperately trying to recall the sequence of letters and numbers that Monica had so specifically given.

It is said ten thousand hours of practice are required to truly master something. By that measure, Ben might not yet have reached the rank of Master, but he was surely a maven. One thing he had quickly learned relating to his gift, was the importance of a good memory. His gift was frustrating enough without recalling partial conversations. The gist of a conversation was fine but codes…pin numbers, access codes, and whatever the hell they were talking about last night, required precision.

From his teens he had exercised his memory, sometimes listening into the most mundane of conversations, and applying associative techniques – connecting something you want to remember with something you are already familiar with. For numbers, Ben used the rooms in the house he grew up in – he had to include the downstairs toilet and upstairs bathroom as rooms. For the alphabet, Ben used the houses down his street or at least as many as were needed. Both sides of the street, starting on the right side then alternating, 'A' on the right followed by 'B' on the left and so on.

But the real skill, and where the practice was required, was connecting everything. It wasn't physical exercise or healthy lifestyle choices, but Marvel characters that made the difference.

Multiple Marvel characters have been written for each letter of the alphabet. Ben chose his favourite for each and uses these characters to connect houses along the street and rooms within his house.

As Ben rested his head on the steering wheel, a cartoon played out in his mind, a patchwork of scenes assembled during the conversation. Characters emerging from a house or a room from within Ben's childhood home. A fight meant Ben was done with the character and when Ben himself appeared, in true Hitchcockian style, the cartoon ended.

Satisfied, Ben drove home.

As the toast popped up, Briggs came up the stairs, sweating and removing airpods from her ears.

"Morning," Ben said, trying to sound cheery. "Toast? Coffee?"

"Sure, thanks. You're up early," Briggs replied.

"That would be thanks to Arthur Havishem and his golf match." Ben hesitated, as Briggs poured herself an orange juice from the fridge. "I heard something last night but have no idea what it might mean. It was an odd sequence of letters and numbers."

"You remember the sequence?"

"Yeah, it ends with Ant-Man coming out of the upstairs bathroom and joining me in the bedroom."

"What? Oh, that's your dumb memory palace. Sounds like I should be thankful the sequence wasn't any longer."

"It's not dumb or a memory palace. And I'd like to see you remember a complex sequence while your half asleep. Anyway, yes, I can remember the sequence, but it's gibberish. I've written it down on the table. I was hoping it might mean something to you."

Briggs sat down with her juice and looked at the paper laying on the table. She looked back at Ben, shaking her head.

"What else did you hear? Any clues as to what it might be?" She asked.

Ben tried to recall the conversation. "James asked for an address, that's when Monica spelt out this. And she called it an onion, at least that's what I thought she said. Weird huh?"

"No actually, it isn't." Briggs replied. "Onion makes a lot of sense. They were talking about the dark web. The code you heard would be a dark web address."

"The dark web?"

"Yes, the dark web." Briggs confirmed. "Estimates are ninety percent of internet traffic occurs on the dark web. Sites on the dark web are protected from tracking and surveillance, hence 'dark'. The part of the internet that you and I use is referred to as the surface web. There are plenty of legit businesses on the dark web but, if you are going to undertake something nefarious, doing it under the cover of dark is always best."

"So, what do we do with this address? Just type it into Google?"

"No, we're going to need a different browser, and a quarantined space in which to work. I know someone we can reach out to. I'll ask them to set us up. I don't think it would take them long and its hopefully something they can do online."

Ben bit into his toast. "You think the site might be legit?" he asked, trying to keep crumbs from escaping.

"No, I don't. I'm going to get showered then I'll make that phone call. Was there anything else?"

Ben shrugged, "Not really. Some stuff that suggested Monica and James may not be a real couple if you catch my drift."

"What? James is gay?" Briggs asked.

"No. But I think Rupert might be. No, I mean, just from the way they were talking. It's more like it's a relationship of convenience. I don't know, more of a cover then something genuine."

"Was anything said about a password? The site might require a password to access it."

Ben shook his head.

"Okay, no matter, we should be able to take a look later today. And Ben?" Briggs asked, checking to see if Ben was still looking at her, "Good job. You're right, it's not dumb. A bit weird, but not dumb," she said as the door closed.

Ben finished his toast and washed it down with the remainder of his coffee. Like a greasy take out, the thought of those people being loaded into the van, had left Ben feeling nauseous. But fatigue was setting in. No longer pumped with the adrenalin of the night before, the lack of quality sleep was taking its toll. Ben leaned back on the couch and with a flicker his eyelids closed, and he fell asleep.

It was a little after ten a.m. when Ben walked down the stairs ruffling his hair and opened the door into the office area. He was surprised to see Briggs in conversation with a rather animated couple, clearly upset about something. Not wanting to interrupt he remained at the door while plotting a path through the office.

The couple were in their mid to late thirties. The woman was tearful, and both wore the look of worry. Ben moved slowly around the edges of the office, trying to appear casual. The man noticed.

Ben smiled and approached. The couple were seated on the couch. Briggs was in a chair that she had moved closer to the couple. She had her back to Ben. When the woman also looked at Ben, Briggs turned and smiled.

"This is my associate Benjamin Grey," she said, keeping her gaze more toward Ben.

"Hi," Ben replied, "sorry for interrupting."

"Not a problem," Briggs responded, "in fact, it would be good for you to meet Mr. and Mrs. Dalton." She signalled for Ben to take a seat.

Adjusting the angle of her chair, Briggs continued. "Mr. and Mrs. Dalton have a fifteen-year-old daughter, Sarah, that has not been seen since yesterday morning. They are understandably very concerned and wondered if there might be something we can do to help."

"Have you contacted the Police?" Ben asked.

"We went there first," Mr. Dalton replied.

"She left the house yesterday morning. She told us she would be out for the day and not back until later in the evening. Will and I had tickets for the Opera in the evening and so we were late back. We assumed Sarah was sleeping by the time we got back to the house. When she hadn't got up for school this morning, we checked her room, and she wasn't there. The bed had not been slept in." Mrs. Dalton said, her voice starting to break. "We started calling some of her friends but all we could found out is that she was meeting a boy. Nobody could give us his name. That's when we decided to involve the Police."

"The Police were very polite and have opened an investigation, but we just felt that they might not start looking into it straight away, you know." Added Mr. Dalton.

"You see, she has done this before. Not runaway, but just not come back the same day. I was so angry. We grounded her for a month. I was so worried. I was sure she wouldn't do it again. But the Police…" Mrs. Dalton's voice trailed off.

"Could you excuse Ben and I a moment, please?" Briggs asked.

Briggs and Ben stood up, and Briggs ushered Ben into a side room and closed the door.

"I thought you might be able to take the lead on this one," she said. Ben frowned. "I know we have the Havishem case, but I also have this corporate case that I need to spend some time on. You've done missing persons before, and you should be able to squeeze in this one. What do you think?"

Thoughts of the hooded teenagers being shepherded away for who knows what, were stuck in Ben's head. Images of Caroline Walters and Louise Larke flashed across his mind. Caroline's body tragically discovered two days after she had gone missing. Louise Larke went missing the day after Caroline. Now Sarah Dalton.

"Sophie, we're running out of time for those kids we saw at the house."

People typically only start a sentence with someone's name when they want to make sure they were listening. Ben was no different. Briggs turned her shoulders toward him and stiffened as she looked back into his eyes.

"We are going to catch these bastards," she reassured. "There's the possibility these are related. Are you okay to do this?"

"Sure, let me take it."

"I'll show them in. Coffee?"

A moment later, Briggs brought Mr. and Mrs. Dalton into the room, then followed up a few minutes later with a coffee and two teas. Ben spent most of the next hour gathering as much information as he could from the Dalton's. He confirmed his rate and made them aware of his hearing.

When asked about what action he would be taking, Ben responded with several lines of enquiry that he considered worth following up. They appeared satisfied.

On the way out Mrs. Dalton asked, "Sophie, Ms. Briggs, said you've experience of missing people cases. How did those turn out?"

"Yes, it was a young girl around the same age as your daughter Sarah," he replied, thinking back to the April Richmond case. "We managed to find her." Images of April and the serial killer Alexander Jones flashed through his mind. "She was fine," he added.

That afternoon, Ben had made some progress on his lines of enquiry with the Sarah Dalton case, and Briggs' contact was remotely setting up the computer for browsing the dark web. Briggs had been on a video call with Imagearium and shortly after, booked a flight and accommodation to Hsinchu city in Taiwan. She was planning to be away for a week.

"Don't you need a visa?" Ben asked. Briggs shook her head. "Someone must be going with you," he added.

"Three others. A lawyer, the CTO and his assistant," she replied. She paused to look at Ben. "Why, are you worried about me?"

"I'm always worried about you?"

"Aww, you can be a bit of a softie you know. I'll be fine, you do know I've been in some properly dangerous situations. Besides, your case is much more likely to turn violent than mine."

"That's not helpful."

"Let's look at what's going on with this dark web site and see what they are up to. If it's dodgy, we'll just hand what we have over to the Police and let them handle it. That will close out our involvement."

"You fly out on Tuesday?" Ben asked.

"Yup, land Wednesday evening local time after a short stop at Hong Kong. We're travelling together, the CTO's assistance made all the bookings, but we'll meet up for breakfast on the Thursday and plan things from there. The meeting with the supplier isn't until the following Monday, so we have Thursday and Friday, and the weekend if needed, to prepare how we want to approach the meeting. The lawyer will be leading the conversation for us. I plan to make some of my own enquiries once I get there. I've been doing a little research on some employees that work in roles related to the manufacturing. I've also found an ex-employee who recently left the company, though I don't yet know his reasons for leaving. Probably nothing but I'll follow up anyway."

"What happens if nothing gets agreed?"

"We're not expecting them to agree to anything on the Tuesday. We'll give our side, they'll give theirs, and with a bit of luck, we'll reconvene later in the week to hammer something out."

"What do we get out of it?" asked Ben.

"The percentage? One percent of the value of any settlement, on top of our usual fees."

"One percent?"

"I know, doesn't sound like much. But the contract is worth several million, so one percent might not be too bad."

A notification sounded on Briggs' phone. "The computer's ready. Let's go take a look."

Once in the room, Briggs placed her phone down on the desk next to the computer. It was showing some instructions.

Ben sat at the keyboard, while Briggs pulled a chair over and sat next to him.

Ben followed the instructions, opening the TOR browser and carefully typing in the address, checking each digit as he typed. As he finished typing, he said, "It's going to need a password."

"Perhaps not," Briggs replied, moving closer to the monitor as Ben pressed enter.

The screen blinked twice before a simple menu was being displayed along with a short message.

The message read, '*Our product is checked and verified prior to and after every use. You can be assured of its quality. Product can only be sampled at one of our locations unless alternative arrangements are agreed – these will be based on volume and total value.*'

The menu comprised of four labelled rectangular buttons.

"Is this for real?" said Ben, "Looks like a kid has built this page. Pretty sure I could do better."

The buttons were labelled, 'Services', 'Locations', 'Payment', and 'Enquiries'.

"What now?" he asked, looking to Briggs.

They spent the next twenty minutes together going through each menu item and each sub menu until they had explored as much of the site as they could. They still weren't sure what the 'product' that was being offered was, but whatever it was, it was available in many countries across Europe, including the UK, and multiple cities within each. It seemed the default for sampling the product was at designated locations that would not be precisely revealed until purchased. Special requests could be made.

"You think this site is connected to the kids we saw or something else?" Ben asked.

Briggs nodded. "It fits."

"So, we hand this over to the Police?"

Briggs slightly shook her head. "There's nothing here to connect anything. We might have enough for the Police to start an investigation but what are they going to do? Their own surveillance? Repeat what we have spent the last couple of weeks doing?"

"What then? We witnessed kids being shipped off to who knows where to do who knows what."

"Yes! It's a shitty job. You need to have enough to make an arrest and then convict these fuckers. They could arrest anyone for anything if these checks weren't in place. So, if you move too soon with too little, you just scare them off and they'll set up shop somewhere else." Briggs was in thought. "You're going to have to contact them. Make an enquiry, act like your interested."

"Me!?"

"Yes, you. We need more. We need to know where at least one of these locations is. We need proof that Rupert and the Stanleys are involved. Do you think you can get back in the house? You still have a camera in that room, right?"

Ben nodded.

"Okay then," Briggs continued. "Let's also make an enquiry now using the site."

They spent the next ten minutes crafting an enquiry, stating that they required the use of at least ten products for a private function. Money was not an issue given the distinguished attendees.

"What happened with the registration plate?" Ben asked.

"Not stolen, but not a registered plate either."

"People just make plates up?"

"Of course, as long as it looks real and the vehicle isn't doing anything to draw attention, no one is going to check it." Briggs turned Ben's chair toward her own. "I know this is upsetting but it's what we knew could happen when we opened this business. You've seen how life can be pretty shitty sometimes. Those emotions can be a distraction, but we need stay focused and use them as motivation. We need to do things right."

Ben took a deep breath, then asked, "Are your contacts in MI5 able to help?"

"It's the NCA that would need to investigate organised crime. I don't have the same currency since leaving the Service. But yes, I have a friend in London who works at the NCA. She can't directly help us, but she knows a guy in traffic surveillance. He kinda fancies her. Anyway, the plate recognition system allows for plates to be flagged should they pass any of the country's cameras. Our request is obviously unofficial and if anyone asks why our plate has been added to the flag list, it will get removed as an error, but hopefully not before we get a hit back."

Ben nodded and forced a smile.

"Now," she instructed, "get yourself over to the house."

It was late afternoon when Ben parked his Corsa at the end of the road behind the Mansion. He grabbed his jacket from the passenger seat and got out. The energy provided by his earlier nap had been consumed and, like the tide, he could feel the fatigue returning.

He was about to traipse across the field when he noticed fresh cigarette butts on the ground beside the gate. Briggs insisted on keeping what she referred to as a forensic kit in the glovebox of each car. The kit was in fact a small pouch comprising a few Ziploc bags, shoe covers, rubber gloves and Covid masks. It made him wonder if it was training that prompted Briggs to think of these things or if it came naturally to her. Ben took a picture before bagging the fresh butts. He kept the kit with him.

From the rear of the property, Ben watched the house for a couple of minutes before stepping out from his cover. Despite his gift, silence had been his long-time companion. And it is possible to become comfortable with even unwanted companion. But like even the best of companions, there are times they can be a real nuisance. He moved along the side of the property, with only his sight to depend on, his head twitched like that of an owl.

Before approaching the rear entrance, he stopped and looked around again. Nothing. He stepped away from the shadows and walked toward the door. He sneaked and peak through the window, then punched in the code to the lock…nothing. He tried the code again, hoping he might have mis-keyed. Still nothing.

He stepped back from the door and look around. He walked farther back, looking up at the second-floor windows and across more of the house. Forgetting his earlier caution, he jogged over to the other doors at the rear of the property, checking each in vain.

"Didn't insist on a burglar kit did you," he muttered to himself.

He moved around the outside of the house looking for any way in. The house may be old and unmaintained, but the original windows and doors these were not. The front entrance doors could stop a tank and the rest of the doors and windows on the ground level were robust enough to keep this amateur out. But the upper-level windows looked older, a lot older. The twelve-foot ceilings were imposing and a nuisance. Ben did another lap of the house before deciding on a window. If he was going to commit breaking and entering, he wanted to be as inconspicuous as possible.

Two minutes later, Ben was pressing the Havishem's doorbell.

"Oh, hello," Olivia answered, "I was thinking to phone you to ask how it went last night."

Ben felt himself wince. "We are making progress and from what we saw last night, the house is being used as some sort of staging post for something very illegal."

Her eyes sharpened. "Oh, well I don't like the sound of that. What is it that is going on?"

"I'm really sorry but I'm a little strapped for time, and I need some help." Ben responded.

Olivia Havishem's expression changed again, the furrows in her brow deepening. "I don't understand, what's going on? What help?"

"I promise I will explain everything, but I noticed you keep a step ladder in the garage. I wondered if I could borrow it."

"What on earth do you need a ladder for?"

"I realise how this sounds. I still have a camera hidden at the house. It may have some really important footage on it. I can't get back in the house because they must have changed the code again. If I can use the ladder, I may be able to pry open one of the upper windows."

Mrs. Havishem took a moment to weigh the options.

"I see," she said. "Yes, we keep the opener just here next to the door." She took the garage remote from a bowl on the windowsill. "You can use this," she said, pressing the button as she spoke.

Behind Ben, the garage door opened.

"Thank you, kindly Mrs. Havishem, I promise I will come back and explain everything just as soon as I'm done." Ben turned and headed to the garage.

"You're not going to break anything are you!?" she called out after him.

The step ladder was resting against one wall. He wasn't sure the ladder was going to be high enough but then he noticed they could be unlatched and used as a straight ladder if needed. Before grabbing the ladder, he rummaged around a toolbox sitting on a shelf. He grabbed a screwdriver and hammer, then collected the ladder. He noticed Olivia was still watching him as he made his way across her driveway.

Ben paused. "Would it be okay if I went through the bushes here? I think I can squeeze through."

"Well, I suppose so," she replied, now with a phone in her hands.

Ben wondered if she was about to call the Police on him.

He pushed through the bushes and between trees, and with some effort, arrived back at the Mansion driveway. He moved quickly across the driveway and down to the side of the house. Ben had never been accused on being overweight, but he wasn't a paragon of fitness either. He was panting though his predicament fuelled sufficient adrenaline that he wasn't about to stop.

He was at the top of the ladder when he felt it move. Looking down, he saw Olivia Havishem looking up at him, phone in hand.

"You could try this code before you go breaking any windows," she said, holding a slip of paper up.

Ben climbed back down the ladder and looked at the numbers on the paper. He looked back at Mrs. Havishem.

"Well, go on then, go and try that first," she encouraged.

Mrs. Havishem escorted Ben around to the back of the house. Ben punched in the code, and the lock whirred.

"Huh, success, thank you."

"Make sure you put the ladder back where you took it from," she instructed, before walking away.

Ben tucked the slip of paper into a pocket and waited for Mrs. Havishem to turn the corner before heading in. He still found himself glancing around for any recording devices Rupert may have placed. He had no desire to test the legalities between knowing the code and trespassing.

Afternoon would soon be evening, and the overcast sky had placed much of the house in shadow. Switching on the phone light, Ben made his way through the house.

With all the commotion, he was confident no one could be in the house, yet he still found himself creeping down the hallways and up the stairs. He felt the hair on his arms bristle as he touched the door handle to the room in which he hoped to find his camera.

Not much in the room had changed, but it had changed. Ben stood for a moment looking around the room. Images of the blanketed figure slumped in the corner, breaking a nail, flashed through his mind. He looked at the open door where the young girls from the night before would have been led down the stairs and out to the waiting Transit. A sourness filled his stomach as he imagined the girls sobbing in the back of the van, probably bruised, possibly tied, and certainly fearful.

He crouched down to look under the desk, hesitating a moment - Certainty is Hope's ruin. The camera was still there. Letting out his breath, Ben quickly removed the camera and placed it into a pocket. Standing he checked the room one more time. Fresh butts. Again, not sure why it mattered, he took a picture and bagged them. Satisfied, he quickly left the property.

After returning the ladder and tools to their rightful place, Ben rang the Havishem's doorbell again. This time Alison answered wearing an apron. The smell of simmering vegetables filled the air. He was shown into the sitting room. Olivia soon entered the room.

Before sitting she said, "So are you going to explain as to what all that was about?"

"Sorry about that, yes." Ben confirmed.

He spent the next few minutes relaying the events of the previous night and sharing what he thought appropriate about the site on the dark web. He left out that they were young girls and the potential connection to missing teenagers in the county.

"Did you get what you wanted? From the house?

"Er, yes," Ben replied, instinctively touching his pocket.

"Well, what's on it?"

"I'll need to get it back to the office to see what's on it, assuming there is anything on it. The dinner smells great. I'd better be on my way."

Leaving the house, Ben suddenly remembered where he had parked. He looked up at the clouds and hoped for a few more minutes. He set off across the driveway, through the boundary to the Mansion, and around the rear of the property. As he made his way across the grounds, there was a crack of thunder above his head and the heavens opened.

Driving home, Ben was both soaked and starving. He arrived back at the apartment with a kebab and chips in hand. Towelling himself down sufficiently to eat, Ben shared his updates with Briggs over dinner. While Ben showered, Briggs loaded up the camera's memory chip to the computer.

"Anything on it?" Ben asked, as he entered the office room.

"Yeah, lots of legs mostly, but it did get this," she replied, doubling clicking on a clip.

They watched as two pairs of legs, both dressed in blue denim jeans passed by the lens. Then a figure slumped down into the corner, this time without cover. A young girl, perhaps thirteen, sat holding her legs to her chest, shaking and sobbing. Her clothing was frayed and marked. Her face clearly visible.

"Shit," Briggs said.

The girl remained slumped for another minute before being pulled roughly out of camera. A few seconds later the clipped finished. Ben grabbed the mouse and moved the clip back to where the girl's face was in view.

"Do you recognise her?" Briggs asked.

"Nope. It's not Sarah Dalton, and Caroline Walters is black."

"Here, if you look at this clip, you'll see there are others."

Briggs took the mouse and opened a different clip. As the video played, at least two other teenager's legs could be seen. "Here, these are the same shoes worn by the girl we see in the other clip, but these," Briggs paused the video and pointed to the screen, "you can see these are different. Again, the legs are not covered, and the shoe size looks pretty small. And these are different again. These are Velcro." Briggs pointed out.

"Open the other clip again. There, she's in school uniform. Isn't that a logo?" Briggs had paused the video. The image wasn't clear, but it was in the shape of a shield divided into three parts, each part showing something different. Briggs copied the image and pasted it into a different application, where she adjusted it. Gradually the image became clearer, a crest with a building to the right side, an emoji style figure of a person at the base, and what appeared to be kernels of corn on the left.

"Okay, so which school?" Ben asked. "Could we do a manual comparison?"

Typing into a new tab, Briggs soon established there were twenty-eight secondary schools in the Milton Keynes area alone.

"We could try, we might get lucky, but we have no idea which catchment area this might be from. Could be hundreds of schools."

Briggs took out her phone, while Ben sat at the computer and started searching school crests in the Milton Keynes area. His initial confidence soon dwindled as he started to pour through the images. Some were images of school crests, but others were pictures of head teachers, school teams, and classrooms. He clicked for more images.

"What the hell is all this?" he said to himself as images now included formula one teams, football teams, and movies. Scattered amongst them were school logos. Ben continued.

Briggs placed down her phone and pushed Ben to the side.

"Sorry," she said as they looked at each other. "This might be faster."

She switched to the image of the crest she had captured moments earlier and attached it to an email. Ben watched as she worked at the keyboard, still talking. He looked at her phone and realised she was on speaker.

"Is this your tech guy?" he asked.

Briggs turned to look at Ben. "He can hear you. And yes, this is Peter, who helped with us with the website."

"Hi, Peter," said Ben.

"Don't be an ass," she said, still looking at Ben. As she turned her attention back to the screen, Ben caught her saying, "Don't respond to him. He can't hear…"

Ben watched from the side, as Briggs sent the email, picked up her phone and continued talking. It must have been less than a minute when she typed *'denbigh high school'* into the search bar. She clicked on the Denbigh High School link and the home page appeared with the crest front and centre. "Bingo!" she said, though not to Ben, "Thanks as always Peter," disconnecting the call. She turned to Ben, smiling.

"Is Peter always available to you? He doesn't seem to have much of a life," Ben muttered.

"Neither do you," Briggs chastened, "and yes, Peter is a bit of a geek. But's he's a good guy and we're lucky he's helping out."

"How did he find the match so fast?" Ben asked, wanting to move the conversation on.

"Some AI program can compare images. What are those?". Ben was removing the plastic bags from his pockets. "What are those?"

"These are fresh-ish cigarette butts."

"I can see that, belonging to whom?"

"I collected these from the road at the back of the Mansion, and these from the room where the girls were being held."

"They can't be used as evidence."

"I know that." Ben replied, lying. "I thought you might be able to do your thing and find out who they belonged to."

Briggs picked up one of the bags and peered at it. "My thing?"

Ben shrugged, "I'm not sure why I picked them up. I thought if we could find out a name, we could put the person under surveillance and catch all of them."

"That's not a bad idea," Briggs agreed.

Ben straightened. Emboldened, he said, "We have several useful leads piling up. We should be able to ID the girl from the video now, we have these butts, and can we chase that registration plate? I want to make the safety of whoever was loaded into that van last night our priority. But I also have some follow ups on Sarah Dalton."

Briggs pinched a smile and nodded, "Agreed. Let me make those calls. I'll need to drop these bags with someone. But then, I have some homework of my own to do."

"Does the DNA take long?"

"If he'll take them, not long, perhaps a couple of days. It doesn't take long to pull a profile, but the profile needs to be put into the system for a match. I'll put the coffee on."

The door to the room swung closed. Ben pondered his next move. He pictured the girl in the video and the hooded figures, no doubt more teenage girls, being bundled into the van. Like sauce on a stove, his anger simmered. Denbigh High School was an hour drive and would not be open until the morning, meaning being out for at least three hours. He was wishing they had hired someone to help in the office.

He looked up at the board attached to the opposite wall and looked at the names he had written up. At the top, Rupert Henshaw, youngest child of Robert and Emily Henshaw who had tragically been killed in a helicopter accident. He had drawn a line down from Rupert to James and Monica Stanley. To the side, he had written Olivia and Arthur Havishem together with a plus sign with Alison Stallworthy. Ben grabbed a marker off the table and threw it at the board, hoping to hit the name of Rupert Henshaw. He missed.

Sighing he got up, walked over and picked up the marker. He wiped a space on the board and added more notes. Rupert and the Stanley's were running a teenage trafficking outfit. Were they responsible for the actual abductions? He wondered. The girls were being handed off to another group. What was the nature of that relationship? Is Rupert in charge of the operation? Or the Stanley's? Or were they just the middlemen, facilitators between supply and demand?

"I guess that would mean those two groups would not be able to identify each other", he said to himself. "But that also means Rupert the Prick can link us to both groups."

Ben finished writing up his notes. The operation seemed simple enough. Someone grabs the girls, hands them off to another group who holds on to them before handing them off again to another group, that presumably, ends up passing them to the scumbag clients. And what kind of demented freak pays for this? He thought. He stepped back from the board and despite the obvious gaps, he couldn't shift the thought something else was missing. Looking at the time he decided he had still had time to make a house call.

As he left home, he indicated to Briggs he was heading out. She was on a call. He selected an address he had put into his phone earlier from the conversation with the Dalton's and drove away.

CHAPTER SEVEN

It wasn't long before he parked up on the street next to a three-bed semi. He double checked the number on the house. Lights were on and he could see at least one person inside. He knocked on the door. The door was answered by an East Asian woman. After confirming he was talking to Mrs. Li, Ben explained he was a private investigator hired by Will and Valerie Dalton to help locate their daughter, Sarah. Jenny, Mrs. Li's daughter, was understood to be a good friend of Sarah's. Ben asked if he might speak to Jenny.

Licencing for private investigators is not yet mandatory, but Briggs had them certify with the ABI – the Association of British Investigators. The membership card served as his Investigators ID card. The card looked official enough and most of the public wouldn't know it had no official purpose.

Ben showed his investigators identity and was ushered into the front room. The smell of cooked noodles filled the air. Mrs. Li turned the television off and called Jenny down. They knew Sarah had not turned up at school and Sarah's parents had called earlier, but as yet, the Police had not been to talk to Jenny. Ben did his best to sound lowkey and reassured that Sarah was not in any trouble.

Jenny explained the Monday had been a teacher training day and a no-school day. She relayed how Sarah had shared that she and her boyfriend had planned to spend the Monday together, and how her friends were all worried when she hadn't shown up for school the next day.

"But then we figured, you know," Jenny said, glancing at her mum sat next to her, "that she might have slept over, somewhere."

"Do you know this boy's name?" Mrs. Li asked.

Jenny looked down at the sofa.

"You need to tell this man who this boy is. Who is he?"

Ben tried to appear sympathetic. He nodded, "It's okay, she won't be in any trouble. We just want to make sure she's safe."

"Rajeev, Rajeev Pandya," Jenny replied. "He's a sixth-former. She asked me not to tell anyone."

"At Sponne School?" Ben asked. Jenny nodded. "So, he's seventeen?" Jenny nodded again.

"An Indian?" Mrs. Li said. Ben couldn't be sure if it was a question or a statement.

"Sarah was scared about what her parents might think, with him being older and…everything."

Ben typed the name into the social media search. A list of matches came up. He passed his phone to Jenny. "Is he one of these?" Ben asked.

It took Jenny a moment before she passed the phone back, saying, "This one."

"Do you know his address?" Ben asked.

Jenny shook her head, "But I know the street name, at least the one Sarah gave me. She mentioned he lives on School Lane."

"School Lane," Ben repeated. "Did she say where? What town?"

"No, but look, his page shows Abthorpe," she said, turning her phone around to show him.

Ten minutes later, Ben had driven the short distance to School Lane, Abthorpe. Abthorpe was a small village nestled just a few miles northwest of the famous Silverstone circuit, and just a couple of minutes drive from the office. The Wappenham road sliced through the village, a narrow B road with hedgerows on each side. School Lane was the first turn on the right and named after the school located at one end. The school dates back to sixteen forty-two and now served as the Village Hall.

School Lane was even narrower than the Wappenham Road, and cars parked along the kerb made sure only one car at a time would be travelling up and down it. Ben parked the car and got out. There were only a few houses on the lane, all stone construction, well maintained and modernised, but very old.

Ben walked briskly up and down hoping to see anyone of Indian descent. He realised there was a driveway behind him, curving left and right providing access to two eighties style family homes. Crossing the road, he stood at the foot of the driveway, peering from house to house.

His phone vibrated, it was Briggs. He accepted the call and could see right away that she was animated.

"We have a hit on the plate," she said, before Ben could say anything. "It was tagged a few minutes ago in Sharpness. We need to get going."

"Sharpness? Where's that?"

"It's next to the Severn about an hour away. They must be using the river to move the kids out. Where are you?"

"I'm just at Abthorpe looking for Sarah Dalton's boyfriend."

"Drive to the Premier Inn at Silverstone. It's on the A43, it's on the way. I'll pick you up from there."

Briggs ended the call.

As Ben put his phone back in a pocket, an older man came out of the house to his left, Indian looking. "Hell," he said to himself, turning away and jogging back to his car.

Ben arrived at the hotel only moments before Briggs. He had parked in a spot farthest away from the hotel's entrance hoping they either wouldn't notice or not be concerned by the minor parking infraction.

On the way, Briggs was explaining why they were the ones driving rapidly to Sharpness and not the Police. Ben was all for reasonable protections for citizens but the question of what it was going to take for the police to get involved, had repeatedly crossed his mind.

Briggs drove quickly but with caution. Last thing they needed was to be stopped by traffic police or for Briggs to lose her licence while speeding past numerous traffic cameras. It was almost ten p.m. and the A43 was quiet. The A43 became the A34, then the A40. After slowing down for roadworks, Briggs eventually asked about Sarah Dalton's boyfriend.

Ben relayed the conversation he had with her friend Jenny. "I'd just found Rajeev's house when you phoned." He said.

"We agreed the van and the safe return of those kids was our priority," Briggs reminded Ben, trying to look toward Ben while keeping her eyes on the road. Ben nodded.

They turned onto the M5 heading south towards Bristol. Still no signs for Sharpness. Ben broadened the navigation screen in the car. They would be turning off shortly. He started to wonder what they were driving toward. If the kids were being transported, were they going to get there in time to prevent it? And how were they going to prevent it? He figured anyone who can acquire people can definitely acquire guns. And while Briggs is very capable, she isn't Jason Bourne. A smirk ran across Ben's mouth as he realised the irony of him finding the silence unsettling.

The navigation showed they were close. Briggs dialled a number hands-free and began talking. 'Harper' was the name displayed on screen. Ben looked at the number, it was a greater London area code. How many contacts does she have? He thought. He watched her mouth from the corner of his eye, while pretending to be looking ahead. He soon gave up, having no idea what she might be talking about. He looked at his own phone instead, his anxiety increasing proportionally as they approached their destination.

Briggs slowed her speed as they drove into Sharpness. A small town or a large village, Ben wasn't sure on the distinction. The smell of the river entered the cabin. They turned onto Bridge Road. It was dark, but Ben could make out commercial units in the direction of the river. Street lighting exposed concrete pillars and slopes – the dock. Briggs slowed the car again as they made their way parallel to the river. She was following the signs to the marina. The road narrowed as they came to a bridge. Briggs killed the headlights. Tram lines emerged from the grassy shoulder, into the tarmac from the side and across the bridge. On the other side and to their left, were large open warehouses storing what looked like industrial sized chemical containers. A large crane stood silently, its chain swaying gently in the breeze.

Briggs parked near the warehouses. They got out. There was no sign of the transit van they had seen at the Mansion, or any sign of life for that matter.

"The marina is just down there, the other side of the bridge." Briggs said, pointing in that direction.

"Okay," said Ben, "what's the plan?"

"Well, we need to see if the van is here, and if it is…assess what to do next."

Ben waved an arm. "After you."

They walked swiftly along the side of the water. There was sufficient lighting on the ground and from above, for Ben to realise they were now on a tiny island, an islet, connected to the mainland by two bridges. The one they had just driven over and a higher elevated bridge that he now noticed, just a short distance from the former. The strip of water they were next to was a canal that ran parallel to the Severn, the longest of the UK's rivers.

Ben knew to stay close behind Briggs. His primary attention was on Briggs, she was his ears. They passed under the high bridge and found themselves alongside another iron warehouse stripped of much of its side housing. Briggs crouched and her pace slowed. She turned and signalled 'quiet'. Ben looked around, he still couldn't see anything of note.

Rather than continuing along the canal, Briggs chose instead to progress along the side of the warehouse and farther into the islet. They soon came to an access lane. In one direction, it curved upwards and around to connect with the high bridge. The other direction provided vehicle access to sheds and warehouses adjacent to the water. Briggs straightened and jogged toward the warehouses. Again, her pace slowed as they approached a larger warehouse, the Boat House, with a rusted sign for Boat Repairs. A new looking eight-foot-tall wire fence surrounded the property, but the entrance gate was wide open.

Suddenly, Briggs ducked and stepped off the land and into the tree line. Ben followed. There was no street lighting here and barely enough light for Ben to make out what Briggs was telling him.

"Voices, just beyond the entrance. Someone is in there, but we haven't seen the van yet."

After a moment, she motioned for them to continue. They snuck past the entrance, keeping to the trees and away from the boat house. There was another smaller building with a decrepit sign saying the 'The Old Sawmill' barely attached to it, then the area opened up. Their sneaking had become creeping.

Ben tapped against Briggs' shoulder and pointed away from the Sawmill and to a van, and two other vehicles, parked at the water's edge. Briggs nodded and put her hand up for Ben to stay in place. Slowly she moved closer to the van. Ben could now see movement, two then three figures. One appeared to step down into where the river must have been, but it was too dark, and he was too far away to make out any detail. He watched Briggs as she moved ahead, slowly almost entirely concealed by the bushes and trees. She paused, then slowly made her way back.

The two remaining figures Ben could see were standing next to each other, he presumed they were talking. Then one lit a cigarette, the flame from the lighter briefly making one man's bearded face visible. Briggs returned and gave a thumbs up. Ben shrugged. Briggs moved past him and back toward the Boat House entrance. Ben followed.

"It's the same van. At least it has the same phony plate." She said.

"Any sign of the girls?"

Briggs shook her head.

"So, what now?" He asked.

Briggs took out her cell and dialled nine-nine-nine. Finally, Ben thought as he saw Briggs say 'Police'. He watched her mouth closely as she informed the Police of a disturbance at the Boat House marina.

"I think someone has been stabbed," she added. "Better get an ambulance as well. Quick." She closed the call. Looking at Ben she said, "That should do it."

"I don't want to just stay here," Ben said. "What if we're too late."

Briggs nodded.

Again, they made their way slowly along the tree line and back toward the vehicles. As they approached, the two figures moved to the back of the van and opened the rear doors. A smaller, hooded figure was pulled from the back of the van and stumbled to the ground, wrists apparently tied together. Other people were being pulled from the vehicle. Soon eight figures the size of small adults, teenagers, were lined up. Ben and Briggs watched as the hoods were removed, and Bearded Man paced along the line up. The other presumed man pulled out a phone and started taking pictures. The flash from the camera, lit each smaller figure in the line up. Girls, all similar in stature but with different hair and skin colour, perhaps between twelve and fifteen. Briggs brought a straight finger to her mouth, Bearded Man must be talking.

Briggs shielded her phone and checked the time, concern etched onto her face. A third figure appeared, taller than the girls but not as large as Bearded Man or his colleague.

"We can't let the girls get on the boat," Briggs signed. Again, she told Ben to stay in position, before she crept toward the vehicles.

Ben watched as Briggs made her way to one of the vehicles. She stopped at a wheel. Bearded Man was now on the phone. Ben looked around hoping to see the flashing lights of the emergency services. Nothing. Bearded Man still had the phone in his hand away from his face. He then pulled it back for a moment, before returning the phone to a pocket. *They were out of time.*

Ben stood up, walked out from the bushes, and toward the kids and Bearded Man. It was the other larger man that noticed him first and he quickly stepped between Ben and the line up.

"Who the fuck are you?" the large man asked.

Ben pointed to his ears and trying to sound drunk said, "Sorry, my ears don't work too well. What did you say?"

The man took another step forward. Standing at least six-four, he was half a foot taller than Ben. And Ben realised he was now within range of being punched.

"I said, who the fuck are you?" the man repeated. "Get the fuck out of here right now."

Ben pretended to wobble. "I'm sorry, I think I'm lost. I parked my car next to a bridge. I think I may have had a little too much to drink."

The man pointed behind Ben. "Now get the fuck out of here."

Ben looked clumsily around and lost his balance. As he got back to his feet, he felt a blow to his jaw that knocked him back down. He was suddenly being dragged away. After a few metres, the man grabbed Ben up and shoved him hard against the fence. Ben struggled to stand, though this time not acting. Strength had gone from his legs and his vision lacked clarity.

"Step back in this direction and I'll kill you."

Seemingly satisfied, the man turned his back on Ben and started to walk away. Ben got back to his feet. His clothes were now wet, and he felt the warmth of blood inside his mouth. He turned and started walking away, not wanting to test the big man's sincerity.

Ben stumbled out of the entrance and looked behind to see where the big man was at. He was surprised to see Big Man running away. *Sophie!* He was about to try to run back in when a Police car passed him, driving through the entrance as if chasing Big Man. Another Police car followed. A cocktail of relief and adrenalin rushed around Ben's body. His head cleared, and normality returned to his legs. He jogged after the cars.

Up ahead the police vehicles had stopped. Ben moved around one of the cars to see the scene unfolding around the van.

Four police, one still holding on to a taser gun with its wires attached to a man laying on the ground. Another was using a radio. Three and four were placing Big Man in handcuffs. *Where was Briggs? Where were the girls?* Ben thought.

"The boat!" Ben shouted. He went to move past the tasered man on the ground and towards where he expected the boat to be moored, but the policeman with the radio approached, placing a hand to Ben's shoulder.

"There!" Ben shouted again, as a boat was making its way through the marina.

Ben felt his arm being grabbed and pulled downwards. His attention remained on the getaway boat. Ben looked around for Briggs.

His shoulder now being shaken. Ben turned to see the officer only inches from his face, apparently, shouting. He felt a blow to the back of his legs, and he dropped to his knees. His arms were pulled behind him and he felt the cold steel of handcuffs being placed around his wrists. Another blow, across his shoulders and he fell on his face to the ground. He felt someone pad him down.

"I'm deaf!" he shouted. "I'm not one of them! I'm the one that called the Police. Please, let me up. There are kids on that boat, abducted!" Ben rolled onto his side and tried to get back onto his knees.

"The boat!" he shouted again.

He got on to his knees and looked around. Big Man was now sitting in the back of one of the police cars. Bearded Man was also in cuffs, sitting on the ground, leaning up against the vehicle Big Man was in. An officer stood over them both, taser at the ready. Bearded Man was saying something.

Ben got to his feet and looked to see where the boat was. He found himself being grabbed again. He turned to see officer with the radio.

"These guys are trafficking teenage girls. The girls have just been loaded onto that boat over there. You have to stop that boat!"

As Ben spoke and the two men looked out across the water, another boat came into view. A bit smaller but following the first and catching it up. Both men stepped closer to the water for a better look.

Up ahead, a small footbridge had been raised, providing the marina boats with access to the river. Boats of all different sizes, and canal boats lined each side of the inlet. The second boat was gaining on the first but there wasn't enough room for it to pass, not before the raised footbridge at least.

"Eight, there are eight kids. Girls, teenagers," Ben said, continuing to watch the boats. He assumed the officer would hear him, but he had no idea if the officer was saying anything.

The second boat was getting closer, much closer to the first. As the first boat reached the footbridge it was hit on the corner from behind by the second. The nose of the boat turned and hit the concrete platform holding the footbridge. With the second boat wedged in behind, the first boat was stuck.

"Get over there!" Ben shouted.

Unsure what was playing out behind him, Ben felt some relief to see Radio Officer racing to the two stricken boats.

Ben and Briggs were not under suspicion but had been separated while making their statements. After they had made their statements they were shown to a waiting area. Ben poured himself a coffee and sat down next to Briggs and the beige fabricated sofa.

"What are we waiting for?" Ben asked.

"Because they haven't said we can go yet." Briggs replied.

"We're not under arrest."

"How's your face? You have a bit of a bruise."

"Sore, but I'll live. They checked me over for a mild concussion."

"Do you still have all your teeth?"

"I'm fine. Anyway, what the hell was that James Bond stunt you pulled?"

"It wasn't exactly James Bond…but yeah, it was pretty cool. Never mind that, what the bloody hell were you doing? You could have gotten yourself killed?"

"We needed time, and you said we couldn't let the girls be put onto the boat. I couldn't think of anything else to do."

A man with a ruddy complexion, dressed in light grey two-piece suit entered the area. He stood six feet, with the shoulders of an accomplished swimmer and the waistline of a darts player.

"Hi, I'm Detective Inspector Burke," he said, offering his hand to Briggs.

"Sophie Briggs."

"Benjamin Grey, Ben."

"Sorry to keep you waiting. I'm with the National Crime Agency, I doubt I need to explain to you two why the NCA have been asked to get involved. This isn't your first involvement with something like this," he said, looking more toward Briggs. "I can't condone your actions tonight, but I do appreciate them. I'm supposed to tell you that you should have called the police and let them handle the situation, but you already know they would not have gotten there in time. Those girls likely owe their lives to you.

They are currently at the hospital being checked out, but as I understand things they are largely okay, physically at least. Listen, I know it's been a long night for you and I don't want to keep you longer, but we may need to follow up with you should we have further questions. I understand your involvement began after you were hired by," he looked down at his notes, "Olivia Havisham?"

"Havishem, with an 'e'," Briggs corrected.

"Right. You were investigating events at a property and discovered it was being used to hold these girls before being moved on. Why didn't you involve the Police earlier?"

"We didn't really have any good evidence at the time." Briggs responded.

"You mean the footage you have."

"With respect, what we have is much more meaningful following tonight's events. It wouldn't have been taken as seriously if we had presented it sooner." Briggs replied.

"Right. Well, you'll be pleased to know the owner of the boat you took doesn't want to press charges, once we explained why you took it. Here I had this info pulled for you, thought you might appreciate it."

Burke handed a sheet of paper to Briggs. It was a list of the girl's names that had been on the boat.

"Their parents are aware of what you did in saving their kids," he said. "I know they will want to thank you in person when you get the chance."

"What happens now?" Ben asked.

"The NCA will handle things from here on. An official investigation has been opened. We'll start with those arrested tonight and move on from there. We appreciate you sharing the evidence you have collected, and the information shared. It'll help. But it's best we handle things now. I assume you'll be needing a ride back to your vehicle?"

"Please," Ben confirmed.

"Okay, you are good to go. Officer Cook is available to take you to your car."

On their way out of the station, Briggs handed the list of names to Ben. There was no Louise Larke but knowing these girls were safe brought a smile to his face.

Briggs said, "I'm proud of you, super proud of you actually. What you did back there was very brave." Ben smiled. "Stupid, but brave," she added, as they got into the back of the police car.

After collecting their car, they had only driven as far as Gloucester before agreeing to stop at the M5 services for something to eat. The services were new and had been built into a hillside. At seven a.m., the main kitchen had just opened.

Ben showered and tried to clean his clothes as best he could. It would have to do and besides, many of the truckers here at this time, looked as dirty as he did. Ben grabbed breakfast and coffee and joined Briggs at a table.

"Do they have shower gel?" Briggs asked as Ben sat down.

"No, just hand soap, but I'm not running that through my hair."

"How did you dry yourself?"

"I turned my top inside out and used that. Not great but it'll have to do," he replied, placing the damp top on the seat next to him.

"Well, you are looking better. That bruise will be there a few days though."

"How's the coffee?"

"Not bad. I quite like this place. And the food's good too." She said, popping a pork sausage into her mouth.

"You know, you haven't stopped smiling."

Briggs suddenly raised both arms in the air and shouted, "Yes!".

Ben felt himself duck and quickly looked around at the reactions of the few others grabbing an early breakfast. Most continued to tend to their own business while one older guy grinned and gently tipped his drink in Ben's direction.

"Isn't it a great feeling?" Briggs asked, though Ben only caught the last two words. "We saved those girls and nailed those bastards." Her expression suddenly changed. "What's wrong with you?"

"It does feel good, yeah good," he said, raising his hands slightly in a much tamer version of Briggs' cheerleading.

"But?" Briggs prompted.

"Well, it's like you said, they are only part of the network. There's still the Stanley's and Rupert."

"Look, in this business you have to learn to take your wins. And besides, the NCA are now involved, that's what you wanted, right? With the information we've provided, it won't be long before they are being arrested."

Ben nodded and looked down at his food. Briggs reached out and tapped him on the wrist. "They'll be put under surveillance, probably before they even realise the girls have been rescued. The site, you discovered, is gold. They'll be able to use that for all kinds of leads."

"I can't shift this feeling that we're missing something."

"Come on, eat up, I'm knackered and really need to get some sleep."

Ben placed some bacon on his toast and ate. "What I really want to know is, how do you know how to hotwire a boat?"

Briggs let out a laugh, "I don't. I found the keys. That was the third boat I was on. I wasn't sure if I was going to have to circle back around and get on to the boat with the girls. By the time I found some keys, I could see the police were on their way, so I just needed to make sure the boat couldn't leave."

They finished up and headed home.

Ben awoke and glanced at the bedside clock, midday. His jaw ached and his body felt like he'd been run over. Not wanting to get up, his thoughts drifted to Sarah Dalton. He forced himself into the shower and got dressed.

Briggs was not around. The coffee pot was still on and half-full. He popped a couple of paracetamol and downed them with coffee.

Slouched in a chair in the office downstairs, he searched online for any news of the previous night's events. He resisted the temptation to open his mobile game. On his way out, he went to change the sign on the office door before realising it was already reading 'Closed'. Before he reached his car his phone vibrated. It was Olivia Havishem.

He accepted the call on audio and switched to speaker. An app on the phone would convert incoming speech to text. It wasn't perfect but usually sufficient to hold a sensible conversation. And Ben wanted to avoid her inevitable questions if she saw the bruising around his chin.

"Good morning, Mrs. Havishem."

"Olivia please," she replied. "And it's the afternoon. Why aren't you on video? Surely, you've not just woken up?"

"Good afternoon, Olivia, how can I help?" he said, ignoring her questions.

"I wanted to let you know Elizabeth is arriving later today. She called me to say that she would be coming to the house. I have invited her to dinner, perhaps you would like to join us?"

Ben sighed, then hoped it wasn't audible. "I'm kind of busy with a few things."

"Well, she did ask if she could meet you. She's been very concerned with what might be going on at the house. I've tried to keep what I know to myself, but she knows me well enough to know something is going on. If you could join us, it would be better if you field her questions? It is her home after all. Can you join us? Chargeable hours of course and you'd be helping me out."

"What time?"

"Six sharp. It's difficult to entertain late dinners as you get older. It's the acid reflux you know. So, you'll join?" she asked.

"Sure, thank you. Yes, I'll see you at six then."

"Will Sophie be joining, or will it be just you?"

Why does the use of the word 'just' always sound like an insult? He had no idea where Briggs was but knew she was going to need time preparing for her trip.

"No, just me," he confirmed. He closed the call and checked the time again.

Abthorpe was just a few minutes drive and Ben soon found himself standing at the Pandya driveway. Clouds were gathering again as Spring struggled to get a foothold. Ben pulled his jacket tighter, walked up the drive and rung the bell.

An elegant woman dressed in a red sari opened the door. A fleck of grey in her hair was the only feature suggesting her age began with a four. She seemed to frown for a moment as she took in Ben's appearance. But then her face softened, and she smiled gently.

"Hello?" she said, as the warm waft of spices hit Ben's senses.

"Hi, my name's Benjamin Grey. Sorry to disturb you. I'm a private investigator and I've been asked to look into a missing person. A student from Sponne School, Sarah Dalton. She's not been seen since Monday."

"And how might I be of help?"

"You are Mrs. Pandya? Rajeev's mother?"

"Yes. How does this concern us?" she replied, her posture noticeably stiffening.

"I understand that Rajeev was friends with Sarah. Sorry I'm not trying to suggest Rajeev is in any kind of trouble at all, but he might have been one of the last people to have seen Sarah."

Mrs. Pandya relaxed a little. "I see," she said. "Well, Rajeev won't be home for another hour yet. He gets the bus."

"I understand. Actually, I came at this time as I had no wish to surprise you in front of Rajeev. I thought it would be better if I gave you a heads-up so to speak." Ben forced a smile.

"I see. Thank you for the consideration. You are welcome to come back closer to five. I will tell Rajeev you are wanting to speak to him. He has to do his homework before dinner so if you come before five, he will be at home."

Ben nodded, "Thank you. I'll come back shortly. Thanks again." He stepped back and Mrs. Pandya closed the door.

Ben walked back down the driveway and to his car parked on School Lane. Opening his phone, he searched for a café close by. He saw there was a pub in the village.

The New Inn was a stone building very much in keeping with the character of the village. A few bench tables lined the limited open space outside. Inside, the décor was a mix of modern and tradition that, to Ben's untrained eye, seemed to work. The place seemed bigger on the inside with nooks and crannies leading to more spaces. A short hallway led out to a covered patio. The pub was quiet, and the female bartender watched as Ben entered, carrying a laptop.

"Hello Luv, what can I get ya?" She asked.

"Just a coffee please, if that's okay?" Ben replied.

"I'll pop a fresh pot on for you. There's a menu on the bar if you do end up fancying a bite to eat."

Ben chose a table near the window and away from the bar. He glanced around to see if there was a sign for Wi-Fi. Not seeing anything, he switched his phone to hotspot and started up his laptop. He spent the few minutes before his coffee arrived browsing the local area.

He grew up in the Southeast of England. His abusive dad left home after Ben had turned seventeen. They could not be considered wealthy, but Ben and his mother made do. Ben hadn't travelled much, in fact he hadn't travelled at all. After the London terrorist attack, it had been Briggs that suggested they go into business together. Despite being on the fast-track, she had become disillusioned working for the government. Ben was meandering, not sure where life was taking him, but the attack and his subsequent employment in tracking a young girl, had given him a purpose. He accepted her offer, which wasn't hard as she was offering a fifty percent share without requiring him to put up any money of his own. They agreed terms and Ben was more than happy to follow Briggs' lead on where Grey and Briggs Investigations should be located.

"Milk or cream?" the bartender asked, placing a mug of coffee down in front of Ben.

"Milk please," Ben replied, assuming she had offered milk as he only caught the word 'cream'.

The woman lingered. "Not seen you around here before."

"No. Though I live not too far away. I'm a partner in a business at Greens Norton."

"Where is he?" she asked.

"Who? Oh, no, my partner is female. We run a private investigation business." Ben showed her a business card.

She took the card and glanced at it. "Which one are you? Grey or Briggs?"

Ben forced a smile, already feeling uncomfortable with the number of questions. "Grey, Benjamin Grey."

The lady pursed her lips, "You don't look like a private investigator." Ben didn't respond, figuring saying nothing was the quickest way to get her to move on.

"Would like anything to eat?" she said, eventually.

Ben quickly did the math. He'd been there less than ten minutes, and the coffee might stretch him to thirty minutes with a top-up. He wanted to be back at the Pandya's at four-forty-five, giving him an hour to kill.

"Sure," he replied. He glanced down at the menu standing open on the table. "Perhaps, I could get the sticky toffee pudding?"

"Sure. You don't want to try the fish and chips? They're fabulous."

"No, thank you. Just the pudding, thanks."

"Huh, Ok. I'll grab your milk."

Ben resumed his browsing, reviewing the map of the area. Sponne School was in Towcester just to the northeast. Silverstone to the south. Milton Keynes and Banbury are the two larger towns within a reasonable bus commute. He imagined what he might do at their age in their position, though he never considered himself typical. Sarah was white and younger than Rajeev who was from Indian descent.

They were at the age Ben had always considered 'tricky'. Tricky because Rajeev was old enough to have sex. Sarah on the other hand, remained under the legal age – would they have waited? A parents and a kid's nightmare. The law attempts to make sense with its 'Romeo and Juliet' exceptions, but sufficiently determined parents might be force an arrest should they choose to press charges - tricky. Ben, and his girlfriend Dawn at the time, were eighteen when they lost their virginity, though Ben was in no doubt, if the chance had come sooner, he would have taken it.

Ben stared at the map. Sarah and Rajeev were being cautious – neither set of parents were aware, and Jenny had been sworn to secrecy. Travelling together would increase the risk of them being seen. Did they meet up somewhere? He sighed as he accepted the vanity of trying to guess where they may have gone. He had to hope Rajeev would be forthcoming.

Ben looked out of the window but from the corner of his eye he could tell the bartender was returning with his pudding. He quickly looked back down at the laptop in the hope she would not interrupt him.

"Here you go, Luv," she said, placing the steaming pudding on the table.

Ben hadn't heard her, but felt obliged to look up to say thank you.

"So, are you working a case now?" she asked.

"I am working, yes."

"What? Something in Abthorpe? Nothing happens in this village."

Ben didn't respond.

"Best bit of excitement we've had round here was when this posh lady was thrown from her horse. A kid was cycling and must have gotten too close to the horse. Must have spooked the horse coz it went up, you know like they do, and the lady fell off the horse and on to the front of this parked car. She was okay, bit shook up mind. She was wearing all the gear, had a riding helmet on and everything. The owner…"

Ben's phone vibrated. He was perhaps never more grateful for the interruption. "Please excuse me, I need to take this call. Thank you," he said.

The woman remained at the table for a moment as Ben took the call. It was Briggs. "One moment, let me put you on video," he said, confident that should be enough to gain him a little privacy. The bartender left the table.

They provided each other a quick update on their movements for the day. Briggs was back at the office having been at the Imagearium offices earlier. Ben shared he had been invited to dinner with Olivia where he was expecting to meet Elizabeth Henshaw. Briggs expressed no desire to join.

After the call, Ben settled the bill, gathered his things, and left the pub. Patrons were steadily gathering and the once lonely bartender was now in her element, juggling several conversations simultaneously. Ben moved his car back to school lane just in time to catch a lanky teenager walking up the Pandya driveway. Ben gave the boy and his mum a few minutes before knocking.

Mrs. Pandya opened the door and showed Ben into the lounge where Rajeev was already sitting. His head hung, elbows on his knees, and his fingers loosely crossed. After introductions, Ben sat across from Rajeev and his mother.

"Sorry again for the interruption. I'm assuming your mother has explained why I'm here?" Ben asked. Rajeev nodded, his head still tilted toward the floor.

"I just have a few questions and then I'll get out of your way." Again, a slight nod from Rajeev.

"I understand that you were with Sarah on Sunday. That you spent the day together?" Ben asked.

There was an uncomfortable silence, and Ben began to think he may have missed something being said. He took his cue from the mother who was looking at Ben, seemingly expecting the next question.

"I'm sorry, I lost my hearing when I was a bit younger than you are now. I rely on lip-reading to get by, unless you know how to sign."

The mother's expression softened. She touched her son's arm. He lifted his head to look at Ben.

"Yeah, we went to the circuit, some of the formula one teams were there testing their cars. We got the bus into Silverstone and met up there. There's a shuttle to the circuit." He said.

"What time did you last see Sarah?"

"It was seven thirty. I had to be back by eight," Rajeev replied, glancing at his mother as he spoke. "We got separate buses. My bus came before hers. She was still at the bus stop when I left. She was fine, I don't know why she wouldn't have gone home." His hands fidgeted. "We picked that Monday because her parents were going out to the Opera it was a teacher training day for us. I would have taken her home, but I didn't have time for the bus ride to her place then back to mine. It would have made me late."

"Which bus stop was that? That you and Sarah were at."

"In the village, the one outside the White Horse, near the memorial. That's where we arranged to meet, and that's where I caught my bus home."

"Do you remember meeting anyone else? Did anyone approach during the day or seem to take an interest in Sarah? Anything out of the ordinary?"

"No. There were people around, doing what we were doing, there for the testing. We'd had a good day, she was happy and laughing, disappointed I couldn't stay longer. I felt bad about having to leave her, but she said she'd be fine. Said she'd been on the bus a hundred times and the bus stops near her house. She lives near the Leisure Centre."

"The Towcester Leisure Centre?" Ben asked.

"Yes. But it's pronounced Towcester." Rajeev said, stressing the word Towcester. Ben couldn't see the difference.

Rajeev grabbed a pen and a scrap piece of paper from off the table. He wrote 'Toaster' on the paper. Ben nodded his understanding.

"Towcester," Ben said, this time saying it the same as he would toaster. Rajeev nodded. "That's all I need for now, thank you, Rajeev, Mrs. Pandya." Ben stood. Rajeev and Mrs. Pandya remained seated. Mrs. Pandya reacted first.

"You don't have any more questions?" she asked.

"No, thank you. I'll contact the bus company, and we can look at the camera footage. We'll be able to confirm Rajeev getting on his bus and see if Sarah got onto her bus or not. We can go from there." Ben replied.

Back at his car, Ben still had a few minutes before he needed to be at the Havishems. He looked up the Stagecoach website only to find the contact centre had just closed for the day.

He felt a pang in his stomach. He had committed to dinner with Olivia, but the sourness of anxiety hit with the thought of Sarah spending another night missing. He called Briggs and asked if she could help find out more information while he was tied up having dinner.

"Tied up?" teased Briggs. "Sure, they should have a control centre, like taxi firms, keeping an eye on all the buses. Let me try to find out where the one for Towcester is."

Ben watched her lips closely as she said the word Towcester. He was now seeing the distinction. She was pronouncing it correctly, though he hadn't noticed before. It seemed he was the only one who pronounced the 'ce'.

"Thanks," he said. "Message me if you find anything. I'll go there after dinner." Ben started the engine and drove to the Havishems.

CHAPTER EIGHT

Ben arrived before Elizabeth. He sat chatting with Olivia in the living room while they waited for Elizabeth to arrive. The smell of roast beef had helped settle his stomach, and the thought of gravy filled Yorkshire pudding was making him hungry.

"Elizabeth is very concerned about what has been going on." Olivia stated, after the formalities had been dispensed with.

"You've told her what has been going on?" Ben asked.

"Of course. I've known Elizabeth a lot longer than I have known you, young man," she replied, seemingly offended by the thought of her own judgement being questioned. "She's a lovely, intelligent, woman. Educated at Oxford you know, economics. She started her own company with her husband, Charles, an American. They moved to America a few years ago but she still visits, occasionally. It's always lovely to see her."

"How did she react to the news?"

"Horrified of course. I don't think I'd want to be in Rupert's shoes right now. Elizabeth is kind but she's a force of nature when she chooses to be."

"I'm sorry Olivia, what exactly did you share with Elizabeth."

Olivia took a breath before replying. "She already knew of my concerns with seeing the activity at the house. She was supportive of employing you to look into matters. She offered to cover the expenses, she's so sweet. But no, this was my concern and besides we don't have much use for money these days. Anyway, of course she enquired about how things were going. I told her it looked like Rupert and the Stanley's were involved in some sort of unsavoury enterprise. She didn't seem entirely surprised, well, you know with the way Rupert is."

"Did you share with her what that enterprise is?"

"No. We don't know exactly what that enterprise is. Do we?" she replied. "I mean, yes, we know it's most likely illegal, but we don't know for sure if its prostitution they are involved in or still some sort of drugs ring. You mentioned younger people might be involved, perhaps they are employees so to speak."

Like a cat about to pounce, Ben felt his muscles tense. He managed to catch himself. It was clear anything he shared with Oliva would end up being shared with Elizabeth, and her proximity to Rupert, however well intended she may be, would not be helpful. Ben took a breath.

"I hope Elizabeth isn't much longer," Olivia spoke, "the beef has been sitting a while now."

And as if right on cue, the doorbell rang. Olivia stood and moved toward the sitting room door. Ben stood but made no movement to leave the room. Before Olivia had left the room, Alison passed by the door on her way to answering the front door. Olivia was soon embracing someone, her head disappearing under voluminous blond hair. Alison passed by again, this time hidden behind a huge bouquet.

Olivia stepped back into the sitting room. She was followed by a striking woman, standing an inch taller than Ben in her black heeled shoes, wearing a sparkling black dinner dress with splashes of white. She was lightly tanned, and her cheeks betrayed additional pounds sufficient to solicit a caution from a doctor. Her lips popped from a red metallic lipstick. She was conspicuous and imposing in equal measure.

"You must be Benjamin," she said, her teeth glowing from her smile as she offered her hand.

"Ben, please, Elizabeth Henshaw I presume," Ben replied, gently shaking her hand and having to adjust his fingers to avoid the point of her diamond ring.

"Please call me Elizabeth. Olivia has told me much about you. I'm awfully sorry, you had to get mixed up in this. But we're very thankful you did."

Alison stood at the door, a reminder that the dinner was waiting for them.

"Please, let us head through to the dining room. The dinner is ready, and Arthur is not good with eating late. He suffers from acid reflux you know."

The bouquet of flowers had been arranged and was now the centrepiece of the kitchen island. Two bottles of wine sat next to the flowers. They sat themselves down and Alison began serving dinner. The conversation over dinner comprised mostly of pleasantries and fond reminiscing. For the first time, Arthur had spoken more than just a few words and was clearly enamoured with the female quest.

After dinner, they moved to the conservatory. Albert excused himself and Ben, shortly after getting comfortable again, felt his phone vibrate twice - a text message. Elizabeth asked how Ben got into private investigating and what training he had. She seemed surprised by his lack of training or any previous experience with either military or law enforcement. Ben explained, his partner Briggs was the one with all the experience, he was more there to help. Olivia admonished Ben for his modesty.

"You may not have had any formal training," she said, "but, you have been involved with law enforcement. You were helping on that London terrorist attack that played out all over the news. A consultant, I was told."

Ben shuffled in his seat. "I did have some involvement, but I'm not sure I would describe myself as a consultant. I stumbled across some information that proved useful to the intelligence agencies. Nothing more."

"That's how you met your partner, Sophie Briggs?" Olivia asked.

"Correct. It was after the incident, that Sophie suggested we try a private investigator partnership." Ben confirmed.

"And how did you come by the information?" Elizabeth enquired.

"Er," Ben replied, buying time to think on how to respond. "I found something, some plans that looked suspicious to me. I shared it with the authorities, and it appears it chimed with something they were already investigating. Sophie, my business partner, was leading the investigation at the time."

"Oh come, there must be more to it than that. I rather doubt terrorists lave their plans lying around. And since when do they pull civilians into terrorist investigations?" Elizabeth probed.

"I think they thought I was good with details, you know, perhaps reading into things that some people might have missed." Ben replied, really hoping that would be sufficient to move the conversation on.

"You are being coy Mr. Grey," Elizabeth responded. "Perhaps, your partner is simply a little sweet on you darling."

Ben felt himself flush with embarrassment.

"Don't embarrass the poor man. Let him keep his secrets. It matters not, because he has been very helpful to us," Olivia interjected.

The segue way gave Ben some relief. "Yes, I'm sorry to say, we do have reason to believe your brother, Rupert, is using the premises for something…" Ben glanced at Olivia, preferring her adjective, "unsavoury."

Elizabeth was holding her wine and looked like she was about to use it as a wand. "Sadly, I'm not surprised. Rupert has never been one for convention." She turned slightly to Olivia, "Do you remember that time he went missing and we found him selling lemonade out on the main road?" Olivia frowned. "The lemons he used, he had stolen from the grocer that used to be on The Green." She paused like a comedian allowing time for laughter. "I'm sorry, not a time for amusement, I'm merely illustrating our Rupert has always been a bit…" Elizabeth seemed to be searching for the right word.

"Odd?" Olivia suggested.

"Yes, odd, thank you." Elizabeth agreed. She paused a moment before continuing. "What is Rupert up to?" she asked.

Olivia looked to Ben.

"Well, I'm sure Olivia shared with you that we needed to set up surveillance of the property to establish what was going on. We have footage of what appear to be teenagers, being lead from the property and loaded into the back of a transit van. We know the transit van had false plates. Rupert and the Stanleys were present at the property. It appeared to be a transaction of some kind between them and the men taking them away."

"Why can't you be sure if they were teenagers?" Elizabeth asked.

"Well, their heads were covered by blankets. They were shorter than everyone else, including Mrs. Stanley, which is why we believe they are most likely young teenagers, perhaps even younger. It was clear they were under duress."

"I see," said Elizabeth. "So, you think Rupert has gotten himself involved in child prostitution?"

Ben nodded. "Possibly against their will." He added.

"Who does willingly go into prostitution, darling?" Elizabeth responded. "Are you suggesting, Rupert is involved with abducting these people and forcing them into prostitution?"

"It can't be ruled out."

Elizabeth scoffed at the notion. "Aiding and abetting is not beyond Rupert. But, what, abducting people off the streets? No, Rupert wouldn't have the nerve for such a thing."

"He is at least a middleman in this. They also have a website. On the dark web though it isn't clear to us yet, the precise purpose of the site."

Elizabeth took a sip of her wine, "I'm meeting him tomorrow evening. Whatever his involvement is, I will be insisting he hands himself in. We'll make sure he is properly represented, but this sort of behaviour is completely unacceptable. What happens now?"

"We have had to share the information with the authorities, of course. We expect they will conduct there own investigation."

"I see," said Elizabeth. "So, your involvement in this is over?"

"Yes, I think so," he lied. He looked at Olivia, "Unless there is anything else you need from us?"

"Let's not talk about this now." Olivia said. Raising her glass, she said, "We are thankful for your assistance Mr. Grey. I know Elizabeth shares that appreciation despite the unpleasant outcome. We'll leave it in the hands of the good authorities." They clinked their glasses in a toast.

Ben's stomach groaned from all the food he had eaten. He was determined to get out there as soon as possible, without giving offence to his host or their guest. Help came in the form of Arthur sticking his head into the conservatory to say he was heading up to bed. Ben made his apologies for not staying longer, and his thanks for a wonderful roast.

Ben drove out of sight of the house before stopping to look at the message from Briggs. She had provided an address for the Stagecoach control centre. He punched the address into the GPS and drove away. On the way, he called Briggs to fill her in on the meeting.

He arrived at the Northampton Control Centre a little after nine p.m. The Centre was a small office attached to a large depot. There was a security booth at a barriered entrance. Ben hoped his P.I. I.D. would be sufficient to get him in.

"Hi, my name is Benjamin Grey. I'm a private investigator. I need to confirm some details regarding a missing girl." He said, holding up his card.

The man in the booth looked like he could have been only just made it out of collage. He clicked a button on his radio and said, "I have someone says he's a private investigator, wanting some information."

There was a pause and then a voice over the radio said, "Does the ID check out?".

The guard opened the barrier and directed Ben on where to park before heading over to the small office building.

As Ben approached the office, a large, older man sitting at a desk next to the window, watched. He got up from his seat but instead of moving to the door, he slid the window open.

"You the investigator?"

Ben held up his card again. "I'm investigating a missing person. Sarah Dalton, she's fifteen years old, went missing on Monday. She was thought to be getting the evening bus home from Silverstone to Towcester. I wanted to confirm if she got on the bus."

"Monday? There was a problem with a bus that evening," he replied, looking Ben up and down before inviting him in.

Ben shared a picture of Sarah Dalton – one he had on his phone from a picture provided by her parents. The man explained the duty bus had a mechanical problem. The root was disrupted for an hour while a replacement was brought online. Ben was introduced to an operator who could help with any footage captured by the bus cameras. They searched the buses arriving and leaving the stop location provided earlier by Rajeev Pandya. It wasn't long before footage confirmed what Rajeev had told him – he did catch the bus ahead of Sarah. Before Rajeev stepped on, they hugged and shared a kiss.

"What happens if the bus someone is expecting doesn't turn up?" Ben asked, taking up a position where he could see both the operator and the screen.

"We provide a number to call and give updates on the website." The operator replied.

"Yeah, but if your standing at the bus stop, how will you know what number to call?"

"It's posted at the bus stop. But most people would probably just call a taxi."

"Do any other buses stop there? Perhaps ones with an alternate route to Towcester."

The operator switched views on the computer and checked. "Yeah, there is another one, would be a few minutes later, the Whittlebury bus. From that stop it goes into Whittlebury, then Wood Burcote and then Towcester."

"I want to see if she got onto that bus."

They watched the black and white footage as the bus arrived outside the White Horse.

"Why is this one in black and white?" Ben asked.

"Not all the buses have been retrofitted with the colour cameras. There, that's her innit?" The operator said, pointing at the now frozen image on the screen.

Ben looked at the picture on his phone for comparison. It was Sarah Dalton getting onto the Whittlebury bus Monday evening.

"Ok, great. We'll need to check each stop for that bus, so we see where she gets off." Ben instructed.

The operator obliged.

Again, it didn't take long before they watched Sarah Dalton get off at the Burcote Wood stop.

"Why would she get off the bus there?" the operator asked. "That stop serves the Wood, you know people wanting to do the trails – during the day."

"Can you bring up the area?"

As he brought up the map, the operator said, "So, you're a private investigator? You look a bit young to be an investigator."

"What is the age requirement?"

Looking at the images, Ben said, "She must have thought that was the easiest route home. She would have had to walk from there across the fields to her home over here near the leisure centre. It's what, just over a mile."

"It's a bit bleak," the operator responded.

After thanking the guys for their help, Ben left the depot and drove to the bus stop where Sarah had exited a couple of days before. He got out and looked around. He was right, Ben thought, it is bleak. The land was slightly elevated, with arable fields all around interrupted by pockets of woodland. He could see the Towcester street lights down in the distance.

Evening had given way to night. There was a chill in the air and the wind picked up speed as it rolled up the hill. What to do? He thought to himself. A search party would work but the knot in his stomach returned as he thought of Sarah having to spend another night out here. Could she have been taken?

Ben looked around again. Nothing but empty side roads and fields. He noted from the footage that Sarah was alone when she got off the bus. She wasn't being followed as far he could tell.

He retrieved a flashlight from the boot of his car and headed out on the footpath he thought Sarah would have taken. A sign marked 'Burcote Wood' six hundred metres ahead, but it looked more of a copse than a wood. He reached he Wood. The trail split three ways, one farther into the Wood, the others went toward and away from Towcester. He turned toward Towcester albeit the town still looked a mile away. The trail ran along the edge of the Wood. The path was rutted by the farm vehicles that must use it for access, to keep the expanse of foliage trimmed. The trail soon turned and appeared to lead away from where Sarah would have wanted to go. More farmland lay ahead. Ben took a few steps off the path and realised the ground quickly slid away. He managed to catch himself before falling but only just. A dyke, not easily seen, sat between the trail and the adjacent field.

It gave Ben an idea. She could have easily slipped and twisted or broken an ankle. It was no use him shouting out across the fields. He thought of phoning Briggs, at least she'd be able to hear Sarah respond, should she be lying in a ditch somewhere. But wouldn't she have crawled out by now? He peered down into the dyke. It was deeper than he expected, perhaps ten feet and certainly enough for someone to remain unseen. There was some water at the bottom, though he didn't think it could be more than a foot deep. Cold, but not life threatening.

He phoned Briggs, explaining where he was and why. She agreed to help but said she needed a few minutes, having just filled the bathtub.

"I won't be long." She said.

Ben made his way back along the trail to his car. He started the engine to warm the car, reclined his seat and closed his eyes. He drifted, a traveller through space as his mind wandered, voices coming and going as his mind scanned the airwaves aimlessly. He could feel the fatigue in his bones, the stress of the last few days in his muscles. He thought of Sarah Dalton, was she close by.

Soon there were only a few voices remaining. All female, not too old, not too young. He listened in, quickly discounting those not in any obvious distress, not the physical sort at least. Then a whisper.

Ben focused. A girl was calling for someone, or something, perhaps a pet. He thought he heard his name, but how could that be?

"Thank you for today," the whisper spoke, and for a moment he felt a slight warmth on his lips. "See you tomorrow," she said. The connection flickered. "Mum, I'm scared. I'm scared Mum."

Ben felt a shaking. He opened his eyes to see Briggs standing with car door open, her hand rousing him from his slumber.

"She's here," he said, "she's close."

They returned to the trail and stood at the dyke close to where Ben had been earlier. An open potato field spread out before them.

"If she was hurt, wouldn't she still be able to make it out somewhere?" Briggs asked.

"She's here. I think she might be really hurt. Not able to move." Ben replied.

Briggs frowned, then said, "Okay, you go that way and I'll go this way," indicating the two lengths of the dyke in front of them. Ben headed left, now walking away from Briggs, his torch lighting the sides of the dyke as he went. After a few minutes, he came to an intersection. Part of the dyke continued, moving farther away from the direction Sarah would have wanted to go. A new trench marked another edge to the field and moved away from where Ben was standing and toward the town. Ben looked back across the field. He could make out the light being carried by Briggs. She also had made the turn along the field's edge.

They moved steadily along each side of the field. Ben was close to the next turn when he spotted a body slumped near the bottom of the dyke. A trail of blood led down from some rusted farm equipment. Ben shouted and waved his light. Briggs signaled back, she had heard him.

Ben scrambled down. It was Sarah, she wasn't moving and had a gash to her head. She had lost blood, a lot of it but it had started to congeal. He reached for her wrist and checked for a pulse. She was cold but had a faint pulse. She was still alive. He moved her feet out of the water when he noticed

Briggs' light shining down. He looked up. She was panting and had her phone in her hand, talking.

"She's cold and unconscious. Her pulse is really weak." Ben said.

Briggs started down, her phone still in her hand, flashlight in the other. Carefully she examined the head wound and looked for any other sign of injury. She was still talking to someone on the phone. Briggs took off her coat, folded it and slid it gently under Sarah's head. Ben removed his jacket and placed it over her shoulders.

"Shouldn't one of us head back to the road?" Ben asked.

"No need. They're sending a helicopter." Briggs replied.

"You can do that!?"

"Yeah, it's my superpower." She replied, putting her arms gently under Sarah. "Take your jumper off."

Ben removed his top. His t-shirt provided little resistance to the cold.

"Here, fold it and put into under here. I want to get her off the ground and keep her level as much as possible."

Briggs removed her own top. She was wearing only a sports bra underneath. She folded her own top and positioned it under Sarah's lower back, carefully straightening Sarah's posture.

"What now?" Ben asked.

"We wait."

Briggs held a hand and gently stroked Sarah's face with her other. "It's going to be okay Sarah, hang in there sweetheart, just a few minutes."

The next few minutes seemed like an eternity. Once they had done what they could to make Sarah comfortable, Ben stood at the top of the dyke.

Briggs had advised against calling her parents until they were sure which hospital Sarah would be taken to.

It wasn't long before Ben could make out the blue flashing lights of two police cars, heading at speed, along the A43 below. He looked around the sky for the helicopter, then he remembered Michael Schumacher crashing at the British Grand Prix and being flown to Northampton General for treatment. He turned toward Northampton and soon located the helicopter. As it got closer, a bright searchlight beamed down. Ben watched as the light moved across the fields like the eye of Sauron. Then he noticed a lesser light shining up from the ground and toward the source of the greater. Briggs stood next to him, flashlight in hand, pointing it at the helicopter. A moment later and the two lights converged and then split apart again.

Ben continued to watch as the helicopter briefly scanned the field, chose its spot, and came to rest some two hundred feet away. Paramedics rushed from the fuselage, greeted by Briggs, she escorted them to where Sarah was laying. Ben could only watch, unsure of how he might be able to help. Sarah was soon being stretchered away and loaded into the air ambulance. Briggs briefly conversed with one of the paramedics, then jogged away as the rotor blades began to spin.

It was then, two uniformed police appeared on foot. After reviewing the scene and being seemingly content a crime had not been committed, Ben and Briggs were invited back to the station to provide full statements. Leaving one car at the police station they drove to Northampton General, eager to understand Sarah Dalton's condition.

Outside emergency surgery, William and Valerie Dalton sat. Will with his head in hands and Valerie clutching tissues. They greeted and hugged Ben and Briggs as they approached. Sarah's condition was still uncertain, only that she was still alive when she went in for surgery. Minutes turned into hours. Not much was spoken. A door swung open, and a doctor appeared and walked toward them, his features like those of a professional poker player.

"She's going to be okay," were the first words he spoke. "She's suffered significant head trauma, she's dehydrated and has mild hypothermia. We won't know if there's any lasting damage until she regains consciousness."

Will Dalton visibly relaxed as if the weight of everything he owned had been lifted from his shoulders. Valerie broke down into tears, from relief or in fear Ben was not sure, perhaps both.

"She's in induced coma for now. We'll likely keep her that way for the next few hours. She'll be transferred to ICU until we understand the full extent of her injuries." The doctor said. He then turned and looked at Ben and Briggs. "I understand you were the ones that found her?"

"It was Ben actually. I just came to help." Briggs replied.

Turning directly to Ben, the doctor said, "You saved her life tonight. Without treatment, she wouldn't have made it more than a few more hours." He patted Ben on the shoulder before turning, hitting a button, and heading back through the door. Ben swallowed as they all embraced.

For the second time, Ben and Briggs found themselves heading home in the early morning hours. In the car ride back, Ben's mood was somber as he considered the fragility of life. Briggs remained silent until they got back to the apartment, take-out chicken-wings in hand.

"You okay?" she asked, "You want to talk about it?"

"I wasn't sure what to do." Ben replied. "I knew she got off the bus, but I didn't know she was out there. When I got there, I almost turned around, I thought maybe organising a search in the morning was the best thing to do. If I had, she would have died out there tonight. It's crazy how such a small decision like that can determine if someone survives or not."

"But you didn't. You saved her life tonight."

They sat for a moment in silence before Briggs asked, "How did you know she was there?"

Ben shrugged, "Whispers. I'm not sure I've mentioned it before but when I do my thing, when I listen to the voices, there are different kinds. The regular voices of people talking – sometimes shouting, sometimes talking quietly. But there's another kind, I think of them as whispers because they are always quiet but they're also different from the regular kind. These whispers fade in and out, they sound different. I learned these are people speaking in their thoughts. I can't hear whatever someone might be thinking but if they think of saying something, then I can here it. If I'm close enough. It's still speech, just muffled."

"Muffled?" Briggs teased. "I'm not sure you'll make a poet. What made you think she was close or that it even was Sarah?"

"I only hear the whispers if I'm close, so whoever it was had to be nearby. Earlier, at the control centre, I saw Sarah say goodbye to Rajeev. The whisper used the same words, 'Thank you for today'"

Ben smirked.

"What?" Briggs asked.

"It was odd. They kissed, at the bus stop and I could have sworn I felt the kiss. Probably just me getting wires crossed. I thought I heard her say my name. But how could she know my name?"

After seeing off the wings, they showered and went to sleep.

Ben awoke later that morning to the smell of eggs.

"Omelette?"

"Sure, thanks," he replied.

"After everything that's been going on, you haven't forgotten I'm flying out today?" Briggs asked.

"No, I haven't forgotten," he lied. "What time do you leave?"

"Flight leaves at nine ten. I plan to leave around five."

"Do you need a lift?"

"No, I'm good, thanks. We're going to meet up at the Imagearium office before heading down. They're paying for business class. They want to make sure we're sharp for the meeting." She paused. "You going to be okay?"

"I think I'll manage. Are you all set?"

"Yup. What are you going to do?"

He wasn't sure. Something continued to gnaw away at his conscience like a dermestid beetle. The national crime agency had taken over the investigation into the child abductions. They were thorough, professional, and yet remained. He didn't know what it was.

"How are the finances looking?" he asked.

"You hoping for a few days off?" Briggs replied. "Much better than we could have expected. Olivia has been paying promptly though we only have one more week to invoice her for. The Daltons tried to pay us before we left last night or this morning or whatever time it was. I told them we'd pick it up with them later. We have a bit of income from Mr. Samir and my time is being covered by Imagearium. Plus, the prospect of a big fat bonus if we can make a deal next week."

The hours passed. Briggs filled her time with an online meeting with Imagearium, some administration, and final packing. Ben was listless, not sure what to do with himself, hoping no one came into the office, while at the same time, equally wishing someone would. He was caught between wanting to rest and being left alone, and the boredom of it. He sat in the room mulling over the Cricklewood case, replaying events in his head. Just before five p.m. Briggs entered the room to say goodbye and made doubly sure he knew where she was staying and how to contact her. He watched from the office window as a Volvo saloon pulled up and drove Briggs away.

Ben sat alone. He thought back to when he first met Detective Sophie Briggs. She stood at the door to his Mum's place, five feet seven wearing a charcoal suit. He was immediately disarmed by her charming smile and that glint in her eyes that drew you in, a quality very few seemed to possess. She was beautiful in an elegant way, graceful. Not something to be lusted over but, appreciated like a fine sculpture. She had never made him feel different or think him crazy. She simply accepted him. She likely had no idea how much that meant to him.

Briggs had brought him into the plot to blow up the Queen Elizabeth bridge, and almost certainly against the advice of her superiors. She kept his gift known only to a few and she was with him through the whole operation. An operation that later played out in front of the world on social media. They parted ways after that, but remained in contact, meeting occasionally. They became friends. Then one time, out of the blue, she asked if he'd be interested in going into business together. Being a guy living at home with his mum, processing insurance claims as a career and asked by a beautiful woman, he didn't need long to provide an answer. He thought it strange he didn't feel anything sexual toward her. He was sure he had grown to love her but as a close, slightly older sister.

Not sure what to do with himself. He got in the car and drove to the Cricklewood Mansion.

CHAPTER NINE

He turned into the cul-de-sac, a Bentley pulled out of the Loredan driveway. Ben suddenly felt exposed and out of place as the driver of the Bentley stared intently as he drove past. At the circle, Ben looked across to the Stanley's house and noticed an additional car parked in the driveway. The same car he had seen outside Havishem's yesterday – Elizabeth's rental. He slowed the car as he made his way around the circle, thinking it odd that she should be at the Stanley's.

'I'm meeting him tomorrow evening' he recalled Elizabeth saying over dinner. She must plan to read the riot act to them both, he thought. *Well, I can be a fly on that particular wall.* Instead of turning onto the Mansion driveway, he did the full circle and headed back toward the main road. The road never seemed busy, but he looked for what he considered to be a quiet spot before parking up. He leaned his chair back and closed his eyes.

It was no more than a few minutes before he located Monica's distinctive accent. From there it was easy to isolate whomever she might be talking to. He listened in. She seemed to be helping in the kitchen, talking to someone Ben didn't recognise, but who he assumed was the help. They prepared and served dinner. Pleasantries were exchanged and it was soon clear the Stanleys were hosting both Rupert and Elizabeth for dinner.

Ben adjusted his focus to ensure he was including each of them in the room. They laughed and seemed in high spirits as they caught up on each other's wellbeing, politics and economic unrest. Ben struggled to remain focussed, until…

Elizabeth said, "I was with Olivia for dinner yesterday. She shared with me what has been going on at the house." Her tone, sharp and pointed.

Ben couldn't see the reactions in the room but sensed the tension.

"What the hell have you been up to?" she asked.

Rupert was first to respond. "I'm not sure I know what you mean."

"You know damn well what I mean. You've always got your fingers stuck into something unsavoury. And you, how are you two involved? The three of you. The police have been informed and if you are not already under surveillance, you soon will be."

"What are you talking about?" James asked.

"You've been seen smuggling people, children no less, from the house into the back of transit vans! Transit vans with false number plates. On my property!"

"It's not your property Eliz…"

"Shut the fuck up, Rupert!" She said, before Rupert could finish the sentence. "You are about to be in a world of trouble, and if you want my help to get out of it, you'd better tell me what is going on." She added.

"They are teenagers," Monica replied, responding after what must have been an uncomfortable silence.

"We…acquire them from someone else. We stage them at the house before passing them on…to another party. That's it." Rupert said.

"And what of you two?" Elizabeth asked, her tone undiminished.

"Well, I don't really see how this is any of…" James was saying before he too was prevented from finishing his sentence.

"It's my house! You use my parent's home to conduct this unseemly business. I find it revolting." Elizabeth interrupted. Again, followed by silence.

"Why?" Elizabeth eventually asked.

"I took an enormous hit," James stated. "The construction business got hammered during Covid, investments took a dive, and the debts kept piling up. I was going to lose the house."

"How long has it been going on?" Elizabeth asked.

"Three years," Rupert answered. "I met someone while on vacation in Romania. I was approached by a lady. We got talking and she shared how her husband was able to finance her lavish lifestyle. She connected me to someone else and from there, I got involved. I knew James would probably want in, and that's how we met Monica. She helped us set the operation up here like some bloody franchise. Monica decided to stay."

"Who were these people?" Elizabeth asked.

"I've never met them. It's clearly operating internationally, what we do here is no doubt a fraction of the broader business." Rupert replied. "Look, we receive…these homeless, drug addicted teenagers, get them medical attention, clean them up, feed them, and pass them on…for a fee."

"Don't make it sound like you're running a bloody charity. You know damn well what those kids are being used for." There was a pause. "And, what about the website?" Elizabeth asked. Again, the question was followed by what Ben imagined to be an awkward silence.

"It's our bit on the side." James finally replied, his voice sounding as though he were responding to his headmistress. "Just getting a percentage wasn't bringing the money in fast enough."

"So, what?" Elizabeth said, "You set up your own side business?"

"It's no big deal." Rupert replied. "Look, we take in the girls. Sometimes we have them for days, even weeks, before they are moved on. So, we may as well make something from it while we hold them. We borrow them, that's all. One might think of it as training."

"You always have been a fucking retard, Rupert." Elizbeth responded. "You have had every chance to succeed, every opportunity. The best education, Mum taking you to every club and class around to see if anything would stick. While Robert and I had to graft the whole time – our silver spoon was taken away, but you, you had all three! And what have you achieved? You've always spent more than you've earned. You're a fucking parasite."

"Elizabeth, you're right." Monica said, her tone conciliatory. "We were wrong. We should not have used the house. We put you and Robert at risk. Any investigation would have to ask how or if you were involved. We did have our own place but had to react quickly when suspicions were raised."

"Then why didn't you use your own home?"

"Elizabeth, the Mansion was empty. We're sorry." Monica replied. "What is it you want us to do?" she asked.

"You've obviously been giving it some thought." Rupert added.

"You'd make a bloody fine Prosecutor," James mumbled.

Elizabeth audibly sighed. "It has to stop. Shut down that website, now. This enterprise of yours must stop."

"We can't just tell these people we're getting out. That'll put us in harm's way." James asserted.

"You three being arrested has got to be a larger inconvenience than pulling out?"

"I'm not sure you understand, Elizabeth, these are not the kind…"

"There is a buy-out." Monica said, interrupting James.

"How much?" Elizabeth asked.

"Well, it's not like there's a written contract or anything." Monica responded.

"How much!" Elizabeth repeated.

Monica continued, "The understanding is, if any party wishes to get out, that party needs to cover everyone's losses."

"For a month or something?"

"Three months." Monica replied.

"Then how much are we talking?" Elizabeth asked again.

"Half a million." Rupert said.

"Half a million!?"

"We don't know how much the others make. Our share is around fifty thousand a month." Monica clarified.

"You make over half a million a year doing this?"

"Not including what we get from the website." James added, almost sounding smug.

"So, you must have money of your own you can use?"

"Some," Monica responded. "Our money is deposited with a furniture company we set up. We buy junk furniture from closures, garage sales, that kind of thing, and sell it to false customers as antique. The overheads are low, and the revenue is in keeping with any respectable retailer selling antique furniture. We each take a small salary, the rest in dividend. But as James has said, we have had debts to address and Rupert…well, he has his hobbies."

"How much would you need?" Elizabeth asked. There was another moment of silence. Ben imagined, the three of them looking at each other, each wondering what figure to respond with.

"Three hundred," Rupert replied.

"Shut it down," Elizabeth stated. "I'll cover what you need. As a loan. You are going to have to pay me back."

"There's something else," Rupert said, sheepishly. "The website, we have a list."

"Oh, do spit it out Rupert. What list?" Elizabeth replied.

"A client list. The site runs on the dark web for obvious reasons. The names are not real of course, but they are traceable."

"Traceable? What are you talking about? We've been making all kinds of reassurances that their anonymity is guaranteed." James said.

"Yes, well it isn't." Rupert replied.

"These are…clients, that use these teenagers for their own gratification. So, we're talking sex with minors, prostitution, and we'll throw rape in for good measure. How do you know the names are traceable? Who are these clients?" said Elizabeth.

"We had help building the site. I mean, we hardly know how to order groceries online. I wanted a measure for my own security if you get my meaning. Something to do with logging I.P. addresses. I don't know exactly how it works, but I know it does. A month after setting up the site I had them demonstrate a trace for me. They gave me the option of just these IP addresses, or for an additional cost, names. Well, the IP addresses would be no good to me in the event I needed some form of leverage, so of course, I paid for the names."

"And who are our clients?" Monica asked.

"Well, given the entertainment doesn't come cheap, it probably shouldn't be a surprise that our clients include the affluent - doctors, business owners, corporate executives, police officials, judges…government officials."

"You recognised some of the names?" Elizabeth asked, Ben sensing the venom dripping from her mouth.

"Enough to know we won't be going to jail." Rupert replied.

"We'll talk about this more in the morning." Elizabeth said.

"Are you staying here tonight? We can have a bed made up for you." Monica asked, politely.

"No, I'm staying at the Fawsley. Frankly, you make me sick."

The conversation moved to awkward causerie before Elizabeth made it clear she was leaving. Ben willed himself awake, his emotions awash. His immediate concern was to move his car to make sure it wasn't noticed if Elizabeth drove past. He returned to his seat and quickly drove away.

During the drive back home, Ben tried to process everything he had heard. He grinned as he considered Elizabeth's ferocity toward Rupert. The arrogant Rupert must have felt an inch tall. But as Ben replayed more of what was spoken, his grin soured. When they saved the girls at the marina and Police took those guys into custody, he was sure Rupert and the Stanleys would soon follow. Now he wasn't so sure. If they shut everything down, would there even be sufficient evidence to make a conviction. What were the chances the Marina smugglers would involve Rupert. Surely, each party would claim not to know the other. Maybe they didn't. Ben tried to recall the night the girls were handed over. Did any of them use names? He didn't think so. The tower of evidence suddenly felt it had been constructed without rebar. And the client list? Someone of influence with something to lose wouldn't need to be blackmailed, self-preservation would provide sufficient motivation.

Ben's thoughts turned to Briggs. Her flight won't have taken off yet. Boarding would probably start soon, but phoning before she'd even left would make him sound needy. He didn't want to be needy, but he did want her advice. He thought about messaging her as that might make it sound like more of a casual update. But then, she'd call him back and he'd sound needy. He called ahead for pizza instead.

Back in the apartment, Ben lay across the couch, Pizza and tea on the coffee table, TV on. He picked up his phone and texted Briggs - 'What's Peter's contact number?' The status of the message soon changed. She was reading it. A reply came, 'He won't talk to you.'

'I need his help. It's urgent. There is something we need off the dark website. They are going to delete the site.'

A pause, then she typed something, then deleted it, then sent, 'I'll message him now, tell him you'll contact him on my behalf.' She included Peter's Whats App contact info.

Ben stared at the message. A smirk took shape across his face, he was on the hunt again.

Briggs had travelled frequently after being recruited by MI5. Being on the fast-track meant training and conferences all over the world. But this was her first time in Taiwan. The hotel was around an hour from Taipei airport, in the heart of Hsinchu and within walking distance of the HGMC, Hsinchu Global Microelectronics Company, headquarters. By Taiwanese standards the company was small, considered a niche player. The niche was the development of the microchips used in printer control systems. Compared to Imagearium, HGMC was huge, over a hundred times larger in just about every measure that mattered. It also has a sister company that specialises in sensory systems needed for 3D printing, laser control systems used within laser printers, and specialised semiconductors. Though Imagearium had suffered losses from delays and problems to its own clients, it remained dependent on HGMC for the supply of its advanced 3D printers, a rapidly growing market.

They checked themselves in and after agreeing on a time to meet for breakfast, headed each to their respective rooms. It was after ten p.m. and Briggs had been travelling for over twenty-nine hours, but she had no intention of sleeping just yet.

From her laptop, she had a video call with Ben. He shared the discussion between Elizabeth, Rupert and the Stanleys, and she shared Ben's concern at the prospect of them walking free away from this.

"Can Peter help?" she asked.

"He said it would take some time, but when I told him about the I.P. tracking that Rupert was doing, he said that might make things a little easier. I'm not sure what he meant by that, and I doubt I would have been any wiser if I had asked."

They laughed as they imagined Elizabeth's ferocity and Rupert's humiliation.

"Do you have any plans for tomorrow?" Briggs asked.

"I have been invited to a 'Thank you' party by the Dalton's. You were invited but sadly…Actually, I'm not sure the party is just for me, or us I should say, I think it's more of a homecoming for Sarah. Doctors have given her the all clear, she's being released from hospital tomorrow."

Briggs smiled, "I'm so proud of you. I know you don't always like to talk about it, but this is exactly the kind of thing I had hoped for when suggesting we went into business. You, doing your thing and saving people."

"And you ramming into boats and jet-setting around the world in business class." Ben teased.

"I hardly rammed the boat. I just made sure it wasn't getting away. And this jet setting, is how we are going to continue to pay the bills."

They chatted for several minutes more before Briggs closed the call. She had a few things she wanted to get done before hitting the pillow. Before flying out, Briggs had sent messages to two ex-HGMC employees that she thought might be able to provide greater insight into the company's manufacturing processes. She now had more homework to do, researching what she could on the two individuals. Before shutting down she plotted a morning run.

The Dar Lon Hotel was located just off the Nanqing Highway and only a block from the Hsinchu Park and zoo. Stepping out of the air-conditioned lobby, she was greeted by a warm slightly humid light breeze. The smell of compost greeted her nostrils. A landscaping business across from the hotel had spilled onto a patch of adjacent land. Various containers, masonry blocks, shrubs and soil looked to be steadily spreading across the open space. The view was in stark contrast to the impeccable order inside the hotel.

She set off on her route. The immediate area comprised mostly of small businesses and mid-rise apartment buildings. The use of concrete everywhere created an area devoid of character – functional perhaps but inspirational it is not.

Briggs jogged through the side streets and onto the Zhongxiao Road which took her under the highway and toward the Zoo. She passed the municipal stadium with its floodlights still shining on the few likeminded joggers taking advantage of the track. Briggs made a turn, running past the Zoo entrance and to the park behind. She ran for an hour, her pace comparable to any other serious athlete. MI5 had come a long way into accepting women into its structure, and though perhaps not dominated by males, it remained heavily biased toward them. Briggs felt to pressure to more than earn her dues, and she did. She worked harder, studied longer, and ran farther.

After showering, she threw on black jeans and a beige top and headed down to breakfast. Colleen, the thirty-something assistant to Arjun Banerjee, the CTO, sat at a table with orange juice and cereal. Briggs made her way over. Arjun was at the buffet and soon returned with a bowl of fruit and a vegetarian omelette. Arjun was tall, lean but not athletically built. Flecks of grey and slight thinning suggested he was into his fifties. Derek Lionels, the Lawyer, was the last to join the table. White, overweight and looking as though retirement years ago would have been his doctor's recommendation. His wild grey hair, deep furrowed brow and blotchy complexion suggested he had accumulated a good few miles and sacrificed more than one marriage during his career.

Lionels opened the morning giving what was supposed to have been a summary of the contract between the two parties, Imagearium's subsequent commitments and associated losses, and confirming what they hoped to achieve from this visit. Briggs presented backgrounds on several HGMC executives, along with the results of her findings on several other business relationships. In the afternoon, Arjun shared the technical specifications of the printers, what they were being used for and how the nature of the failures had manifested. Colleen's doodling hit its creative peak during Arjun's presentation.

To Briggs, the case seemed thin, and Lionels obvious frustration did nothing to build confidence. Briggs was able to share confirmation of her meetings with the ex-employees – one this evening, and the other at eleven tomorrow morning. They agreed Briggs should meet them alone.

The two meetings yielded little. By all accounts HGMC operated a reputable and efficient business. There was no evidence to suggest a corporate cover up or that the defects didn't sit well inside accepted industry tolerances.

Briggs spent the weekend sightseeing. She and Colleen attended the zoo together on Saturday. On Sunday, Briggs took an Uber back into Taipei, spending the day at the National Palace and sampling food markets. She checked in with Ben each day. He remained waiting for news from Peter.

A text from Arjun had delayed their start on Monday morning by an hour. Over breakfast, Colleen shared that he'd been called into a meeting with the other Imagearium execs. The day passed slowly and ended with Daniel going over how he expected the initial meeting with HGMC tomorrow to go. 'Let us hope HGMC are feeling charitable', Lionels concluded.

Briggs and her companions were greeted cordially by HGMC. Only one of the executives attended, accompanied by members of middle management, a HGMC company lawyer, and a translator. As Lionels thanked HGMC for agreeing to meet, he was politely but assertively advised, the meeting would be kept strictly to one hour. Lionels usual rambling, had been replaced with a much more concise and direct delivery. Briggs sat off centre, making it clear that Banerjee and Lionels were going to be the talkers.

HGMC listened to Banerjee's full presentation before asking questions and responding. A production line manager with responsibility for the circuit boards was invited by the HGMC executive to provide an overview of their processes.

Part way through the presentation, Briggs interjected, "Sorry, you said you follow ISO quality management standards?" She waited for the Translator. The manager looked across at the executive, seemingly looking for direction on how to answer.

"Yes, we follow ISO 9001 standards," he confirmed.

Briggs sensed an opening, like a fighter whose opponent had been jarred by a jab. "So, you are accredited?" she asked.

Again, the manager looked to the executive. "Well, no, not as yet," came the translation, "though our processes are fully compliant."

Lionels leaned in, "but you claim to be accredited."

The executive was first to reply, in English. "We have been clear in our contract Mr. Lionels, which states, 'HGMC complies with ISO 9001 quality standards', we do not claim accreditation. A copy of the contract was placed on the table, its page turned to show the relevant paragraph.

Derek Lionels reached inside his briefcase and produced a HGMC brochure. He turned a page while responding. "Your brochure does state, and I quote, '*Hsinchi Global Microelectronics Company is accredited, complying with all quality management principles as contained within the ISO9011 standards.*' You are claiming accreditation."

Briggs looked at the HGMC executive who visibly winced at the brochure.

"Please could you excuse us for a moment," the executive asked in English. The HGMC employees left the room.

"We have 'em," Lionels said quietly, clenching a fist. He turned to Biggs and asked, "Why did you press them on the accreditation? We've all read the same material, there was no reason to ask explicitly about the accreditation."

"They kept using the same expression, 'we comply with'. Mr. Liu, I can't pronounce his first name, the guy I met on Friday used the same expression, like they've been told to say it."

Lionels looked puzzled.

"If you've actually been accredited," she continued, "wouldn't you prefer to say 'accredited'? I guess the marketing folks were a bit premature."

"Is this sufficient? Does this show culpability?" Arjun asked.

"No, but it might be enough for some form of compensation." Lionels replied. The three of them smiled. Briggs did not.

"What's wrong Sophie?" asked Colleen. The two men stopped congratulating themselves and turned to Briggs.

"Look, I think it's clear HGMC operate as well as any other supplier. Probably better. I'm clearly no expert on this, but all machines fail, and a percentage of anything built has defects. By all accounts, these chips operate well within accepted tolerances. Imagearium has been unlucky. You got the ones with the defect. Shit happens."

"So, what? You don't think we're entitled to compensation?" Arjun asked.

Briggs pinched her lips, "Entitled, no. If they do come back with something, I think we should consider ourselves fortunate their marketing screwed up. But let's not act like we've caught someone committing a crime."

Lionels cleared his throat. "Yes, well, we have been employed to represent our client. Our client has suffered financial loss resulting from a fault in these machines. Some form of compensation is not an unreasonable request."

A few minutes ticked by as they waited for HGMC to return to the room. When the door did open, only their lawyer and the translator came into the room.

Via the translator, the lawyer said, "The fault in the HGMC components supplied to Imagearium is of course unfortunate, but well within the expectations of both companies. HGMC is not at fault. However, in the interests of maintaining healthy business relations and as a gesture of goodwill, HGMC is willing to make a contribution towards the losses Imagearium has experienced. We will cover the cost of the impacted contract. We also understand Imagearium is interested in purchasing two of our latest 3D printers?" He waited for Arjun to nod before continuing. "HGMC, as a gesture of goodwill, will offer Imagearium a discount of fifty percent when they order the first printer. Of course, we would not expect to hear or read of anything where your company suggests the performance of HGMC components is anything less than exceptional. This offer is available until twelve p.m. on Thursday after which it will be retracted entirely. No other offer will be made, and we will not negotiate on this offer. It is more than generous given there is no liability here." As soon as the translator had finished, they left the room.

"What's that worth?" Briggs asked.

"About one point five million," Arjun replied.

"I think that more than covers the flights and accommodation," she said, standing and collecting her things.

By the time they had returned to the hotel, Lionels and Arjun were in agreement to recommend acceptance of the offer. When they joined up for the dinner that evening, Arjun confirmed the Board's acceptance and was asked to pass on the Board's gratitude. Before dinner, Briggs had run the numbers. HGMC's revenue over the last twelve's was more than three billion dollars. The one and half million offered to Imagearium would still be less than one week of marketing budget. To Imagearium, it represented around three weeks total revenue for the year. And to Grey and Briggs Investigations, their percentage would cover a full quarter.

Ben was sitting on the couch eating take out noodles, when Briggs called.

"Just about to watch the match," he said, as her face appeared on video.

Briggs relayed what happened during the meeting with HGMC.

"How much is that worth to us?" Ben asked.

"About seventy-five thousand, I think, assuming we get credit for the discount on the new printer."

"Well done. I can't quite match that, but I did get a rather nice surprise earlier today."

"Oh yeah?'

Ben held up a banker's draft made out for fifty thousand pounds. He was smiling smugly into the camera.

"Fifty thousand! Where do you get that from?" she asked.

"From the Dalton's, along with a rather lovely handwritten note. Here let me read it to you –

Dear Mr. Grey and Ms. Briggs,

Words cannot adequately express our immense gratitude for saving our daughters life.

There can be no doubt that without your intervention Sarah would not have been found alive. We agree with Sarah in calling you our heroes.

Though we could not possibly repay the debt we now owe you, we ask that you please accept this cheque as a token of our appreciation.

Forever grateful,

Signed Val and Will Dalton."

"Wow," Briggs replied. "You do know you can't accept it."

"What!?" Ben replied incredulously.

Briggs laughed, "I'm just pulling your leg. Well done and thoroughly deserved." After a pause, she asked, "Has Peter come back to you?"

"Yeah, he has. But he won't send it to me. He insists on speaking to you."

"Why, did he say?"

Ben shook his head. "No. I assume it has something to do with the names on the list. I don't know."

"Okay, I'll try to contact him from here."

"So, are you flying back early?"

"It looks that way. They will formally accept the offer tomorrow and Colleen is trying to arrange alternate flights back, though I think she would have liked to have stayed longer."

"Well, you could stay longer if you like. I have everything under control. I even remembered to put the open sign on this morning."

"Amazing. Has anyone actually come into the office?"

"Not that I am aware of."

"And have you secured any new business while I've been away?"

"Err. No, no I haven't. But I have got a cheque for fifty thousand pounds," he said, waving the draft at the camera again.

The merriment of the call soon wore off as thoughts returned to Rupert and the Stanleys. Ben hadn't shared that the dark site had been taken down. They were clearing shop, and he had no idea how the police investigation might be going.

Briggs set her alarm to wake an hour earlier than usual. She wanted to catch Peter before he went to sleep.

"Sophie, it's after ten," Peter said, picking up the call. The tiredness apparent in his voice.

"I know, I thought it better to call you after work, and I didn't want to interrupt what little social life you have."

"That's how you ask for help?"

"Oh come on, I was being considerate. Ben brought me up to speed, he said you wouldn't share the client list. That you wanted to speak to me first."

"I'm doing this because you helped my sister. But this…this is big, Sophie."

"I know this isn't always easy for you, the risks you take. But isn't this why we got into this game in the first place? To scrape up the scum from off the streets?"

Peter sighed. "The scum is always going to be there. And this scum…these people are untouchable."

"No one is untouchable. Look at Epstein, Weinstein, hell, Frankenstein for all that matter." She could sense Peter's anxiety. "Look, we knew there were going to be some big names. Our immediate goal is to make sure these fuckers we have been investigating, don't walk free. They think the people on this list will enable them to walk free. Well, that swings both ways, we can use the list as leverage to ensure can't. Peter, if there's any blowback, it's all on Ben and I."

"People use the dark web because of its complex routing and non-indexed addresses. Ben mentioned he thought they had inserted additional tracking into the site. He was right, the site has a sub-routine that executes another program, like a virus would. It traces the IP addresses back and adds them as a string of numbers to a CSV file hidden behind the site. I had trouble finding the routine that discovers the address owners listed in the file. The odd thing about this routine is that it looks remarkably like our code, the tools we use inside the NCA. Anyway, it's a reverse lookup that accesses the relevant service providers for the information."

"Peter, are you going to send me the list?"

"Yes. It'll be encrypted, you won't be able to share the file with anyone, and your service provider won't be able to see it. They will only know something was attached."

"Why wouldn't we at least give it to the NCA?"

"It's too dangerous, to me, to you, to Ben. And besides, we can't be sure someone on the inside isn't involved. Just write some of the names down and hand that to them."

"How many names are on the list?"

"Over two hundred."

"What the…I'm not writing down two hundred names." She said.

"There are some obvious ones you might want to include. Others perhaps best left excluded. Choose some, hand them to someone you trust, and leave it alone."

Briggs found herself nodding in agreement. "Okay, send it to me, and thanks Peter. It means a lot."

A few moments later, the message with a file attached arrived.

Ben awoke to two messages from Briggs. The second, confirmation she would be flying back today, landing tonight local time. The first confirming Peter had sent her the client list but that she was unable to share it with him.

"What the hell!" he said out loud. The message tried to explain why but it did little to appease.

At the kitchen table, Ben browsed the news while eating scrambled eggs. He was about to switch to the game, closing background apps to reduce the possibility of the game crashing, when he noticed he had several previous searches still open. He opened them up and found himself looking at the pictures of Caroline Walters and Louise Larke, and the article about the protests. Was this what was bothering him about the case - the itch?

The article was written by a reporter for the Milton Keynes Citizen, which had also been reporting on the ongoing investigations for the two teenagers. According to the Citizen, both these girls came from loving families, attended school, and had no history of delinquent behaviour. Some four hundred teenagers go missing each year in the Milton Keynes area alone. But how many were girls under the age of sixteen?

On the way out, Ben went to adjust the office sign only to realise he hadn't set it to open anyway. The drive down the A5 to Milton Keynes took about thirty minutes. The MKCitizen had a small office inside the Regus House building, a modern, largely concrete building that backed onto Atterbury Park, east of the city. It didn't take him long to traverse the city and reach the building, courtesy of the H5 – the number five horizontal road, running east to west.

Ben spent the morning gathering what information he could on the cases of the two girls. They lived in separate parts of the city and there was nothing that suggested they knew each other. Caroline Walters strangled body had been discovered by a walker at the edge of a park in the Bradwell area, a little over a mile from where Ben was now sat. Louise Larke had been last seen heading home from IKEA, south of the city.

The Thames Valley Police were able to provide a better breakdown of the missing teenagers, by demographic. He learned of the four hundred that typically went missing each year, in the MK area, a third were female. And of those, a third of those were under the age of sixteen. That dropped to a fifth for under fifteen or around twenty-five girls under the age of fifteen.

Ben sat in silence, alone with his thoughts oblivious to the sounds of the coffee machine or the shoppers busying themselves with the affairs of the day. His mind pictured the girls being herded into the back of the van, just a few nights ago, then shifted to the countries listed on the web site, and the client list. How many teenagers are needed to drive this…industry?

The apple Danish did nothing to sweeten the taste in his mouth. Of course, no operation would be stupid enough to abduct kids from the same area, and thousands must go missing across the country – and many will have nothing to do with abduction – hell, Sarah Dalton went missing simply due to a bus not turning up.

Still, twenty-five a year in an area the size of Milton Keynes was likely not a large number in the context of running organised crime on an international scale. Ben was not one for conspiracy theories, but he had to wonder what proportion could realistically be down to trafficking, organised child prostitution and paedophilia.

"Let's find out," Ben said to himself, collecting his keys and standing.

CHAPTER TEN

Ben spent the next few hours retracing Caroline's last known whereabouts, two days prior to the discovery of her body. She was last seen after getting off the bus on the V6 stop, just before the Walgrave Drive turning. She said goodbye to two of her friends following an afternoon of shopping and skiing at the Snozone. Her home was less than a five-minute walk away. She was wearing black leggings, converse shoes, and a black puff jacket.

Caroline's body had been presumed dumped, thrown from the H3 overpass, some six hundred metres as the crow flies, from where she had got off the bus two days earlier. CCTV covered much of the city centre and major roads, but the H3 overpass was a blind spot – the closest camera only meters away but pointing in the other direction.

Ben drove to the Bradwell Bowls Club, parked, and took the footpath across the sports fields into the park land. The trees and shrubbery were thick, though the footpath was maintained and clear. A couple of dog walkers gave polite greetings as he made his way to the spot where the body had been discovered. He was standing directly below the underpass. Dragging a body through the parkland would have been both high risk and exhausting. There could be no doubt, whoever was responsible, would have pulled up on the overpass, lifted her body and dropped it the fifteen feet or so below. It would take all of a minute.

Other than death by strangulation, the body had little other evidence. Some bruising and minor abrasions. The bruises could only have been caused antemortem and suggested she had been in a struggle. The abrasions perhaps from the struggle or from the fall. No evidence of sexual assault.

Ben watched as the car's clock changed to three fifteen. The disgust and anger that he used as fuel, had been temporarily replaced by empathy and heartache, albeit only a fraction of what the family across the road must be experiencing. Mrs. Aretta Walters had agreed to meet him.

She was a large lady, wearing a purple and pink dress adorned with various flowers all in differing shades of red.

Before they were seated, she said, "We choose to celebrate life rather than mourn the loss, Mr. Grey. In Nigeria, reds and whites are a celebration of life. My Caroline was a light, like sunshine, she could brighten any space she entered."

"I'm so sorry for your loss Mrs. Walters. I can't imagine the pain you and your family must be feeling."

They sat down.

"I agreed to meet with you, Mr. Grey,"

"Ben, please, I prefer Ben."

"Ben, I agreed to meet with you because the police are no closer to finding out what happened. My girl stepped off the bus just yards from her home, only to be taken and dumped like garbage off the side of the road. We came to England for a new life, a better life. Caroline had just been born, and I had completed my engineering certificates. Life has been good to us, we were able to find work, get this home, find a good school…" Tears welled in her eyes.

"What is your interest in Caroline, Mr. Grey, sorry, Ben?" She asked.

Ben had been deliberately vague on the phone, not sure if Mrs. Walters would decline his request to meet if she knew he was investigating child trafficking.

"I've been investigating organised crime in the area, involving child abduction." He replied.

 "Child abduction? Organised?"

"Yes. It's a bit of a long story but suffice to say, I was hired to investigate disturbances at a certain residence. One thing has led to another, and we uncovered what we believe amounts to a cartel. People that abduct teenagers for illegal purposes."

"My daughter has been buried for two weeks, and the police have no leads to go on. You are the first person I have spoken to that might have a theory about what happened to her. Please speak plainly."

"The people we have been investigating, operate in this region. We believe the organisation consists of at least three groups."

"You keep saying 'we'. Who is 'we'?"

"Sorry, my business partner and I. We run a private investigation firm. Briggs, my partner, is currently out of the country but has been assisting me on this case. Anyway, we believe one group is responsible for the actual abductions. They then pass the children off to another group that holds them, by all accounts cleans them up, and passes them onto another group that moves them to different locations. While these groups obviously interact with each other, they may not be known to each other. They seem to be linked via some overarching hierarchy that is ultimately selling these children to buyers."

"We are not talking illegal adoptions, are we?"

"No, we are not."

"And you think, this group may have abducted Caroline?"

"Possibly. Frankly, I have no idea. It is as you say, just a theory. I've run the numbers, and I believe the chances certainly make it a possibility."

"But if they took her in order to sell her, why would they kill her?"

This was the obvious question to ask, and one Ben didn't have a good answer for.

"I'm speculating the children are abducted to order so to speak. Like someone placing an order. Perhaps a mistake was made, or the client changed their mind."

"My child was murdered because someone changed their mind? Couldn't they just have let her go?"

"I don't know, it's speculation on my part. Having taken her, it would have been unlikely they could just let her go. The numbers are horrible. Four hundred kids go missing in this area each year. Of those, as little as twenty-five might fit the profile these people would be looking for, over a year. We know these groups are moving kids on a regular basis. Even if we assume they are covering a much larger area, it could still mean as many as ten of these children could have been taken by this group."

They sat there for a moment, seemingly digesting the conversation.

"So, what is it you want from me? Why are you here Ben?"

"If this group, the one responsible for the abductions, are prowling the area, they would likely patrol the same routes – places they would consider low risk, without CCTV and low-traffic areas. They may also look for routines, kids walking back from swimming club, that kind of thing."

They spent the next few minutes in conversation discussing Caroline's weekly routines. She had two regular activities outside of the school run - Saturday afternoon with her friends where they would meet up at the mall. The other was her weekly clarinet lessons, across town and to which her mum would drive her. They moved to Mrs. Walter's PC for a better view of the area.

"She would meet up with her friends a few times during the week. She'd come home, do her homework, eat and then sometimes go out. I mean they always met up on Saturday's but also during the week, especially if the weather was okay. Here, here's the bus stop, just up and around the corner. The police confirmed she'd got off that evening because you can see her on the bus's camera." Mrs. Walters was pointing to a spot on the V6, Grafton Street, just before the Walgrave Drive turning.

Ben zoomed in and changed to the street level view. He clicked each arrow, following virtually the route Caroline would have taken.

"We can check for CCTV to see if she was being followed, but I think this would have been the spot to take her." Ben had moved the view, turning into Walgreen Drive along to the mini roundabout. Here," he said, leaving the picture of the roundabout on the screen.

"That's just around the corner from here. Surely the police would have checked."

"Maybe. There's no path on this side. You either have to cross to the path on the other side or walk along the grass verge. If she crosses, a vehicle stopping here at the crossing before the roundabout would block anyone from seeing anything."

"Okay, so what?"

"Well, we could see if any of your neighbours close to the roundabout have security cameras of their own. Maybe we can catch a glimpse of the vehicle."

Ben got up and thanked Mrs. Walters for both her time and help.

"Where are you going now?" She asked.

"To talk to your neighbours next to the roundabout."

"Then I'm coming with you," she said, grabbing a light jacket before he could object.

Standing back on the driveway, Ben was struck by the uniformity of the hedges that bordered each property. The homes were early eighties brick, semi-detached and all being well maintained. The owners cared. Cars lined much of one side of the road, his own included.

A slight curve in the road, meant the roundabout couldn't be seen from the Walters home.

"We'll start with the houses nearest the roundabout," he said.

Mrs. Walters may be a substantial lady, but she set off with determination that would have made any major proud.

They discovered, Mr. Arnott, the neighbour across from the roundabout had a driveway camera. The camera showed only half of the roundabout, with the crossing just in focus. The video comprised of snap shots taken every second, twenty-four seven, and stored for a calendar month. The timestamp from the bus footage provided a precise window.

Ben's hunch proved correct. Caroline could be seen, crossing the road when a white transit van, the same model Ben had seen before, drove up, narrowly missing her and blocking the crossing. The van was stationery only moments, before setting off again, around the roundabout and back out toward the V6.

"The police never asked you about this?" Mrs. Walters asked.

"Sure, they asked us if we'd seen or heard anything. But of course, we hadn't."

"You didn't show them this?"

Mr. Arnott flushed with embarrassment. "My wife told 'em the camera doesn't work. You see, we don't do anything with it. I just leave it running. I wasn't here when they came round. And I had forgotten about it. I was going to tell them but what are the chances she would have been taken from here. It's such a quiet neighbourhood. Nothing happens around here, except the odd the fox causing mischief."

"My daughter was taken yards from your house, Mr. Arnott, and you forgot you had a camera?"

Before Ben left that afternoon, Aretta Walters, embraced him.

"Thank you," she said, tears returning to her eyes, squeezing him with the arms of a shot putter. "I know this won't bring my baby back, but it's the first time I've felt like I'm doing something to help find the creatures that did this."

They now had a headshot of the driver of the van, and while Ben had no idea if the plates were legal or not, they were able to provide the police with the first leads.

That evening, Ben sat at the computer in the office. A half-eaten kebab, chips and an empty can of Stella on the table. He was researching the disappearance of Louise Larke. Louise was fourteen years old, five foot four with shoulder length straight mousey hair. She was wearing blue jeans, a red top and white jacket when she left home, the day after Caroline Walters was reported missing and the day before Caroline's body was discovered.

According to reports, Louise left home telling her parents she was heading to Ikea. She travelled using an electric scooter, a present from her parents the Christmas before. Her route would have taken her from her home on Tavistock Street to the cycle path that ran between to a metal recycling shop and a Building merchant. She would travel past Tesco and likely have turned on to Denbigh Road, no relation to the Luton secondary school. A pedestrian crossing provided access to IKEA and the ASDA superstore on the other side of Bletcham Way.

Ben checked the time. It was late and tiredness had crept up like a calm incoming tide. He checked Heathrow arrivals. Briggs was half an hour from landing. Add an hour for customs and yet another for the drive home. He yawned, switched off and headed upstairs to the apartment.

Ben flicked between TV channels. When he was kid there were only five channels to choose from. Now there were hundreds, with thousands more titles available to stream. And yet the result seemed the same, nothing to watch. He settled on rewatching Interstellar – because it was long enough to fill the time to Briggs returning.

Unaware, Ben's eyelids slowly closed, and his head lolled. Voices drifted in, parents discussing their kids, a couple arguing, some guys with slurred speech talking about football. If Ben searched for sleep, he closed his eyes, watched the phosphenes behind his eyelids and travelled through space. When his body craved sleep, it brought him here, to the meadow.

Behind him, the road back to consciousness, ahead the cliff's edge and the drop into the sleep abyss. An unseen force, pushed, no encouraged him to drift toward the precipice. While on the footpath he somehow knew he had the choice to turn back. He also knew the closer he got to the edge, the clearer the voices would become. It required effort to stand at the edge, sifting through the voices and listening in. Eventually, despite his efforts, he would wobble, lose his balance and fall into the darkness.

Over the years, excitement had turned to curiosity, which became indifference, which in turn had soured into distaste. His space travel was powered by urgency, a desperate search for some revelation. The meadow had no such urgency, just a natural desire to sleep, interrupted by the voices of those he could not otherwise hear. The end of the meadow was man's monotony, the tedium of life, sometimes its savagery, his propensity to harm, if not physically then to wish for it. Standing at the edge, the fall was no longer something to resist, but rather a leap to be embraced.

Ben stood at the edge, surrounded by voices. These were the voices of his neighbourhood, his gift thankfully limited in reach. He peered down into the abyss and stepped forth.

He was awoken to Briggs shoving his arm.

"You only just got back?" he asked.

"No. I've just got up. You have spent the night on the couch."

"Where are you going?"

"Out for a run. I can bring back a bagel if you'd like. I'll be about an hour though."

"Sure. We have a bagel shop?"

"A bakers opened on the high street. Lucky for me, they open early."

While Briggs was out, Ben got himself showered and changed. He had two things on his mind, and they both involved the police. Where was the Thames Valley investigation with respect to Louise Larke, and what was the National Crime Agency up to with respect to the child abductions.

"Has the office phone been going to voicemail since I've been away?" Briggs asked, as she climbed the stairs knowing full well she wasn't going to get an answer.

Ben noticed Briggs appear at the top of the stairs.

"Did you check the voicemail?" she asked.

Ben glanced down at his phone.

"On the office phone."

"Sorry, no. Thought it better for you to do that."

"You have an app on your phone. You can play back the recordings and have it translated for you."

"Sorry."

Over a breakfast bagel and coffee, Ben shared his events from yesterday.

"You've given the camera footage to Thames Valley?" she asked.

Ben nodded.

"And they hadn't worked that out for themselves?"

Ben wasn't sure what she meant by that, but it felt like an insult. "Are you suggesting what I did was an obvious thing to do?"

"Oh, sorry, no, I meant it's something that we might have expected an experienced detective to have covered."

The offence subsided, pride restored, by the comparison to an experienced detective.

"I want to know how the NCA are getting on?" he said. "We can't let Rupert get away with this. Why haven't they been arrested at least?"

"Leave that with me. We need to tread carefully. And before you go getting yourself upset, I mean, we need to find someone we can trust with the client information. They are probably securing enough evidence for the arrests, but at some point, once the CPS gets involved, if Rupert draws on his leverage, it will be difficult to know what is being tainted by whom."

"I also want to know how the search for Louise Larke is going."

"You know the odds of her disappearance being connected are not high. And what are you going to do? It's an active investigation, the police aren't going to let you near it. And think about it, if she was taken by this gang, she would either have been one of the girls we rescued, which she wasn't, or she's been moved on already."

Briggs was right. Even if Louise Larke had been adducted and routed via Rupert and the Stanley's, she must be out of the country by now – moved in an earlier shipment. The chances of her being found, almost zero.

"I have to go in for a debrief at Imagearium this morning. Why don't you go through the voicemails and see if we have any requests to follow up."

After Briggs had left, Ben pressed 'play all' and left his own phone to record and translate the messages. He returned to the investigation room, the itch still present, annoying and as indestructible as a fruit fly. He started to write – What do we know as fact? What don't we know?

He went over the notes they had gathered and made a list of things they knew to be fact. It was a short list. Much of what they thought they knew – Rupert being approached while on vacation, the involvement of a larger organisation, groups operating without knowledge of each other – all came from the admissions they made in conversation with Elizabeth. They had also told Elizabeth it involved child runaways and the homeless. That was a lie but perhaps Rupert may not have been aware. Probability dictated the van used in the Caroline Walters abduction had to be the same group, yet this was not fact.

And what of Louise Larke? Two young girls going missing around the same time in the same town. Louise being reported missing the day after Caroline had been abducted. Coincidence possibly but absence of time made design much easier to believe.

Ben spent the rest of the day in Milton Keynes retracing Louise Larke's last known steps. Tesco cameras overlooked the parking lot. Security easily located the footage of Louise scootering by. Though the Police had taken a copy, Security had been instructed to retain the original footage. The cameras along Denbigh Road were owned by the city council. They were reluctant to provide access to the footage despite his PI card. 'I'm acting on behalf of her parents, alongside the police investigation,' he had lied.

The Ford Transit Van is sold in two guises. They held the two top spots for vans sold in the UK, outselling the next competitor by four to one. The two transit models were similar – the Transit Van proper and the Custom. The Custom was noticeably smaller. The one Ben had been seeing was the larger regular model. And sixty percent of vans sold were white. The group had chosen well.

As soon as footage from the camera started to play, Ben realised he was not going to be watching an abduction. In less than a minute, Louise entered from the east, travelling west up along the pavement, dodging a pedestrian and cars making a turn into the commercial units that lined one side of the road.

"Did the police ask about a transit van?" Ben asked.

"You're having a laugh. A transit van?" replied the operator.

"A white one, the regular one, not the smaller custom model."

The smiled dropped from the operator's face as he replayed the footage. "You think a transit might have something to do with her going missing?"

"Go back say, five minutes before Louise arrives," Ben instructed.

"Well, that's one going past now on the other side of the road. There are three, all white, parked in there," the operator remarked, pointing at the parking lot. "Those units are mostly residential services, plumbers, electricians, that sort of thing. They all use transit vans. And look there's another one just driving past."

Ben didn't reply. He had his doubts. The footage did confirm the route Louise took. It was consistent with her going to IKEA, and the police had been gathering all the CCTV footage. But they would have been using it to confirm proof of life and establish her last verifiable location. It was unlikely they would have been looking for a white transit van.

"There's no footage of Louise after this?" Ben asked, knowing the answer.

"No. The police said she was seen on the cameras leaving IKEA, but she didn't come back this way."

Ben returned to Denbigh Road and walked the stretch Louise had taken. A path along one side gave access to the various commercial units. Trees and bushes lined the other side of the road. Where Louise would have crossed, the tree line had been cleared to allow for a cycle route from Denbigh Road, to cross the Bletcham Road dual carriageway. There were crossings for IKEA and another farther up for ASDA, both serviced with pedestrian traffic lights. Ben stood at the IKEA crossing. It was the afternoon and though the roads were busy with motorists, there was little in the way of pedestrians or cyclists. He crossed the Denbigh Road and stood at the median. To his left, the path was clear to the lights a couple of hundred metres away. To the right, the path went behind the tree line to the crossing a hundred metres away.

If Louise was heading back home when she was abducted in the same way as Caroline Walters, this was the best spot. But a van stopped on the Bletcham carriageway would have attracted immediate attention. A van stopped on Denbigh Road could probably be there minutes before being noticed. But Louise was in IKEA over half an hour.

Ben crossed back over the road and stood looking at the tyre shop opposite.

"Can I help you?" said a man stepping out from an open bay.

Ben could tell he was saying something but not what.

"Sorry, could you repeat. My hearing is poor, works better if I can read your lips."

The man, dressed in overalls that had seen its share of oil and grease, came closer.

"Can I help you? You looked like you might be looking for something."

"I noticed you have a security camera up there."

"We have three. That one there covers the car park. We got one in the office and one that covers the bays."

"Have the police asked to look at them?"

"Why would they do that?" he asked.

"Because Louise Larke is missing. She was last seen leaving IKEA."

Minutes later Ben was with the man in the office reviewing camera footage. Turned out the man was the owner.

"We've seen the police around, last week or so. There wasn't much of a presence. Figured it was perhaps a theft or summit."

"The camera only covers the car park. You can't see the pavement?"

"Anything turning can be seen, but yeah, it covers our parking spots out front. Sometimes we have vehicles towed, the cameras can be used to show how long they've been there, you know, if there's any trouble. Any break-ins would be picked up by the internal cams."

"And do you have many break-ins?"

The owner shook his head. "This road is pretty quiet. None of us keep much cash on the premises, so its just tooling and inventory really. And in our case, we only keep the tyres for a day or two. Got no room for anything more."

Ben watched the timestamp on the footage as it approached the time Louise would have been going by on her scooter, just a coupe of metres out of view.

"Sorry, that's all we got. There's a street cam that covers the road, she'd be on that, assuming its working."

Ben only caught some of the words as he tried to keep an eye on the footage that was still running.

"What's that there?" Ben asked, as a white transit van came into view. The van turned into the lot and parked facing the Denbigh Road. "Is that one of yours?"

"We have a blue one. Most of our suppliers are white, like that one, but that one's clean. If it was for us, it would have Pirelli, or Michelin on the side."

They continued watching. Several minutes went by before a man stepped out from the passenger side, athletic build, bald, with a beard. Ben paused the frame but didn't recognise the face onscreen. He let it continue to play. The man walked away from the lot and out of view. Ben checked the time stamp.

"That happens too," the owner said. "People park on this side, then grab a sandwich or such from IKEA."

"Why would they do that?"

"Cause Bletcham Road is a lot busier. If you want to stay on this side, then parking here and walking over is likely a lot quicker, especially if its not raining."

The recording continued. "How long are we going to be watching this for?"

"Louise was in there about thirty-fives minutes." Ben replied.

"Here let me fast-forward. I do have a business to run."

"Slow it down again." Ben asked, as the clock spun past the thirty-minute mark.

"That bloke hasn't returned yet." The owner pointed out. "Normally they're only ten minutes or so, even when its busy."

"He's not going to," Ben replied.

"How would you know that?"

Just as the owner asked the question, the van reversed out of the spot with some urgency and left the car park.

"Because I've seen that plate before. They've just snatched Louise Larke. Here can I get a copy?" Ben asked, slipping a USB device from his pocket.

"Do I need to give this to the police?"

"Up to you, but I will make sure they get a copy. Thank you, you've been very helpful."

That evening, Briggs proposed eating out at a Korean restaurant. They sat in a booth while marinated meats and a variety of vegetables were brought to the table.

"You have to cook yourself?" Briggs pointed out, after the server left the table.

"What's the point in coming out to eat then."

"Just try it."

Ben had shared his discovery. Though he had no footage to confirm it, Briggs agreed that Louise Larke had been taken by the same people that had taken, and killed, Caroline Walters.

"Louise was taken only a few days before those at the Mansion were loaded into the back of the van we saw."

"So, we just missed her?" Ben asked.

"No, dummy, you had been at the house nosey-ing around at least a couple of times before then. You're deaf not blind."

"Oh, thank you for reminding me. What are you saying?"

"If they were keeping her, she would have been at the house when you were taking a look around."

"Okay, so she never made it to the house."

"You think she's also been killed?"

Briggs shook her head, "You think Caroline may have been taken by mistake."

"In error."

"In error then. Taken but not wanted for whatever reason. They can't keep her, so they," she said, glancing around and not wishing to finish her sentence.

"Do we assume, Louise was taken in preference to Caroline. If so, why the fu.., sorry, why the hell, would Louise not be on the boat?"

"You don't think they killed her too?" he replied, in what he hoped was a whisper.

"Exactly. These people may not be professionals-r-us, but they are not going to want to make the same error twice."

Ben shrugged. "So where is Louise Larke?"

As they ate, Ben agreed with Briggs that there was something odd about Louise Larke being taken and then being a no-show at the Mansion. Caroline's death had been one of efficiency. They surmised Caroline had likely killed in the van as soon they realised and error had been made, and then promptly dumped. They chose a site where they must have known the body would be discovered within a few days, but it was also a camera blind spot and instantly accessible. It was efficient.

Briggs confirmed she had reached out to an old acquaintance she trusted at the NCA. She hadn't shared the client list only asking for the name of someone in authority that could also be trusted.

"Give it to the papers," Ben said.

"We do want to catch these bastards."

"Who is on this list?"

"Everyone is represented on this list. Everyone, lawyers, politicians, councillors, fucking barristers."

"Celebrities?"

"Premier league footballer, does that count? A bloody BBC weather reporter. I haven't looked at all the names."

"Yes, you have. I would."

"Okay, I have, but I don't recognise most of the names."

"You don't recognise most of the names?"

"Look, its better you don't know. You get pissed off when Rupert and his cronies have not been arrested within a few days. Imagine how'd you'll be knowing some celeb is carrying on for months or years, while a case is built."

"You said you had news to share," Ben reminded Briggs. Which she had used as the excuse for eating out.

"Yes. I wondered if we should look to hire someone to manage the office?"

"Done."

"Aren't you supposed to ask me if we can afford it at least?"

"Nope. You wouldn't have suggested it if you didn't think we could afford it. And besides, from what you've said, the numbers are looking pretty good already."

"And I can't keep having these calls directed to my phone. And as you're not checking the voicemails, we could be loosing more business than an employee would cost us."

"Done. I don't need convincing. It's a great idea. Let's do it."

"Well, I have someone in mind."

"Who?"

"Her name is Harriet. I bumped into her at the Imagearium office. She works on reception. She's young, but she's bright and seemed quite enthusiastic when she knew I was a PI."

"Is she pretty?"

"I'm not trying to find you a girl friend. And she's only twenty or something, not long graduated. Actually, she's a bit chubby, but she's lovely, I think she'd be fine. I'd like to see if I can poach her."

"Fine. Do you want to vet her?"

"Vet her? Oh, you want to do your thing on her? Check out what she's thinking?"

"Not really. But I could. I have a superpower."

After a moment, Ben said, "You know you've never asked if I've, you know, listened in on you."

"Have you?" she asked.

"No. And I wouldn't. I learned the hard way."

"Not even tempted?"

"With you? No. What would I find? Interests in dodgy Scottish crime thrillers, shoes and some unexplainable lack of interest in football and computer games."

She was staring at him.

"What?"

"Your dad walked out on you. Your mum thought you were going nuts when you tried to talk to her about your gift. You grow up with these voices in otherwise silence. Then you stumble on something. Something massive. It scared you and yet you had the courage to tell someone about it, knowing they would have to ask questions about how you came by such information. Hell, for a moment, some thought you were involved."

"But not you." He said.

"Ben, you are very brave, you have a good heart. You're a good man, and I am happy to trust you with my life if needed. I am not for a moment, going to get hung up on whether you might secretly be listening to my thoughts or whatever else it is that you can do."

"Okay, you can shut up now, you're going to make me cry."

The next day they were at a Costa Coffee interviewing Harriet on her lunch break. They offered Harriet the job for a slight increase on what she was currently earning and with the incentive of more paid holiday. She would start in two weeks.

It meant the afternoon was spent at the accountant's signing papers that agreed to them conducting payroll. They now had another excuse to eat out in the evening – their first employee.

The following day, Saturday, Briggs spent the morning going through the voicemail. Three were potential cases – another missing person, another potentially cheating spouse, and the other was from a barrister's office. The barrister's office was situated in Buckingham and would not be open until Monday. The message was an enquiry into whether Grey & Briggs could provide investigative services to their cases. She assigned the missing persons to Ben.

Sunday passed slowly which is how Ben liked them. Getting up late, poached eggs on toast and some gaming. Briggs would be out at Tae Kwon Do and then busying herself with something, and so not around to roll her eyes or interrupt. The afternoon would be football on the telly followed by more gaming in the evening.

But his plans for this Sunday evening were interrupted. Briggs bolted up the stairs and insisted he switch on the local news.

A reporter stood outside a house they both immediately recognised – the Stanleys.

A joint operation between Thames Valley Police and the National Crime Agency has led to the arrest of more than a dozen people accused of being part of an organised crime syndicate responsible for the abduction and trafficking of children. I'm outside the home of James and Monica Stanley who were included in the arrests, and allegedly at the heart of the syndicate. It is not yet clear how far back the crimes might go, but some believe it could be several years, involving more than a hundred children between the ages and ten and sixteen. The investigation is continuing.

"They've finally made some arrests." Ben said, sitting down.

"And credits to Thames Valley and the NCA for the bust. No mention of Grey and Briggs." Said Briggs, still standing.

"How did you know this was on?"

"That detective we ran into after the boat episode tipped me off. I'm meeting him tomorrow. You can come if you'd like?"

"Where will they take them?"

"Who? The Stanleys? They'll want to keep them all separated so likely the cells of several different stations. Case like this, they probably have forty-eight hours to charge them or let them go. Assuming they are charged they could be released on bail or remanded until they appear in court."

"But could you find out where they will be held, where Rupert is being held?"

"Are you okay?"

"Perhaps I'll get a better read now they're sitting in a cell with just their thoughts. Something's been bothering me almost from the beginning. I don't know what I is, but it's been nagging from almost the beginning. It's my itch."

"Your itch? You think we've missed something?"

Ben shook his head, "I dunno. And I want to make sure he doesn't know anything about Caroline Walters or Louise Larke."

"Yes, I can find out where he's being held." Briggs replied, turning to make her way downstairs.

"Aretta Walters was right."

Briggs stopped.

"When she said the police weren't taking her daughter's case as seriously as Louise Larke's."

"We don't know that, Ben. Sometimes people just screw up. Resources are tight and the Thames Valley detectives are almost certainly going to be overloaded. They send some inexperienced traffic bobby to knock on neighbourhood doors and take some statements. The wife says the camera doesn't work, it's not checked, and all the detective in charge is told is, 'it doesn't work.' It doesn't mean race has anything to do with it.

Sure, there were those that thought that me being black or a woman, or both, was the only reason for me being fast-tracked to promote diversity and all that bullshit. But I worked my arse off, and I was good. And I came to be accepted. Look, there are plenty of assholes in the police, it attracts jerks that want to wave a badge around. But even the bad ones want to catch bad guys. It was a mistake. And you got to put it right."

CHAPTER ELEVEN

Ben parked next to the Banbury Bowling club at People's Park. He was less than two hundred metres from Banbury Police Station. A sign next to his spot read 'No Overnight Parking Permitted' but he saw no cameras to suggest the lot was being patrolled.

He angled his seat back, closed his eyes and slowed his breathing. He would not be in the meadow. Ben was on the hunt. He was the space traveller. His muscles relaxed, his head became heavy, and the voices emerged. He sifted and filtered, quickly dispensing with the irrelevant and obvious, narrowing his search, sharpening his focus. He heard someone speak the name 'Rupert Henshaw'.

"Rupert Henshaw. Do you remember a few years back that crash at Silverstone?"

"There are a lot of crashes at Silverstone."

"Helicopter crash smart arse. Says here he lost his parents in that crash."

"You want me to feel sorry him?"

"Why do you have a stick up your arse tonight? You not getting enough from your missus?"

"I'm not getting anything from my missus, now go and check on him."

Ben assumed he had been listening to two officers. He continued listening. There was a short silence then…

"Hey, you need anything before we call it a night?" Said one of the officers.

"No, I'm great thanks. Can you turn off those lights?" Came the reply. Rupert's now familiar voice.

"You know, I have a daughter, she's twelve years old. Get yourself a good night's rest now."

"What happened to innocent until proven guilty? And turn the bloody lights off! Bastard."

"Yeah, yeah, Dickhead."

The airwaves fell silent again. Ben yawned but remained determined to keep focussed and keep listening. More silence, and then a whisper – Rupert was thinking to himself.

"How the shit did this happen?" How did they know about the drop? How did they connect us to that? They wouldn't have given us up. It must have been that fucking PI snooping around, bloody Olivia's lapdog. All they know is some bloody girls passed through our hands. They have nothing to say we took them or caused them any harm. Well not all of them."

An image of Louise Larke flashed into Ben's mind almost jolting him from his slumber.

"Ah, there you are. They had better let me out of here soon or you will soon be looking the worse for wear. I'm sorry Uncle Rupert isn't there right now to comfort you. To stroke your hair, to touch you, caress you."

Ben felt revulsion as he sensed Rupert's excitement build.

"There you go. Awe don't cry."

Ben's instincts shouted at him to tune out, but he needed something, anything that might help locate Louise.

"Does this feel better? I bet it does. You know you are much better off with me. I treat you nicely, feed you, give you what you need. Even had this basement converted for you. You see how good I am to you." Rupert's whisper became raspy, more urgent, his excitement building.

Ben felt his own disgust, nausea in the pit of his stomach. He was floating, moving. He was suddenly awake grabbing for the door handle and leaning out of the car, sure he was going to vomit. Nothing came and the nausea started to pass. Drops of sweat dripped onto the pavement. Ben touched his head as if in disbelief.

He got out of the car and stood leaning against it. The cool night breeze helped to clear his thoughts and dry the sweat. He took his phone out and called Briggs.

"He has Louise Larke."

"Rupert has Louise?"

"I think she's still alive. Trapped in some basement. He must have kept her himself. He's a fucking monster."

"Any idea where?"

"I'm not sure. He said he had converted the basement for her."

"I thought you said he was gay, another stupid lie of his. Okay, so it must be a place he owns. He obviously doesn't stay at the Mansion."

"Where does he live?" Ben asked.

"One sec. Let me take a look. Bugbrooke, small village not far from the Mansion. Come here first, we'll go together."

Ben was back at home in under thirty minutes. Briggs was waiting on the driveway for him as he pulled up.

"We can take mine." She said.

The drive to Bugbrooke would take less than ten minutes, though Ben had hardly spoken a word.

"We can't go in there." Said Briggs.

"What do you mean we can't go in there?"

"You can't just break into someone's house."

"Soph, we have no idea what kind of condition she's in."

"We don't know for sure if she's even in the place. If we break in and she's not there, then we are definitely screwed."

"Then come up with a plan because I'm going in there."

They turned off the A5.

"The address is next to the marina."

Briggs slowed the car. The road was narrow with no lighting. A tall hedge lined the right-hand side. They approached a small car park.

"I guess that must be for the marina." Briggs said.

"No. It's a pub," Ben replied, pointing to two parked cars. "Where is the marina?"

"According to the map, on the other side of that hedge. Here, we must need to turn in here."

They found themselves on a gravelled access road that curved behind the pub.

"Are you sure this is right?" Ben asked.

She wasn't but continued driving at a crawl around the corner.

At the back of the pub there were several other buildings.

"Barn conversions," pointed out Briggs.

"Don't tell me he owns that." Ben remarked, as a substantial pre-war townhouse-style building emerged from behind the conversions. He can't be complaining about money and own that."

They parked at the front of the townhouse, got out and walked over to the entrance.

"This has been converted, into apartments." Briggs said. Beside the entrance were three buttons with three names against them. "Henshaw. Rupert has the ground floor."

"I'm going around."

Ben paced off, looking around the outside of the building. Briggs went around the other way.

Ben had just reached the rear of the building when Briggs came trotting towards him.

"Over here," she said, before turning and heading back where she came from.

Ben followed. He turned the corner to see what had grabbed Briggs' attention. The light from her phone shone upon a small, lunette window, built into the wall at ground level.

They looked at each other and in unison said, "a basement."

"That's enough for me."

"Ben, we can't just break in."

As she finished her sentence, Ben kicked at one of the glass panes. It didn't break.

"They're not going to put a window at that height unless it's really hard to break."

"We need to get in there. What about the bay window at the front?"

"Sure, that'll break and attract the attention of the whole neighbourhood."

"Then what!?"

"Move the car."

"What? Why?"

"Because if you break in, I will need to call it in, and I don't want the police finding my car parked outside the front."

Ben moved the car to the pub's car park and jogged back. Briggs had found a good-sized rock. She was about to throw it when a light came on in the apartment above. A man's face peered between curtains. A moment later the entrance light came on and a short heavyset man appeared at the front steps.

"Can I help you?" he asked, in a tone designed to express suspicion.

Briggs had dropped the rock and had her PI card in hand. "Hi, yes, we're wondering if Rupert Henshaw lives at this address?"

"Why do you want to know?"

"I'm Sophie Briggs, this is my business partner Benjamin Grey. We are private investigators working on behalf of Louise Larke's parents. Louise went missing just over a couple of weeks back. She was seen with Rupert Henshaw."

"Well, you're not much good at your jobs."

"Oh yes, and why is that?" Briggs asked.

"He's been arrested. Was all over the local news. Something to do with human trafficking. Disgusting really. Anyway, he's not here."

"So, he does live here? Before his arrest."

The man stepped back into the entrance and reached his hand back. A lamp came on lighting the front of the building. The man took a step down and seemed to be assessing his chances against Ben and Sophie should trouble ensue.

Ben smiled, it's not me you need to worry about, he thought.

"We know he's been arrested. We were the ones that put him there." Said Briggs.

"I see."

"Does his flat have access to a basement?"

"Yeah, but it isn't furnished. Just storage space. I was offered it but took the second floor instead."

"I don't suppose you'd happen to have a key?" she asked.

"Why would have a key? Besides that creep kept to himself, and now we know why. You think he has someone in there? What, one the girls?"

"Maybe."

The man seemed to be considering his options. "This place is owned by the guy that runs the pub. We could ask him. He must have a key."

The man was wearing slippers and took the lead in walking across to the pub. They went in a rear entrance where the man in slippers rang a bell. The three were soon joined by an older lady who seemed to be trying hard to avoid the onset of age. A floral perfume mixed with the smell of beer and battered fish. After a brief explanation from slipper man, the owner was summoned.

Ben struggled to keep his frustration in check as the owner bumbled around looking for the apartment keys and then a jacket. *You're only walking ten yards.*

"Shouldn't we call the Police?" the owner asked as they walked back over to the apartments.

"No need. You're the owner. If you are okay to let us in, we can take a quick look round. If it's all clear no harm, no foul. If there is someone in there, then the sooner we find them the better." Briggs replied.

The owner seemed satisfied. "He'd better still be paying his rent, you know, while he's on remand or whatever they call it." He said, inserting and key and turning the lock. "I'll just step inside with you. Please don't touch anything."

"How do you get to the basement?" Ben asked.

"From the kitchen. Head inside and then to the back, round the corner and there's door."

"Thanks."

The owner stepped inside first and switched on a light. Slipper man chose to remain at the entrance to the apartment. Ben and Briggs slid past the owner and into the apartment.

The orange shade around the faux candle lights hanging from the ceiling did little to light the room. The walls were brown and created a sense of being underground. A red leather sofa faced a large screen Tv. A brass carriage clock sat on the mantelpiece with a print of Rembrandts Christ in the Storm hanging above.

The lounge space opened to a dining area where a walnut table stood accompanied by four chairs. Beyond the table an archway led into another space. Around the corner from the table was the kitchen. It was a large, farmhouse style, with cabinets across the top and drawers along the bottom. An island provided yet more storage and another place to eat. The apartment was tidy. Very tidy.

Ben let Briggs take the lead. He stood back as she reached for the basement access door. She turned the doorknob and frowned. The door took some effort open, the reason why becoming clear as it swung open.

"What the fu…?" she whispered. A bed mattress had been nailed to the inside of the door.

"Can you hear anything?" Ben asked, hoping he was whispering.

Briggs shook her head. She stepped cautiously down the narrow staircase.

At the foot, they were greeted by another door and another mattress. Briggs glanced back at Ben and opened the door into the space beyond. Ben hit the light switch.

Briggs stepped into the light. Ben watched as she turned and looked around, then quickly moved out of view. He followed to find Briggs crouched down, cradling someone's head. The partially clothed body of a girl lay strewn on a dirty mattress on the floor. Ben's heart was in his mouth as he moved to see the face. It was Louise Larke. Her ankle was held by a cycle chain attached to part of the plumbing that had rubbed layers off the skin. Then her eyes opened. She was breathing and started to speak though Ben couldn't make out what she was saying.

Briggs turned to Ben. "She's going to be okay. She needs water."

Ben quickly looked around, nothing. Briggs was pulling out her phone. He turned and ran back up the stairs to the kitchen.

The owner called, "Is everything alright!?" but of course Ben didn't hear him.

Ben poured some water into a glass and rushed back down the stairs. He returned to find Louise sitting up, sobbing as Briggs held her.

Morning broke as they got out of the car. Ben had witnessed as many dawns in the last couple of weeks as he had in the previous ten years. A shaft of yellow light escaped the clutches of the clouds and raced across the purple, gray sky. It was soon extinguished as the clouds tightened their grip. For Ben, that about summed the world up perfectly.

They entered through the back of the office. Ben had said very little – answering when asked questions by the Police, though Briggs did almost all the talking, and not speaking at all in the car afterwards. He went straight to his bedroom, closed the door, crashed onto the bed and fell asleep – no meadow, no short walk, just straight off into the abyss.

Ben awoke to the smell of coffee and bacon. The clock said it was fifteen minutes to noon. His stomach groaned. In the kitchen, Briggs was standing at the hob, her back to him. She had her ear buds in and jigged as she flipped the bacon. She turned.

"Morning," she said, glancing to see if it still was morning. "I was just about to wake you. Bacon butty?"

Ben put his hands through his hair, "Yeah, thanks."

"Take a seat, it's almost ready. Cheese?"

They sat at the table.

"You stink," said Briggs.

"Thanks. I suppose you've run ten k and showered."

"And opened the office and followed up with the NCA," expecting Ben to bite at her last remark. He bit instead, into the sandwich. "Are you okay?"

Ben took a swig of his coffee and placed the mug back on the table, a little too firmly. "I'm not sure I want talk about it."

"Talk about what? Saving Louise? What can be more rewarding, more noble than saving someone's life?"

"Not having to save someone's life. This gift you are so quick to praise is a…bloody nightmare." A tear escaped from the corner of his eye. "It's not like I'm just given her location. I have to listen. I have to stay listening in the hope of getting a sliver of information that might be useful. That bastard, Rupert, sat in his cell replaying his fantasies. I was there. I had to listen to it all." His voice cracking. "I don't know how, but I could somehow sense his excitement. It's like wading through a sewer." He wiped his face.

Briggs reached across and took his hand. "I don't know what to say. You're right it's not a gift. A gift is given, it's free, no strings attached. Your ability comes with a cost. I'm sorry Ben, I had no idea. But if you hadn't have used it Sarah Dalton would not be alive, and Louise Larke would have been left to perish. And those arseholes would still be out there kidnapping and murdering children. Ben you are thirty years old, we could be doing this for another twenty years, you need to reconcile yourself with this. We can operate without you having to listen in, but how are you going to feel if it could have prevented a death? Or deaths? No one else can do what you do, and there can be no doubt you are saving lives because of it. Look, I'm sorry you are the one bearing this burden, but in all honesty, I wouldn't want it any other way. I can't do this for you, but I can be there with you, every step of the way. Always." She wiped a tear from her own eye.

They sat in silence for a moment until Ben took another sip of his coffee. "Twenty-nine."

"What?"

"You said I was thirty. I'm twenty-nine. I'm in my twenties."

"Jerk."

Briggs refrained from reminding Ben about the missing person case she had assigned to him. She stood watching him as he sat with his head down, facing his phone, thumbs pressing on the screen. Perhaps he was the prized stallion, to be mothered, cared for, and only brought out for the big occasions. The paradox of the loafer sat in front her wasn't lost. She threw a candy at him.

"I'm off to that Barristers in Buckingham. Coming?" she asked.

"No, thanks."

Briggs didn't move and kept her gaze on him.

Ben looked back her before adding, "I have that missing persons case to make a start on."

Satisfied, she headed out.

The remainder of the week felt like a return to normality. They had been added as a preferred investigator to the office Mrs. Carole Phelps OBE. She represented matters of immigration, probate, and reserved instruments, which Briggs understood involved mainly land ownership, transfers and registration.

Ben's missing persons case only required standard investigation techniques. The parents of Bobby Blithe reported their nineteen-year-old son missing after he had not been home for two days. Ben had managed to track him to a hostel in East London with help from the Salvation Army. He was working as a dishwasher at a nearby Chinese restaurant that paid in cash. At nineteen, he was entitled to his privacy. It seemed house rules, argumentative parents, and the breakup from his own girlfriend caused him to leave. Bobby had no desire to return home. He was safe, healthy and of sound mind, and Ben reported as much back to his concerned parents.

The weekend, the office was closed and that gave the Briggs the excuse to rearrange a few things ahead of Harriet's arrival. And on the Sunday evening, she insisted Ben join her for a surprise. Briggs drove him twenty-five minutes around the city of Northampton to the village of Moulton, parking outside a stone schoolhouse.

"It says, 'Institute of Agriculture'" Ben pointed out.

"Oh, does it, I've not been here before."

They got out of the car as several other vehicles arrived. People were grabbing large sports bags from the boot of their cars and fencing Epees. Briggs grabbed a small bag from the back of the car.

"You're not taking up fencing?" Ben asked.

"Not me, you." She replied, smiling.

They followed the others behind the main building to a sports hall. Inside people of various ages were walking around in various states of attire.

"Before you start with all your objections and before moving on to all the reasons why you can't try this, I've already signed you up for the beginner's course. Six weeks, prepaid. If you don't do it, I don't get my money back."

Ben watched as new arrivals put on their equipment. Briggs tapped him on the arm.

"This about sight not sound. You're not at a disadvantage. None of them can hear much under those helmets."

Briggs was interrupted by a man in his forties, fully dressed and holding his mask.

"You must be Benjamin?" he asked.

"Ben. Hi."

The man held out his hand, "Pleased to meet you Ben, I'm Colin. I'll be your instructor. Do you have a change of clothes?"

"Sorry, what?"

"Oh, my bad," said Briggs, "I forgot to mention, your first lesson is today, well, now actually."

"Dressed like this?"

"Here," she said, sliding the bag towards him, "I packed these for you. And don't worry," mouthing only the words, "they know you need to be able to read heir lips. They'll loan you the gear."

"Then why do I need a change of clothes?"

"You'll see," she said.

A few minutes later, Ben was changed and fully equipped. The lesson was limited to sixteen, and after a safety briefing and equipment explanations, Colin had them practicing their first techniques.

"It gets friggin' hot under all this." Ben remarked, with the lesson only part way through, sweat dripping from his locks.

At the end of the lesson, she asked, "So, you're gonna come back next week?"

"Yes. It wasn't too bad."

She even got a 'thanks' during the drive home.

The following day Ben and Briggs attended court for the bail hearings. Rupert, James and Monica were being heard by the same judge to avoid any appearance of inconsistency. They sat toward the back with a few reporters as the Crown Prosecutors shared a lengthy list of charges with the residing judge. The NCA lead detective entered and sat down next to Briggs.

Ben and Briggs fully expected bail to be granted and so were pleasantly surprised when bail was denied. They were all to be retained at his majesty's pleasure while awaiting trial. A trial date was deferred. All parties were given another seven days to submit preferred timelines with explanations. The judge would also decide then on separate trails for the defendants. Given the numbers of charges and the complexity of the case, the trial would be months away.

As they exited, local media had gathered outside. A reporter stopped the detective to ask for his view on the bail hearing and if he expected any further charges to be made in the coming weeks.

Briggs told Ben they were heading to a pub where they would meet back up with the detective.

They reached the pub first. Being a Monday afternoon and too late for lunch, too early for dinner, the place was quiet. They took a booth away from the few customers at the bar and ordered two pints.

The pints arrived just before the detective. He approached and slid into the booth next to Briggs, facing Ben. He was around the same height as Ben at five ten. He was Chinese Western mix, his short black hair longer on top than at the sides, just long enough to lean forward like pine trees covered in tar. He looked young but for a few telltale wrinkles at the corners of his monolid eyes.

"Detective Chief Inspector Robert Golovitch," he said, holding out his hand. "We've seen each other but not been formally introduced. You met my partner, DI Burkes."

"Benjamin Grey, Ben."

DCI Golovitch must have sensed the momentary delay it took for Ben to shake his hand. "I know right. My mum is Hong Kong Chinese, and my dad was from Serbia. They met here while at university."

"You still on duty?" Briggs asked.

"Yes. But I'll get a water." He held out a hand until a waitress came to take his order.

"Sophie mentioned you know each other."

"Yes, well kind of. Briggs, sorry Sophie…"

"Briggs is fine," she interrupted.

"Briggs and I attended the same training a few years back. She joined after me but already had a bit of a reputation, out working and out scoring everyone else. Anyway, I wanted to thank you for your input on this case. It must have shortened our investigation by months, and who knows what might have happened in that time."

"You're welcome."

"Though something a bit more public might have been nice," Briggs responded, lifting her pint to her mouth.

"You probably have some questions about the case?"

Ben nodded.

"I can't normally share anything about an ongoing investigation but as you already know a lot, it's more of an update than me sharing information. You might have noticed the Caroline Walters murder charge was missing from the list of charges. That part of the investigation is ongoing. We're sure they were involved, it's clear they knew about the abductions, but the CPS wants more before a charge is made. In addition to the arrests you know about, we have charged two others connected with facilitating human tracking, transporting the minors to a network within Europe. We don't have much information on that network unfortunately, but we're sharing what we have with Europol. Thames Valley have also made arrests connected to the abductions. We believe one of those arrested was responsible for Caroline Walters death.

The other information you provided, the footage with the tattoo, the cigarette butts. The tattoo is used by an east European gang with ties to all sorts of illegal activities, it helped immensely in narrowing our search. Obviously, we charged the individual but it's not clear how far into the gang's activities we may be able to get. The cigarette butts will help secure a conviction. DNA places them at the house."

"You can use them as evidence?" Briggs asked.

Golovitch glanced around before answering. "We're off the record, right?"

Ben nodded as Briggs said, "Of course."

"Suffice to say, the butts made there way back to property so they could be logged and photographed."

"DCI Golovitch, that is naughty," Briggs said, smiling.

Golovitch adjusted himself, "Yes, well, it's a small thing under the circumstances and saves time for everybody."

"We were surprised Rupert didn't make bail," said Ben.

Golovitch nodded. "We were expecting they would to. But then the sister, Elizabeth Henshaw came to see us. She provided a signed character statement stating she considered it likely that Rupert would try to flee the country." He laughed, "I guess he must have stolen her dolls or something when they were younger."

"Anyway," Golovitch said, drinking some of the water. "The Chief Super is aware of your contribution and has agreed to make mention of your valuable contribution at the next media briefing tomorrow evening. Perhaps it will help your business." Golovitch stood. "Can I ask you a question Mr. Grey, sorry, Ben? How did you know Louise Larke was at Rupert Henshaw's property? The presence of the white van just before she went missing is a little suspicious, but any connection at the time to Rupert would have been highly speculative at best. And even then, how would you know to look for her at his apartment? The neighbours didn't even suspect anyone was there."

Ben looked across at Briggs.

"Ben thought it was statistically viable that Louise Larke had been taken by the group. If she had been taken and not moved with the girls on the boat, then it was also possible she had been killed or kept for some other purpose. If so, by whom? So, we went to check on Rupert's place." Briggs responded.

"Statistically viable?" repeated Golovitch.

"Sure. Simple math really. The number of missing kids, minus those that would have been too old. Two girls missing in the same week from the same area. Yes, probably unrelated but at the same also statistically viable, say greater than one in five." Ben added.

"I heard you also found the Sarah Dalton girl. Good for you. You are starting to get a reputation for yourself. Anyway, have yourselves a good day. Will see you around."

Ben waited for the detective to leave before asking Briggs, "Does he know about the list?"

"I doubt it. I haven't told him, I'm still trying to find the right person to share it with."

"The right person?"

"I told you, someone senior enough to be able to do something with it. But also, someone who want fold under pressure. In my experience people are not born corrupted. Most become corrupt, careers, money, loved ones, they can all be threatened or rewarded. It's easy to judge but it can be hard for people put in that position."

"Corrupted? You make sound like we've found the one ring. Why are you sticking up for them?"

"I'm not sticking up for anyone, people make their own choices. I'm just pointing out that we are all capable of doing horrible things. The difference is only how big a shove is needed. You might sit there being all noble, but what if someone threatened me to get you to do something?"

Ben shrugged, "They probably picked the wrong person to threaten."

"Jerk."

In the weeks that followed, Grey and Briggs, with the help of their new receptionist, Harriet, carved out what they now considered to be a routine. Ben took most of the missing-something cases as Harriet labelled them, while Briggs attended to contractual cases from Carole Phelps QC, and spousal-spying.

Grey and Briggs Investigators received a Certificate of Appreciation from the Mayor of Milton Keynes in recognition of their role in bringing human traffickers to justice. The Mayor of Northampton responded with an award for Business Excellence. Harriet proudly framed both awards and hung them at reception.

But Benjamin Grey's itch remained.

EPILOGUE

"Mr. Grey. What are you doing here? Are you boarding the same flight?"

"Actually, no I'm not flying today. I came to see you. You were my itch." Ben replied, taking a seat next Elizabeth at the departure gate. "I didn't know it was you at the time, but I had this thing that just wouldn't go away. Like a crease on the bedsheet when you are trying to get to sleep, not enough for you do anything about at, just a nuisance. My itch. But when it's there the next day and then the next, and so, it becomes harder and harder to ignore. That was you."

"What on earth are you talking about Mr. Grey?"

"Early on, you made a mistake. Obviously, I didn't catch it at first, hence the itch. But it came to me a couple of weeks after the arrests. I was expecting you to help your brother out, but it you really didn't like him did you. Offering to loan them the money for their buyout was genius."

"Rupert was a cretin. Always up to something. I'd had enough of his stupid antics. He got what he deserved."

"No, it was more than that though, wasn't it. You set him up. He didn't know it, but he was working for you. You probably had someone approach him while on vacation, I imagine that much of his story was true."

"I have no idea what you are talking about."

"You knew he'd be interested. Monica was put in place to help them set the operation up. Tell me, did Monica know she was working for you?"

"I don't know what you are talking about. And I am not liking your tone, Mr. Grey. I have a plane to catch shortly, and I'd like it if you left now."

"How many of these operations do you have going, Elizabeth?"

"If you are accusing me of somehow being involved in their disgusting activities then you are very mistaken. I have cooperated with the police from the very beginning."

"Yes, you have. You must have really hated Rupert. I think you were always prepared to offer him up if it became necessary. You probably enjoyed it."

Elizabeth glanced around, "I'm going to ask that you remove yourself before I call security and tell them you are harassing me."

"I'll leave you very shortly, don't worry about that. Don't you want to know what your mistake was?"

"I don't know what you think you know, but whatever it is, it is you that have made a mistake."

"The code. The code to the back door of the Mansion."

"Yes. Like I said, I've been cooperating all along. Even when Olivia first had you snooping around."

"The code first changed after Rupert became aware of our involvement. But then it changed again. I went back to the house, the morning after we watched those children being loaded into the back of a van, tied and hooded. The code had changed within the last twenty-four hours. I was thinking to break in as I still had a camera in the house, but then Olivia appeared with the code. It made me wonder how you could know the code so quickly. I guess it could have been possible for Olivia herself to have been in on things. But that little detail bothered me. That was my itch. And like every itch, it wouldn't go without a good scratch. How did you know about the new code so quickly? Again, it's possible Rupert was telling you as soon as he changed it

– I assume it was changed by Rupert, but given your somewhat hostile relationship, it didn't seem telling you anything was high up on the list of his priorities."

"What is your point?"

"Someone else was telling you. You had someone on the inside, some way of knowing. Was it Monica? Then we discovered Rupert had kept Louise Larke for himself, tragically connected to the murder of Caroline Walters. The abductors took the wrong the girl. Caroline was not what he wanted. About the right age, very similar slender build, both had long hair with curls. But Caroline was black. What happened, didn't Rupert tick the right box? Neglected to say, he wanted a white girl? Anyway, I can imagine what you must have thought on finding that out. Stealing the merchandise and a murder, that was enough to require your personal attention. And then there was the website."

Elizabeth's eyes flashed.

"The website you might have tolerated but not the list. Naughty Rupert, he really couldn't be trusted to just follow orders, could he. Well, anyway, even after the charges had been brought, the itch still remained. It made me wonder. Rupert really didn't know who he was working for. He wasn't aware of your inside man, or woman. We did some homework, and the circumstantial evidence started to mount. Your spending and assets far outstrip your income despite your shell companies. Your travels have little to do with your legitimate businesses and they aren't exactly most people's vacations of choice…Albania, Serbia, Bosnia."

"Those are very beautiful, and for the most part, uncrowded."

"Yes, I'm sure they are. But be that as it may, it was sufficient to start pulling your phone records. I imagine if we took a look at the phone you carry in that Chanel purse of yours, we'd find some interesting contacts and messages."

"You have nothing, Mr. Grey. Empty conjecture and hollow speculation. My brother is an idiot, and he only has himself to blame. My affairs are my own." She glanced around again. "What? Are you going to make a citizen's arrest or something. You have nothing. Even if I was involved, you think I'd sit here and confess all to you? Finding those girls on that boat was quite impressive for a private investigator. Finding that girl Rupert had been keeping, was very impressive. One might think you had an insider of your own, but I'm about to get on my plane. And though I can't say it has been a pleasure talking to you, it will be nice not to have to see your unkempt hair with your dirty converse sneakers again. I won't bid you good day."

Elizabeth stood, clutching her bag she turned and walked toward boarding.

"Oh, I did I mention Monica? She has something interesting things to say about you."

As Elizabeth held her passport out for the stewardess, another hand reached out and took it.

"I can take that," said Briggs.

"Who the hell are you?" asked Elizabeth, looking between the stewardess and the stranger that had just snatched her passport. "What's going on?"

"These lovely people are going to arrest you. Please, let me introduce DCI Golovitch and DI Burkes of the National Crime Agency. You probably recognise them." Briggs said, smiling. She handed the passport to Golovitch as he approached Elizabeth from behind.

The Cricklewood Mansion remained deserted for several months before being sold under auction purchased by representatives of a well-known media presenter. The Stanley property soon followed.

On the afternoon of the seventh of November, the office phone rang. Ben happened to be sat on the couch supposedly reserved for waiting clients. He was looking beyond Harriet at rain falling outside. Harriet reached over to answer. She had her back to him so he couldn't make out what she might be saying, but he assumed she opened with a cheery, 'Good afternoon, Grey and Briggs Investigators, how may I help you?'. She very quickly stopped twirling the pen between her fingers and started making notes. At the end of the call, she placed the handset slowly back into its cradle. She turned her seat around and saw Ben looking at her. She tore off her notes and walked over.

"Have you seen Sophie?" she asked.

Ben pointed to his right to the office room with the large glass window.

"Oh, sorry, yes. Just a moment, I'm coming back." She opened the door to the room and Briggs soon stopped what she was doing, got up and followed Harriet back to where Ben was sitting.

"We just had a call." Harriet started, glancing down at her notes. "From a Thomas Haydn. He said he was the Musgrove Family solicitor. Sounded real posh. He said Alistair Musgrove, the founder of Musgrove Investments, commonly known as Butler Musgrove, had been found dead. The police believe he was murdered. The family want to hire Ben to investigate the murder. Is that the one that was on the BBC last night?"

"I expect it is one and the same," Briggs replied. "Until this year he was famous for being the youngest billionaire in the country."

"Isn't he old?" Harriet replied.

"I mean, he first became a billionaire at the age of twenty-six having established a private investment company a few years before. Or something like that."

"And they have asked for me?" Ben asked.

"Yes. Sorry Sophie. He said the family wanted you and would pay whatever fee you felt appropriate along with any expenses. He wants you to call him back to confirm. I think they want you to start right away. I wrote down the number here," she said, handing her notes to Ben. "Does this mean you'll be on tv?"

"Do you want to take it?" asked Briggs.